UNDERCOVER HEART

By Pamela Stone

Undercover Heart

Undercover Heart

ISBN: 978-0-9894100-4-5

Copyright © 2013 by Pamela Stone

This book is a work of fiction. Names, characters, places and incidents are the product of the writer's imagination or are used fictionally for the purpose of this book.

All rights reserved. No part of this book may be reproduced, scanned, redistributed or transmitted in any form or by any means, print, electronic, mechanical, photocopying, recording, or otherwise, without the prior written permission of the author.

Printed by Create Space

Pamela Stone

Acknowledgements

I'd like to dedicate this book to my good friend, Kay Fenter, who years ago helped with the original draft. And as always, thanks to my most amazing critique partners, Linda Steinberg and Juliet Burns.

> Roberta,
> I hope you enjoy. This one is a little darker and a little sexier, but truly a book of the heart. Plus it's set in Galveston.
>
> Enjoy,
> Pam

Undercover Heart

Chapter One

"Excuse me, Jameson?" Dani rushed down the worn stone steps of the business academics building toward a small group of college students, focusing on the tall blond. This guy hardly looked twenty. The man she was searching for was twenty-six. But yet...

"Jameson?" she called again.

He adjusted his back pack and kept walking.

She quickened her pace. "Jameson Shayne, could I talk to you a minute?"

He stopped, glanced at the group of students he'd been walking with, and let his gaze take a leisure stroll up and down her body.

Up close, there was no doubt this was James' son. He was a younger version of his father. James would be thrilled to find him after searching for two years. Well, providing she could keep Jameson Shayne from disappearing before her brother-in-law had time to drive to Dallas.

"Hello." Smiling, she closed the distance between them. "You have no idea--"

"Shhh." He yanked her against him and growled into her ear. "I don't know who you are, but I'm kind of in the middle of something. Do us both a favor. Slap the shit out of me and walk away."

"Excuse me?" Her brother-in-law had lost the trail twice. If this was Jameson Shayne Kelley, she would not let him slip away again. "I just want to talk."

"Get out of here." His tone was gruff but his eyes were almost pleading. "Play along. Just turn--"

"Hey, Tucker!" One of the college kids he'd been walking with yelled. "You gonna stand around all afternoon with Miss Priss or you coming with us?"

Tucker? Adopted parents' name? And what about her outfit said Miss Priss? Okay, so her capris and shirt matched, unlike the grungy jeans and baggy shirt Jameson Shayne seemed to prefer.

Without warning, Jameson jerked her against his chest and planted a hard kiss on her lips. She clamped her lips together, but he ran the tip of his tongue around them.

She bent her elbows, wedged her arms between their chests and shoved. "What are you doing?" She wiped her mouth on the back of her hand.

"Nice job, sweetheart," he whispered, his back still to his friends. He winked. "Now get the hell out of here. Please."

"What?" She stared into intense blue eyes, trying to put any sort of logic to his actions.

His gaze roved over her yellow capris and crisp striped blouse. "And for the record, my name's Shayne. Just Shayne."

Dani stood stunned as he strode off to catch up with his friends, her heart still pounding from that kiss.

"Who's she?" A guy with dusty hair and a scraggly mustache cast a backward glance at Dani, but spoke to Shayne.

"A friend of mine from back home."

"Why'd she call you Jameson?"

"My old man's name," he replied. "She calls me that when she's pissed off."

Dani swallowed. Close enough. His father's name was James.

He wanted her to play along? No problem. He'd already cast her in the role of pissed off girlfriend.

"J-Shayne. Wait up." Dani undid a button on her blouse and sauntered after James's son and his five friends. "I came all this way and you think you can just walk away from me?" she asked Shayne. "We have to talk. And I'm not leaving until we do."

Shayne's glare was meant only for Dani. "I'm headed to a party."

"So bring her along." Mr. Scraggly Mustache waved her into the group. "Aren't you going to introduce us, Tucker?"

"No, she's--"

"Hi, I'm Dani." She flashed Shayne a warm smile. "Dani Cochran." No chance that he'd recognize her name. Dani's sister Patty had married James Highland fifteen years ago, long after Shayne had been adopted and disappeared from the system.

"I'm Brent," Scraggly Mustache said. As a preppy little blond pushed her way into their circle, Brent stepped aside and made room. "This is Courtney."

The girl focused her burning green-eyed glare on Dani, then flashed Shayne a cunning smile. Dani slipped her arm around Shayne's waist and tilted her head to study his face.

Shayne narrowed one eye at her then glanced at Brent, ignoring Courtney altogether. "So when's this going down?"

Dani's heart stopped. *When's* what *going down?*

"Who the hell knows? Can you give us a ride? My car's at the apartment." Brent squeezed a redheaded girl's rear end.

Three of the kids, including the platinum haired Courtney, climbed into a silver pickup. Shayne fished a key chain out of his pocket and pushed the button. When the alarm on a black Mustang next to her chirped, Dani jumped. Shayne shot her a warning glance.

"I'm fine." She tried to calm her pounding heart. If a car alarm spooked her, how was she going to pull off this charade?

She had no choice. For James' sake. Her sister and brother-in-law had invested a fortune looking for this guy.

Shayne helped Dani into the passenger seat and mumbled, "Just stay cool and I'll get us through this."

Get us through what? Dani wondered as Brent crawled into the backseat, pulling the little redhead with him. The girl wiggled her way into the guy's lap and his fingers fumbled for the buttons on her blouse.

Dani diverted her eyes and attempted to ignore the shrill giggles coming from the back seat. What had she gotten herself into?

She tried not to stare at Ja--at Shayne as he slid behind the wheel and started the engine. Having no idea what he expected from her, she kicked a wadded up fast food sack out of the way and tried to make sense of the last ten minutes.

Shayne pulled out of the parking lot and fell in behind the pickup. When his hand slipped off the stick shift onto her thigh, heat flared from his touch. She caught herself and glanced out of the corner of her eye.

Shayne's profile was like his father's. But the thick,

tousled blond hair he kept shoving out of his face made him look young and rebellious. He hadn't shaved this morning and the scruffy shadow accented his tan complexion and sensuous mouth. She ran her tongue across her top lip, wondering whether he'd try to kiss her again.

What was she thinking? Turning toward the window, she reminded herself she was here to reunite Shayne with his father, not get involved with the guy.

Shayne coasted the Mustang to a stop in front of a red brick apartment building in the center of the block and killed the loud engine.

"You two want to drop by my place after this? The four of us could have a hell of a party," Brent suggested.

Shayne glanced in the rearview mirror and Dani glanced over her shoulder just in time to see Brent pull his hand out from beneath the girl's minuscule skirt.

Shayne squeezed Dani's thigh, turned his head, and winked at her. "Not tonight, man. Dani and I are overdue for a little one on one."

Her cheeks were flaming hot. One on one? Her imagination kicked into overdrive.

Shayne yanked the emergency brake and crawled out. Dani gave herself a mental shake, took a deep breath and followed.

Just keep your distance and don't let him out of your sight. What was so hard about that? When he tried to take her hand, she adjusted her purse strap before following him upstairs into a second story apartment.

The room, packed with laughing, partying kids, reeked of smoke. The floor vibrated beneath her feet from the heavy bass thudding from the stereo speakers. The blinds were closed and Dani squinted to see in the dim light. Typical college apartment with furniture courtesy of someone's garage sale. The type of stuff passed from student to student

She stayed close to Shayne, not sure why he made her feel secure. For all she knew, he could be the devil himself. But he seemed safer than the rest of the crowd.

This apartment and its occupants all reeked of trouble. The smoke had a sweeter odor than cigarettes purchased at the corner convenience store. James was not going to be pleased with the man his son had matured into. Or, possibly matured wasn't the correct term.

Shayne high-fived a couple of guys and someone stuck a beer in each of their hands. He took a swig, threw his arm around Dani's shoulder and led her across the room. Backing into the corner, he slid his arm around her waist and pulled her against him, shielding them from the crowd.

The only way she could avoid his touch was to make a scene. For now, she stood plastered against his chest, but he ignored her, scanning the room instead, as if searching for someone. Or something.

When she'd charged off without waiting for James to get home to follow up on the latest lead, Dani hadn't bargained for this. If she'd had any idea of the situation Shayne was leading her into, she would have bolted, like he'd suggested. This apartment was a ticking time bomb. *When are you going to learn to think before you leap, Dani?*

She pushed against the restraint of his arms and raised her voice to be heard above the stereo. "Maybe you could give me your phone number and we can talk later."

"Be still." He smiled, but held onto her arm and his response was dead serious. "You should have left when you had the chance. We're staying, at least until someone I need to see shows up."

"Who? A drug dealer?" She was in way over her head.

Undercover Heart

Shayne glanced away, took her untouched beer, placed both bottles on the tile floor, and then tightened his arm around her waist. "Trust me," he whispered in her ear. Nibbling her neck, he slid his other hand beneath the hem of her shirt. "You're doing fine, just play the part a little longer."

Dani's skin burned beneath his fingers and her legs wobbled. She almost turned her head and tasted his lips. The guy had her off balance.

She'd been hearing stories about Shayne since she was nine years old. But this man was no longer the two-year old child James Highland and his teenage girlfriend had given up for adoption. Shayne was a full-grown, one hundred percent male and too sexy for his own good.

Her own good.

By sheer force of will, she shoved away. But his incredible blue eyes snared her. Dark sooty lashes and brows heightened the vivid color. Those eyes didn't miss a thing.

Shayne moved his lips to the corner of her mouth. Her nostrils filled with the scent of soap and shampoo, no trace of over-powering aftershave. Resting on his chest, her fingers tingled. His low-riding jeans and oversized Dallas Cowboys T-shirt might reflect college adolescence, but the muscular, six-pack beneath was no kid's.

Dream or nightmare, Dani was sunk if she didn't put an end to this madness.

Glancing past his shoulder, she found the blonde from campus glaring from the doorway. Reality check. Was this all an act for the girl's benefit? When Shayne tried to kiss her, Dani clamped her lips shut, pushed away, and nodded toward the other girl. "Girlfriend?"

He glanced behind him. "We've passed some time in a back seat or two."

She swallowed her growing dread. "Is that why you're still in college at twenty-six, so you can get high and seduce young girls?"

He lifted a brow. "They're of age."

"How reassuring." She tried to move from between him and the wall, but he grabbed her wrist.

"Stop making a scene," he demanded, lowering his voice and growling into her ear. "You need to loosen up." He pressed her hands against his chest and leaned close.

"I doubt anyone is sober enough to notice." He was somewhere over six feet. She stood flat footed and her eyes were on the same level as his shoulders. She tugged against his vise-like grasp.

Pulling her tight, he spoke into her ear. "Behave." Soft voice or not, his delivery left no room for argument.

Shayne nibbled her earlobe and kissed his way around to her chin. "Just play along." His lips felt as warm against her cheek as his voice sounded in her ear. Being this close messed with her common sense. "Kiss me, Dani, like we're lovers."

As Shayne's lips touched hers, she stared into his cobalt eyes. The kiss was soft and persuasive, a drug in itself. If he'd had more than one sip of beer, she couldn't taste it.

Focus, Dani. She backed away and broke the kiss. "I'm not your lover. I'm here to talk."

Shayne's eyes widened, but he loosened his hold. Given the effect he had on her, she got some measure of satisfaction that his breath was uneven too.

He stared, his gaze burning into her. He ran one long finger down her nose. "Later. When this is over," he promised, tucking a strand of hair behind her ear.

Undercover Heart

Dani blinked and avoided the intensity of his eyes. When what was over?

As Shayne shifted, she spied one of the guys from the group on campus standing in the doorway, just behind them. No doubt enjoying the entertainment.

Shayne followed the direction of her stare and eased around her. "Don't go away."

She was smack in the middle of a situation of at best, underage drinking. At worst, a drug bust waiting to happen. But if she left now, they'd never find Shayne again.

Shayne spoke loud enough that she could pick up pieces of his conversation. "Look, Brent, is this going down or not? I didn't expect my girlfriend. She's not in the best of moods right now and I'm a little anxious to get her home and chill her out, if you know what I mean?"

Brent leered at her like he wouldn't mind taking her home himself. "I'll bet. But hey, I'm not sure when he'll show. I thought he'd be here by now, you know?"

Enough of this. She had no idea how to get back to her car, but she refused to be part of a drug deal. Dani started for the door, but before she'd taken two steps, a jock dressed in jeans and a varsity jacket blocked her path. He brushed one arm against her breast. "Hey, Babe. You tight with Tucker, or you open for other options?"

Dani's skin crawled. She could smell the alcohol on his breath. She stepped to the right to move around him.

He shifted to his left, puffed out his chest, and forced her back against a chair. "How about you and me slip into one of the bedrooms?" He ran the back of his hand along the side of her breast.

Repulsed, she knocked his hand away. "Back off!" Did he think all it took to impress women was wearing his football jacket in ninety degree weather?

"You heard the lady," Shayne threatened from behind his shoulder.

The jock yanked his hand back so quick he almost tripped backward over Shayne.

Shayne nailed him with an icy glare.

The guy's gaze darted between Dani and Shayne. "Uh, sorry man. Didn't know it was like, serious, ya know."

Shayne's scowl followed the jock until he disappeared down the hall. He narrowed his eyes and took a step toward Dani just as the front door opened and two guys strolled in. They were both young and clean cut, wearing tennis shorts and carrying athletic bags.

"Shit," Shayne muttered. "Stay right here. Do not move."

Shayne and half the crowd followed the two guys into the kitchen. Dani's blood turned to ice. She no longer cared whether James ever met his son. In the haze of her throbbing head any lingering doubt had cleared. Jameson Shayne was a druggie.

She pushed through the crowd, maneuvering around a group of teenage girls who looked too young to be nursing beers and exchanging lewd jokes. Did any of these kids' parents have a clue? No matter. She'd be down the block before Shayne returned.

She opened the door and screamed as a policeman charged through and grabbed her arm, propelling her backward inside the apartment. A team of armed, uniformed officers pushed in behind them, ordering everyone to stay where they were. When the cop released her arm, Dani covered her face with both hands. Why hadn't she left earlier? She lowered her hands and stared at the two officers blocking the door.

A struggle broke out in the kitchen. Everything

happened so fast. She'd been transplanted into the middle of one of those real life cop shows. Everywhere she turned there were more blue uniforms with guns.

Shayne raced back into the living room and focused on the spot where he'd left her. Frantically, he scanned the crowd. Dani knew the instant his gaze locked on her.

One of the two officers who'd been blocking the door joined his partners in the kitchen. Shayne focused on the remaining officer. He edged toward Dani, clamped a hand around her wrist and waited until the officer was distracted by two girls attempting to convince him to let them leave. Shayne tugged Dani along as he eased his way to the door and then slipped outside.

Her heart raced faster than her feet.

They bolted down the stairs, but footsteps pounded close on their heels. Dani was afraid to look back. Was it the officer or just more of the kids making a run for it?

"Halt!"

Dani glanced over her shoulder at the policeman. "Shouldn't we stop?"

"Run!" Shayne pulled her along.

Spurred by adrenaline, Dani forced her legs to keep pace with Shayne's. She was a decent runner, but he was faster. Her pulse pounded and her lungs ached. Why hadn't she listened to her sister and waited for James to get here?

They were five feet from the Mustang and escape when the officer jumped Shayne from behind. The two men scuffled and the officer punched Shayne in the face and shoved him against the car.

Holding Shayne's head against the hood of the Mustang with one hand, the officer pointed the gun at Dani with the other. "Don't move, lady."

Chapter Two

*H*andcuffed! Arrested! Dani cringed as the officer snapped the cold metal handcuffs on her wrists then searched the contents of her purse. She watched, frozen in terror, while another policeman frisked, cuffed, and loaded Shayne into a van along with the other kids being escorted out of the apartment.

The van carrying Shayne pulled away. The officer pointed Dani toward a second van and shoved her into a seat. Tears stung her eyes, but she refused to give way to panic. She was going to need an attorney. Her life had just taken a downward spiral and all because of one Jameson Shayne Kelley, or Tucker, and his drug habit.

She studied the other occupants as the van bumped along. Most of them sprawled arrogantly on the bench, showing none of the mortification she felt. She tried to wrap her arms across her churning stomach, but her hands were cuffed behind her.

The ride to the police station didn't last long. They carted Dani along with the other women to a large holding cell. There was no sign of Shayne.

At least an officer removed the handcuffs before locking them in. Dani rubbed her chafed wrists, shoving down an overwhelming urge to scream and bang on the door.

Brent's girlfriend, the voluptuous redhead, flopped down on the bunk. "This your first time?"

Undercover Heart

Dani nodded, trying not to stare at the gold ring through the girl's right eyebrow. The jeans she had on probably cost more than three pair of the ones in Dani's closet.

Dani rubbed her eyes. "I think I'm going to be sick."

"If it's your first time and you weren't holding, there ain't anything they can do. They'll just try to scare you."

The tactic was working. "You've been in here before?"

"Only twice, in high school. I didn't have anything today, so they can't charge me and they know it." She chortled. "My grandpa's got money."

Detention officers called the occupants out one by one. An eternity passed before they called Dani for her turn in the interrogation room. The officer listened to her story, but looked skeptical when she said she had just tagged along to the party with a friend. He kept asking her the same questions over and over, like he wanted to trip her up. Every time she tried to elaborate, he reminded her to just answer the question. He had her so flustered, she wanted to confess to something, anything so he'd allow her to make her one phone call. Eventually the guy was convinced of her innocence or just gave up.

The phone rang three times and Dani prayed that Patty would answer before it rolled to voicemail. After she heard her sister's voice, there was another long pause while she accepted the collect call. Dani's sentences came out so jumbled she had difficulty making her sister understand.

Dani took a calming breath. "I found Jameson Shayne. We got arrested."

"Arrested? For what?" Patty asked.

"Drugs, but it's not like you think. Please, come to Dallas and get me out of here."

"Wait a minute. You took off work this close to the end

of the semester and went to Dallas?" Patty demanded. "Explain."

"Later. I only have three minutes." Dani took a breath. "Just get here. Please."

"I can't believe you did this. I told you to wait for James."

"If we waited until James found time to take off and follow up on the lead, the semester would be over and he'd lose him again. So I came. Shoot me."

Patty let out a deep sigh. "Are you sure it's him?"

Dani closed her eyes. "Patty, his hair is a little longer, but other than that he looks just like James did in your wedding pictures."

"I'll call James back and see if he can change his flight to Dallas instead of Houston. You stay away from that guy and let James handle this. Do you understand?"

"Yes." Dani felt better after hearing her sister's voice, even if she was angry. At least she didn't get the, 'Don't you ever think before you act?' lecture. She wasn't convinced Patty really wanted James to find the son he and his high school girlfriend had given up twenty-four years ago. The guy didn't have enough time to spend with his and Patty's two kids as it was.

Dani folded her arms across her chest and fought tears as the cell door clanked shut behind her. Her head felt like it might explode and she would've gladly paid $100 for two aspirin and a cold bottle of water. She dropped onto one of the bunks. This was a nightmare.

She should've just followed Shayne and waited for James to make contact. But what if he'd vanished again before her brother-in-law could get here?

The only facts the P.I. had uncovered was that the initial adoption had fallen through and Shayne had lived in foster homes until age eight. After that, information got scarce and he'd had only minimal leads to help locate him.

The blonde strolled over to the door, turned, and glared at Dani. "You aren't his type, you know."

Dani pressed her fingers against her throbbing temples. Why give up this bizarre game at this stage? "After today, I tend to agree with you."

Green eyes flashed. "So you're the sweet, innocent, girlfriend from back home he's supposed to marry and live happily ever after with?" She huffed. "He likes 'em wild and he likes variety. He'll be in bed with someone else before you've been married a week."

What a little witch. Shayne and the green-eyed blonde deserved one another. Dani took a deep breath. The girl was young and needed some good old fashioned parental guidance, as did Shayne. Still, given the current situation, Dani wasn't about to give her the pleasure of thinking she intimidated her. "I bet I can keep him happier in bed than you did in the back seat of his car."

"You'd better be more creative than a bed, if you plan to keep Shayne Tucker interested," Green Eyes taunted, flashing a wicked grin and studying her chipped chartreuse fingernails. "He changes girlfriends more often than he does socks."

The night loomed like an endless horror.

For the next three hours, Dani managed to ignore Green Eyes and the other cellmates, as one by one disgruntled parents arrived to collect their delinquent offspring. The bars closed in around her and she gained a whole new respect for the caged animals at the zoo.

It seemed like forever before an officer opened the cell door again. "Danielle Cochran?" At her nod, he motioned for her to come.

She followed him down the hall. A lady with bleached blond hair and a hot pink scrap of fabric for a dress yelled from one of the cells. "Hey, hon, get me out of here and we'll go shopping. You ain't never gonna catch no man in them clothes."

Dani quickly turned her head and picked up her pace. Where was the officer taking her? Her brother-in-law hadn't had time to get here from his business trip.

She stopped in her tracks.

Shayne stood in front of the desk signing papers. He shoved a persistent lock of straw-colored hair out of his eyes and frowned. "We're free to go."

"What?" Dani asked.

"I called my old man and his lawyer got us out, unless you'd rather spend the rest of the night in here?"

Shayne acted so nonchalant Dani wondered why he'd even bothered to bail her out. She assumed by 'old man' he referred to Mr. Tucker, his adoptive father. If the fancy car and choice in colleges were any indication, the Tuckers had money. Shayne was attending one of the most prestigious schools in Texas.

His father probably had an entire team of lawyers on retainer just to bail Shayne out of trouble. At Shayne's age, Mr. Tucker should have told him to get out of his own mess and let him rot in jail. The more she got to know Shayne Tucker, the more he seemed like a spoiled, rich brat.

Joining Shayne at the desk, she waited for the officer to hand over her belongings. She fought to keep her fury under wraps long enough to check her stuff and sign the release. Everything was there, including her small canister of mace.

Shayne frowned as he waited for her to replace the contents of her purse, then took her by the arm. "Brent talked his dad into driving us back to my car."

She followed him out front where Brent and his father were arguing beside a white Lincoln. Brent studied the toe of his sneaker while his father lectured. The kid didn't look so cocky now. He looked more like a little boy who'd just knocked a baseball through the neighbor's window.

Dani joined Shayne in the back seat, but when he brushed against her, she stiffened and slid to the other side. At least he was smart enough not to make an issue out of it. The Lincoln still had that new leather smell. Why couldn't parents realize that instead of giving their children every material convenience, they could benefit a lot more from a little love and discipline?

Brent's father ranted in the front seat and Dani wondered if the man ever took the time to actually listen to his son. She held her tongue and waited until they could get back to Shayne's car. She could throttle him for getting her into this mess, but maybe it wasn't entirely his fault. How had he been raised? She wasn't dealing with that child James remembered. Shayne was a grown man, and more than slightly dangerous. A trait that, for some reason, made him even more intriguing.

In a daze, Dani stared out the window into the moonless night. How was she going to get out of this with any dignity left? One more excuse for Patty to lecture her about not stopping to think. Patty. Dani reached into her purse and turned her phone on to boot up.

The Lincoln glided to a stop beside Shayne's Mustang and she opened her door and bolted out. At the moment, she didn't want any help Shayne might offer.

Brent's father lowered the window and glared at Shayne. "Stay away from my son. Do you understand me?"

Shayne captured Dani's hand before she could escape and raised one eyebrow at the older man. "Why you yelling at me? I didn't exactly drag him along."

Brent slouched in the front seat while his father turned and addressed Dani. "If I were you, young lady, I'd be more discriminating about the company I kept."

She tilted her head and frowned at him as the window went up. "Maybe you should spend more time with your son."

No sooner had the Lincoln pulled away, leaving them alone, than Dani turned on Shayne. Her patience and the initial spell of his charm were beginning to wan. "It's obvious that you're screaming for attention too!"

"Don't start with me." He rubbed his palm across his forehead and pressed a button on his key chain, but nothing happened. Mumbling about cheap batteries, he forced the key into the lock, opened the passenger door, and propelled her into the seat.

The door slammed and he trudged around the car. In no mood to do him any favors, she didn't even unlock his door. Shayne fumbled with the keys and slid in. The loud engine vibrated through her already pounding head. Dani was ready to fight and judging by his stormy expression Shayne would be more than willing to comply.

She fumed. "How serious is your drug problem?"

"I don't have a drug problem." He turned and glared. His soft tone failed to hide his impatience. "Just calm down. I know a little all night diner where we can talk."

Calm down? "You got me arrested!"

"I'll take care of it."

"Take care of it? How are you going to take care of a drug record? Thanks to you my career is ruined, not to mention my reputation. Do you really think my school board will understand?" She gulped air into her lungs.

Undercover Heart

"School board? You're a schoolteacher?" He chuckled. "Elementary, I'll bet."

His amusement only increased her fury. "Middle school. Is there something wrong with that? Some of us work for a living. What do you do besides deal drugs?"

Shayne shoved his hair back and exhaled. "First, why don't you fill me in on why you were looking for me?"

Because being locked in that dingy cell had given her time to think things through for once. And it was up to James Highland, not her, to confront his delinquent son. "I'm not sure you deserve to know after today."

"All this insistence about talking and you're going to clam up now?" He changed gears and accelerated.

Her phone beeped and she unlocked the screen and checked her four new texts, all from Patty. James had landed at DFW! Already. He had a rental car and was headed for the police station. She quickly answered Patty's text. "Look, I haven't slept in twenty hours and I don't trust myself to drive. Do you mind just dropping me at my hotel?"

***

Shayne had no idea how Dani'd known his real name and age. His nerves were jumpy. In all fairness, she'd been a good sport and had every right to be ticked off. But he needed to know why she was here.

He downshifted, and stopped at a light. "I'm too wired to sleep tonight after all this. You are going to talk to me now."

He'd run her name at the station. She'd lived in Galveston almost three years. No priors, not even so much as a speeding ticket. How the hell did she get a copy of his class schedule and a snapshot of him on campus taken with a long distance lens?

"Where are you staying?" He already knew she had a

card key for the Radisson.

    She hit send on a text, leaned back and closed her eyes. "Downtown Radisson."

    Shayne raised one eyebrow, but turned back toward downtown. He figured she thought the worst of him, but until he knew her game, he had no intention of breaking his cover. "Texting your boyfriend?"

    "Sister. Is that okay?" she snapped.

    Jeez, was he fishing to see if she had a boyfriend? Talk about juvenile. He pulled into the hotel driveway before he realized he should have parked in the garage. Damn, he was wiped. "Let me park and then—"

    Dani stepped out and turned back to him. "I cannot believe the mess you've made of your life. You need to seek help for your habit." Before he could get out, she'd turned and headed for the revolving door.

    "Wait!" Dammit. He jumped out, grabbed the valet ticket, and caught up to Dani midway through the lobby. "Hey!" He grasped her arm and jerked her around. "We talk now, sweetheart."

    She yanked her arm out of his hold and scowled. "Why should I talk to you?"

    Shayne nodded toward the deserted hotel bar. "Two years looking and you're going to just walk away? In there." If this was a setup, he'd rather face it now than be blindsided later.

    She rubbed her temple and glanced at the hotel entrance. He checked over his shoulder, but there was no sign of anyone else there. Not even a clerk at the front desk at this hour.

    Dani turned and paced across the lobby, away from the deserted bar, twisting her purse strap. "I thought I could do this, but I can't."

Undercover Heart

"Can't do what?"

She stole another glance at the front entrance and crossed her arms beneath her breasts. Her shoulders slumped and she looked like she might freak out. She was expecting somebody.

"Tell me, Dani."

"Why?" She seemed to get a second wind. "You dragged me to that...that crack house where you held me prisoner, pawed me, and got me arrested. I've been frisked, finger printed, booked, and interrogated. I was arrested for possession of illegal drugs!"

"You weren't arrested. They hauled you in on suspicion."

"Well pardon me if I'm not as familiar with the legal system as you are. I haven't had much experience with being arrested." She paced to the other side of the lobby.

As a rule, he was immune to emotional women, but something about this one had him spinning. Feisty, sexy, a little flaky. Still, that could be the idea, especially if this was a setup.

And the way she nibbled her bottom lip. The woman possessed an amazingly kissable mouth.

Shayne captured her wrist to stop her from pacing. "All part of the game. Now for the last time, calm down. You want the hotel to call the cops?"

"No." Again, her eyes cut to the side to check the door.

What the hell was her game? Had this been her scheme all along? Lure him back where some scumbag he'd busted was waiting with a bullet? Whoever she was expecting, he intended to stay and get reacquainted. "You know what? Enough of this crap. I'm outta here. Have a nice life." He turned and headed for the entrance. He was almost to the revolving doors. *Come on, baby. Show your hand...*

"Wait!"

Shayne stopped and slowly turned, folding his arms. *Worked every time.*

"Can I buy you a drink?"

Shayne nodded toward the dark bar. "It's two o'clock in the morning. The bar closed an hour ago."

Her lips tightened. Yet, something in those whiskey eyes told him Dani felt more vulnerable than he did. "A soft drink out of the vending machine?"

He stalked back to her. "Talk to me."

Her quick intake of breath and wide eyes alerted him to the arrival of her mystery guest.

On instinct, Shayne spun and crouched, retrieved his Glock from his boot and leveled it on the man standing inside the door.

"No!" Dani yelled.

Wearing a business suit and tie, the guy appeared more distraught than threatening. Thick blond hair. His blue gaze locked on Shayne. As did Dani's. Her lips moved, like she wanted to say something more, but not a single sound escaped. She chewed her bottom lip.

Shayne's fingers flexed around the butt of the gun as he slowly straightened. "Somebody enlighten me."

Dani shook her head and covered her mouth with both hands. She closed her eyes, then opened them.

He changed his focus to the suit. He'd never felt eyes bore through him like this guy's. He was tall, blond, somewhere between forty and forty-five. Shayne's instincts kept him tense, ready for battle. He didn't lower the gun as he returned the man's stare. Something about him

Undercover Heart

seemed...familiar.

Dani touched Shayne's arm. "I should have explained, but you..." She nodded toward the guy.

Still focused on the Glock, the man took a step forward and extended his hand. "I'm James Highland, your--"

"I know who you are." The name tore through him like a slug in the gut. Whatever warmth he'd felt toward Dani before vanished. Shrugging his arm out of her grasp, he snapped the gun back into its holster and focused on one thing. Getting the hell out of here.

Highland moved toward him. "Wait a minute, son. Jameson, just slow down and listen."

What did the asshole expect, for him to rush into his waiting arms? Call him daddy maybe?

Shayne glared at Dani and shoved past Highland. "I'm not your son and I sure as hell don't go by Jameson."

Dani reached out to him, but he jerked his arm away. "Who are you? Some kind of investigator?"

She shook her head. "James is married to my older sister."

Highland took another step forward. "Jameson, I've never stopped worrying about you for one minute, but I didn't want to confuse or upset your life. I didn't feel I had the right."

"Confuse or upset my life?" Shayne turned to Dani and raised one eyebrow. "Now there's a guy with a heart."

Dani winced, but he didn't care.

Highland held up both hands, palm forward. "Just settle down and listen a minute. We need to talk. I've always loved and cared about you."

"You were loving enough to get a fifteen-year old girl

pregnant and caring enough to throw away your two-year old kid. What a guy!"

Highland looked like he'd been doused with ice water, before the anger kicked in. "And your morals are so much higher? You just got an innocent girl arrested."

Before Shayne could respond, Dani jumped to his defense. "James, take it easy." She turned to Shayne. "He does love you."

"Obviously."

She stepped closer. "He's put a great deal of money and effort into finding you."

"I'm impressed, really! After twenty-four years he decided to check on me. Every kid dreams of such a father. Let's nominate him for Father of the Fucking Year."

"And I'm sure he's so impressed with a druggie for a son!" she returned, her big brown eyes shooting sparks.

"Stay the hell out of my life." Shayne pushed through the revolving door and waved to the valet.

"Let me talk to him," he heard Dani say as she dashed after him. "Slow down. Wait a minute."

He handed the valet his ticket and waited until Dani came face to face with him. Why couldn't she just leave it alone?

"Tonight never happened. I'll make sure your record is wiped."

Dani titled her head. "How?"

He arched a brow. "Don't worry about it. I'll take care of it."

Dani shouldered her purse and studied him. "You have a half-brother and sister. When my folks were killed four years ago, James made sure I knew I wasn't alone. I was part of their family. But even with all of us to care for, he couldn't forget you. He talks about you so often. He always worried about what kind of family adopted you and if you were happy."

Shayne narrowed his eyes. "If he cares so damn much, how come he waited until I was twenty-six to look me up?"

She bit her lip. "Like he said, because he didn't want to interfere in your new life."

"That's crap. He didn't bother because he didn't want to take any responsibility. Maybe he didn't want to have to explain his bastard."

Dani backed a step away. "Not true. He's not like that. He loves you."

"Don't tell me you believe in that shit."

She set her jaw. "Love isn't shit."

"The man didn't even give me his name. I went to the orphanage under the name of the girl who gave birth."

"Your mother?" she clarified.

"The girl who gave birth," he repeated.

"I've never met her, but I know James." At least she let his comment pass.

"If he's so anxious to know me, why did you come instead of him?"

"He was away on a business trip. Since the last two reports didn't pan out, I didn't want to wait for him to get home."

"What reports?"

Dani's brow wrinkled. "The first time, the P.I. claimed you were a junior at Stephen F. Austin."

"When was that?" he asked.

"April a year ago."

Shayne hid his astonishment behind a shrug. How could they have gotten so close without him picking up on it? He was losing his edge.

"When James arrived, they'd never heard of you, same with the University of North Texas, last fall."

Crap. The investigator was better than Dani realized. He couldn't understand her devotion to Highland though. Shayne watched the expressions chase across her face. He'd never met a woman so easy to read. In less than twelve hours, he'd seen confusion, fear, anger, and even lust in those eyes.

Illuminated by the red hotel marquee and the late night breeze stirring her dark, silky hair, Dani seemed out of place. He stared at her mouth as she nibbled that bottom lip, a nervous habit of hers he'd already learned in just the few hours they'd been together.

"Don't leave. Please come back inside." She looked as confused as he felt; yet her mouth beckoned his. "Give us a chance."

Not a mistake he could afford. Still, he ran the back of his hand down her cheek. "You can't fix this, sweetheart."

Those velvet brown eyes closed and her lips parted from the caress. So innocent. He was losing his judgment. He straightened and eased away, remembering that his biological father was standing just inside the door.

"After all this, you can't leave," Dani whispered, opening her eyes and staring into his.

Damn, she was vulnerable. Vulnerable was a dangerous trait. He'd learned that lesson before he could read and write.

Undercover Heart

He recognized the deep throated rumble of the Mustang and shook his head. He ran his thumb over her lips. "Sure I can. I don't care how damn tempting you are."

He turned and handed the straight-faced valet a couple bills, got in the car, and accelerated out of the drive. When he looked in the rearview mirror, Dani was still standing alone on the sidewalk staring at the back of his car.

He dropped it into second at the stop sign and floored it, tempted not to stop until he put as much distance between himself and James Highland as possible, maybe all the way to the damn Pacific Ocean. The car idled up to a red light and he fought to control his raging emotions. Of all the scenarios that had crossed his mind, coming face to face with his biological father wasn't one of them.

Why in hell would the loser decide to look him up now? Twenty-four damn years later. And what was the guy doing right this minute? Hiding in the hotel lobby like a whipped dog?

His mind wouldn't work. He couldn't fight his way through the flood of pummeling emotions. He'd gotten where he was without any help and he sure as hell didn't need anything from some asshole who'd suddenly decided to play daddy.

His knuckles were white from gripping the steering wheel. You had to be insane to let people get close. He didn't need the complications that came with relationships. Sure as hell not with James Highland.

Or the guy's sexy, meddling sister-in-law.

Chapter Three

*H*ow could the Dallas police have no record of Dani being involved in a drug bust the day before? She hadn't dreamed up that little nightmare.

"Anything you can tell me about Jameson Shayne Tucker. Or anyone by the given name of Shayne!" Dani flinched as James Highland drummed his fingers on the front counter and barked at the female officer behind the desk.

The woman maintained her cool stare. "I'm not authorized to give out that information, sir."

"I want to talk to your chief." James fingers clenched. Dani felt for him. He'd finally found his son and this woman was throwing up a roadblock. She knew something she wasn't telling.

"He's not available at the moment. I'll see if he has any free time to speak with you today."

Dani dropped into a chair, but James paced back and forth, his leather soles tapping on the polished tile floor of the stark waiting room. Dani was agitated and Shayne wasn't even kin to her.

For a second, in the wee hours of this morning, she'd glimpsed that little boy, so young and innocent, yet Shayne was neither. He'd pulled a gun!

No matter how tough he acted though, he had to be reeling from what he'd just learned. She understood the hostility, yet father and son deserved a chance to know one another. Family was important. James could help him.

She and James were left cooling their heels for almost an hour before a young officer entered. "Mr. Highland?"

James stood and extended his hand. "Yes."

The officer looked him up and down. "Will you come with me, please?"

James held the door for Dani and they followed him down a hall and into a barren office. There was no Chief of Police plaque, or any other for that matter, but hopefully they were going to talk to someone with authority. There were a few neglected books on the shelf and nothing on the desk except an empty metal inbox.

The middle-aged black man standing behind the desk wore a suit instead of a uniform. He extended his hand. "Mr. Highland. I'm Lieutenant Richter. I understand you're interested in finding Shayne Tucker?"

"If that's Shayne's name now, yes." James shook his hand. "Anything you can give me. Phone number. Address."

The worn leather chair creaked as Lt. Richter sat and indicated they should do the same. "Are you a relative?"

"I'm his father." James' Adam's apple bobbed. "Well, not legally. I'm his biological father, but his mother and I gave him up for adoption when he was a toddler. We were just kids ourselves."

Lt. Richter raised his brows, but listened to Dani recount the events from the day before. "No charges were filed against you, Ms. Cochran."

Dani leaned forward. "Look, I'm delighted I don't have a criminal record, but I'd like to understand what happened last night."

"Are you authorized to give me any information on

Shayne Tucker?" James interjected. Dani had never seen him like this. His temper was on the verge of exploding.

Lt. Richter stood. "I need to see some identification."

James pulled his driver's license out of his wallet.

Lt. Richter studied it then handed it back. "Wait here," he instructed and left the room.

"Something's not right. This is a vacant office." James ran a finger across the dusty desk, leaving a shiny streak. He turned to Dani, adopting the same fatherly tone he used on his kids. "Dani, are you sure there isn't something you're forgetting?"

"There's still one piece I can't figure out." Dani shook her head. "I mean, I know he's almost twenty-six, but he looks twenty, at most. Did you notice?"

James blew off steam. "He stormed out before I had a chance to notice much of anything. I was in shock. I'd like to know what he was doing with that gun and where it was when he was in jail."

Dani gulped. Just one more piece that didn't fit. "I hadn't even thought about that."

"Couldn't you have stopped him last night?"

"Sure, I could have thrown myself in front of his car." Dani hadn't slept the night before and she wasn't exactly in the mood to be accused.

How was Patty reacting to all this? She knew her sister wasn't excited about the prospect of James finding Shayne. Patty never let up about how little time James spent with Kyle and Molly and didn't understand why he was compelled to find a grown son he didn't even know. Dani was more sympathetic to the search. How could you have a child and not at least know they were safe?

James squeezed his temples. "This is the third time

Undercover Heart

I've been so close, only to have him vanish. At least we saw him this time."

Lt. Richter returned and stepped behind the desk. He looked from one to the other, then focused on James. "In all my years, I've never run across a situation quite like this." He nodded toward the door.

Following the man's direction, James turned and froze. Dani clasped her hand over her mouth. Shayne stood in the doorway, dressed in tight jeans and a black, long sleeved T-shirt, with bright yellow letters, D. E. A. across the chest. His hair was combed back away from his face. He looked older than he had in the early morning hours. His mouth was set in a grim line.

Dani did a double take. They were staring at James sixteen years younger.

It took a minute for reality to register. Dani's perception of what had happened the day before shifted.

Shayne's gaze lingered a second on Dani then turned to James. Taking a step forward, he extended his hand. "I'm Shayne Kelley." No smile. Any lingering emotions from earlier were expertly concealed behind a blank stare. His entire demeanor radiated a quiet threat. An invisible wall.

"Kelley?" James took a step closer. "Hello." His hand trembled as he reached out to shake his son's hand. "I can't believe it's actually you."

Lt. Richter silently left the room, granting them privacy.

Shayne dropped James' hand and shoved his in his pocket. "Look, Mr. Highland."

James frowned. "Don't you think Mr. Highland is a bit formal?"

"You prefer Daddy?"

Ignoring the barb, James offered a smile. "How about calling me James?"

"Fine." The total lack of emotion in Shayne's tone left a chill in Dani's heart.

James' gaze traveled up and down his son. "You don't understand how long I've wanted to see you, to know you're okay. I would've never pictured it like this."

Shayne's steel blue eyes narrowed to slits. "What did you expect to find, a two-year old?" His voice remained quiet and deathly controlled.

"I don't know." James closed one eye and studied him. "I just can't believe you're standing here. You work for the Drug Enforcement Agency?"

That not only explained the gun and his strange actions yesterday on campus, but possibly why they'd had such a difficult time finding him.

Dani stepped forward. "You were undercover yesterday?"

Shayne turned to her. "Yeah, and you almost blew three months of hard work setting up that bust when you came waltzing up out of nowhere. I had to shut you up."

"So you made me part of your cover?"

To her amazement, Shayne grinned. "You didn't leave me much choice. I couldn't afford for anyone to get suspicious."

Dani returned Shayne's grin and held his stare, acquainting herself with the new reality of Shayne Kelley. "So you still use your mother's maiden name, not Tucker?"

"Tucker's a cover."

James shook his head and held up a hand. "You were never adopted?"

"No." Shayne motioned for them to sit, and then leaned his lanky frame against the desk. "The only way I know to say this is straight out." He focused on James. "I appreciate that you made the effort to find me, but I'm not in the market for a family. It makes my job easier if I'm alone. I change identities and locations regularly and complications make things messy. I only agreed to talk to you to ask you to back off."

James held his ground. "I won't get in your way or interfere with your job, but I've worried about you too long to just walk away."

"You did before." Shayne took a deep breath, and his tone returned to controlled. "Look, I'm sorry Dani had to go through that bust yesterday, but I asked her to leave. She didn't listen. Being involved with me could put you in danger and it could put me in danger."

"You must be curious about--" James began.

"I'm not."

A Dallas police officer knocked and stuck his head around the door. "Kelley, we're ready. You coming?"

Shayne pushed himself up from the desk and shoved both hands into his back pockets. "It's been...enlightening."

The officer held the door for Shayne. Dani glanced up. "Wait a minute. You're the officer who searched me." Her brow wrinkled. "And you hit him."

Nodding at Shayne, the young officer's grin stretched from one freckled ear to the other. "With a face like his, can you blame a guy for wanting to mess it up?"

"Keep looking over your shoulder, Thornton," Shayne advised, easing toward the door.

Dani realized Shayne was about to escape at the same time James stepped forward. "How can I contact you?"

Shayne shook his head. "There's no reason."

James reached into his pocket and handed Shayne a business card. "Just in case... I printed our address and phone number on the back."

Shayne looked like he wasn't going to take the card, then stuffed it in his jeans pocket and slipped out of the office.

James curled his fingers into his palm and let out a breath.

"Are you all right?" Dani asked, touching his shoulder.

"I can't believe we found him. Or that he's chosen such a dangerous career." He stared at the door and his voice cracked.

Lt. Richter stepped forward as they exited. "Mr. Highland, I'm Kelley's lieutenant."

A loud commotion sounded from the next room as a team hustled out the door. Bulletproof vests bulged beneath their shirts and their shoulder holsters and guns made the scene look surreal. The danger Shayne faced knocked the air out of Dani. The thought of someone shooting at him sent her into a panic.

Without a backward glance, Shayne disappeared out the rear door with the rest of the team.

James stared at the door.

Dani wanted him to do something. How could he just stand by and let his son walk straight into danger? She blinked. Evidently Shayne had been doing it for some time. Maybe ignorance was bliss.

"They'll be fine." Lt. Richter said.

James flinched, still staring at the door. "What are the chances one of them will get shot?"

Undercover Heart

Dani wasn't sure she hadn't been more comfortable with the idea of Shayne being a druggie or even a small-time dealer.

"Slim. They're well trained. Come on, let me get you a cup of coffee." He led the way to a sterile break room and seated them around a serviceable wooden table in the corner. "Actually, he didn't choose the career, we chose him."

James stared at the oversized, brawny man. "Why?"

The lieutenant placed a Styrofoam cup of coffee in front of Dani and handed James one. "Tell me what you know about Kelley."

"Nothing since he was two and a half. His mother and I wanted a better life for him. Signed the papers for him to be adopted. That's the last we knew. I hired an investigator a couple years ago, but the few leads didn't pan out."

Shayne's lieutenant shook his head. "He, uh, he doesn't want anything to do with you. It's nothing personal. He's a loner. His freshman year in college we recruited him for a special unit we were putting together. Shayne had signed up for a self-defense class and the instructor was so impressed that he approached us. With his youthful looks, he was perfect to go undercover in high schools. He had the skill to defend himself and even better, he needed the money for college."

"So he's been doing this since he was what, eighteen?" James asked.

He nodded. "I was in on the initial interview and when I learned he had no family and no emotional ties, that cinched it. We trained him and placed him in a Houston high school. He had a knack for the work and put himself through college. Kelley's like a secret weapon. Don't be fooled by his appearance."

Dani shook her head. "He doesn't look that tough."

"He's tough and he's detached. Perfect candidate for the job."

James stared at the lieutenant. "So he has no family?"

"None. He spent his life in group homes and in and out of foster homes. He prefers being alone."

"But, his job is so dangerous," Dani said.

Lt. Richter met her gaze. "Only if people recognize him like you did yesterday. He's the best I've got and part of the reason is that he doesn't have commitments. He knows the law. He knows the game and the lingo. He has natural street smarts and even better instincts. Best of all, he has no fear. There's nobody at home waiting for him, so he doesn't panic under pressure."

"What you're saying is, he isn't afraid to die," James clarified.

"I've never thought of it exactly like that, but maybe. Not having a family gives him an edge. Nobody to worry about."

Ending the conversation, the lieutenant stood up. "Look, I just wanted to explain, because I know Kelley, and he won't. You deserve that at least. But, I do agree, it would be best if you forget you ever met him."

"Forget my son is risking his life every day and has no fear of dying? That's a pretty tall order."

"He's content and well paid. He's been doing this job almost eight years. Let him be." He glanced at his watch and reached to shake James' hand. "They're wired and I need to be by the radio. Don't worry. We'll take care of him."

James held tight to his hand, delaying his departure. "I need his address and phone number."

"That's classified."

Undercover Heart

"I'm his father."

Lieutenant Richter tilted his head. "Even so..." He eased his hand out of James' grasp and left the room.

"An undercover cop?" James led Dani back to the lobby.

She figured he was still trying to grasp the turn of events as much as she was. The gun should have given them a clue, but she'd been so focused on finally finding Shayne that it hadn't registered.

"Dani, hey."

Dani nodded at Brent and his father from the night before. "Brent."

"You here to get a copy of your police report too? My dad needs it for my attorney," the kid explained.

James stepped forward and stuck out his hand to Brent's father. "I'm James Tucker. I presume your son was involved in that fiasco yesterday too."

Dani snapped her mouth closed and didn't rat him out. Evidently Shayne wasn't the only one who could adapt to different roles.

Brent's father turned. "Charles Turnbeau."

"Mr. Turnbeau." James let out a deep breath. "I've got a problem. My son moved and refuses to give me his address. Shayne's out of control. But as long as I'm paying his tuition, he's damn well going to listen to what I have to say." He focused on Brent.

Charles Turnbeau glared at his son. "Do you have the address?"

Brent shuffled his feet. "Yeah, but Shayne'll be pissed."

"Tell the man where his son is," Charles ordered.

Pamela Stone

***

Dani concentrated on the lyrics to a popular song one of her students had chosen. The assignment had been to choose a song to analyze and compare to one of the classic novels they'd been studying this semester. This song had been at the top of the charts for the past month or so. Typical taste for a tween girl awakening to the thrill of first love, or evidently first heartbreak. A sad tale of love gone wrong. Abby led the class in every assignment, but that hadn't worked in her favor with the boys. "Good choice, Abby. What classic story would you relate the lyrics to?"

"Romeo and Juliet." Abby flashed a sideways glance at Eric, the class hottie, if a seventh grader could even be classified as a hottie. "They loved each other so much, but I guess it was destined to end."

"Well, at least the people in the song didn't die," Abby's friend piped in. "I mean at least they get a chance to find another love."

"True." Dani nodded. "Romeo and Juliet is one of my all time favorite love stories, but it is very sad. Anyone remember what we call a story like theirs?"

"Dumb," Eric offered. With his blond hair and lethal smile, all the girls in the class had crushed on Eric at least once over the year, but only recently he'd begun to show an interest in one specific girl. A feisty little redhead who didn't seem as enamored with his mischievous blue eyes as the rest of the girls.

"A tragedy," Abby answered.

"Shakespeare was famous for writing tragedies." Dani smiled at her students. "Well, that was the last song. Did everyone enjoy this assignment?"

"Analyzing songs is a lot more fun than reading old books that someone wrote centuries ago," Eric said. "I know you say they're great, and some of them were sort of entertaining, but I still don't understand what reading them is supposed to teach us."

"History sometimes repeats itself," Abby said.

"Well, I think we're all smart enough not to kill ourselves just because we can't be with somebody we think we love." Eric glanced at the redhead next to him. He'd been sitting with her at lunch all week. "No offense, Kaitlyn. I mean, I like you a lot, but I wouldn't expect you to off yourself if I was a jerk or something."

"Romeo wasn't a jerk like you." Abby glared at Eric. "He was misguided."

Eric nodded. "No kidding."

Eric reminded Dani of Shayne, both in attitude and looks. Who was she kidding? Since her trip to Dallas, everything reminded her of Shayne. The guy was stuck in an endless loop in her brain. She went to sleep each night and woke up the next morning thinking about him. Whether he realized it or not, even at twenty-six he could benefit from a family and a father. People needed people. They needed love.

"Tomorrow is the final. Is everyone ready? The exam will be twenty-five multiple choice questions worth two points each plus five short essay questions worth ten points each. Pay attention to the facts when answering them as there will be certain elements I'm looking for." She grinned. "And I may add a bonus question."

Kaitlyn cocked an eyebrow at Eric. "You mean so maybe Eric can pass and you won't have to put up with him again next year?"

Eric grinned at her taunt. "You'd miss me next year if I failed."

Kaitlyn looked him straight in the eye. "Like you so charmingly put it, I wouldn't off myself over you."

Abby narrowed her eyes and stared out the window.

Eric just might have met his match In Kaitlyn.

The bell rang and Dani took a breath. "Study hard tonight and get plenty of sleep. Class dismissed."

As the students gathered up their belongings and shuffled out the door with about as much grace as a herd of cattle, Dani rubbed her eyes. Just one more day of class, then a week of averaging grades and cleaning out her classroom for the summer.

"Hello, Ms. Cochran," the superintendant said as she entered. "Are you ready for school to be out?"

"Oh yeah. I think the kids are already mentally on summer break. It's been a challenge just to keep their interest the past couple weeks."

"Same every year." She glanced around the classroom. "Have you decided to take on the summer class? I think your enthusiasm could work wonders with them."

Dani shrugged. "I can handle them. They're just kids who need some special attention, right?"

The superintendant nodded. "See, that positive spirit of yours is just the thing to get them caught up. Of the six, four are on probation. If you don't mind, I'll give their probation officer your cell number. You'll be required to keep him apprised of their progress and of any issues. Both he and I will need to be notified of absences. This class is their only chance to not fall behind a year in their studies."

Dani grinned. "They'll do great. With only six students, I can give each one the individual attention they need to get caught up. It'll be a fun challenge." Not to mention provide a little extra cash to spend on renovating her house.

***

Undercover Heart

During the next couple of weeks, Shayne tried to forget the encounter with James Highland. It was more difficult than anticipated. When he was young, he'd dreamed of his parents coming back and rescuing him from the loneliness of the orphanage or foster home. But life was no damn fairytale.

Still, it was hard to forget James Highland now that he had a face to put with the name. The possibility that the guy might be a decent person didn't set well either. He knew better than to trust him. Besides, what did he need with a father? He was a little old for softball games and trips to the zoo.

The Dallas case was about wrapped up. All things considered, it had been a relatively simple assignment. They'd brought down two levels of dealers. And one of them they'd used as bait to get the big boss. The only real hitch had come when Dani had happened on the scene the day of the initial bust. Until he'd found out who she was, even that had only added a little challenge.

Driving back to his apartment, he considered where they would send him next. He was past due for a change, the chance to become anonymous again, a distraction from the nagging thoughts. Changing identities and existing in new environments was what he did. He was comfortable where nobody knew him.

He pulled into the drive and frowned. A teenage boy sat hunched on the bottom step of the garage apartment. Shayne crawled out of the car, watching for any sudden movements. "You need something?"

The boy's belligerent gaze scaled him. "You Shayne Kelley?"

Shayne narrowed his eyes. "Who wants to know?"

The boy stood up and shoved his hands into the pockets of his baggy denim shorts. "Kyle Highland."

Chapter Four

*K*yle Highland? The name brought Shayne to a dead stop at the bottom of the stairs. "Really?"

"I decided to check out Mr. Perfect."

The kid had the kind of tone that tempted cops to toss them into juvy without even hearing their story. "What does that mean?"

"You're Mr. Perfect and I screw everything up."

"Why don't we take this conversation inside?" Easing around his uninvited visitor, Shayne led the way upstairs and unlocked the door.

Kyle followed him into the garage apartment and turned up his nose. "Why don't you rent a real place?"

Shayne opened the refrigerator and grabbed two soft drinks. He pitched one to Kyle and popped the top on the other. "How'd you get here?"

"Bus."

"Where did you get my address?"

Kyle was preoccupied scrutinizing the apartment. "Dad wrote it in the address book by the phone. All he talks about now is how well you've done. Shayne this and Shayne that. Shayne's done so much with his life. Shayne's in danger."

Shayne studied his quarrelsome half-brother. He had

dark hair, but his father's blue eyes. "Do your folks know where you are?"

Kyle smirked at the dusty, portable television abandoned by the previous tenants. "You don't even own a big screen."

"Don't watch much TV. Do they know you're here?" Shayne repeated.

Kyle shook his head. "Are you kidding? They don't even let me go to the mall by myself. They treat me like a kid."

"Do you have a cell phone? Call your mother."

Smirking, Kyle met Shayne eyeball to eyeball. "I left it at home so they couldn't track my location."

Shayne handed his phone to Kyle. "Call 'em."

Kyle pitched it onto the sofa and flashed a challenging glare. "They don't give a shit about me. Why should they care where I am?"

"Doesn't matter whether they care. You're a minor and they have a right to know."

"Dad doesn't care, as long as I'm out of his hair. All he ever does is gripe. He's a jerk."

Shayne shrugged and took a swig of caffeine. "Well, we agree on one thing at least. Look at it from my perspective, at least he raised you."

Kyle wandered over to the boom box, also left behind by some college kid. "Do they still make these things?"

"Kyle, why are you here?"

"I wanted to meet my half-brother, the big, important DEA agent." He spat out 'brother' as if the word left a bad taste in his mouth.

"That's crap. You don't feel any more brotherly toward me than I do toward you."

Kyle started around the room for the second time, cutting his eyes at the weight bench. "Well, that's two things we agree on."

Shayne admired the kid's guts, but didn't care for the antagonism. Why had James told Kyle what he did for a living? That kind of knowledge could be dangerous given this kid's mouth. Grabbing his cell, he pulled out his wallet, and searched for Highland's business card. Keeping one eye on Kyle, he dialed the number.

"Hello." The woman who answered sounded frantic.

"Hello, is this Mrs. Highland?"

"Yes. Who's this?"

"Shayne Kelley. I have Kyle."

"What are you doing with Kyle?" Her tone was just short of accusing him of kidnapping.

Shayne took a deep breath and counted to ten. As if anyone would choose to have Kyle. But he didn't want to start a fight. "He was camped on my stoop when I got home from work. Says he took a bus."

"Oh." Her voice softened. "Probably paid for the ticket with the two-hundred dollars he stole from his father's wallet."

Kyle looked away and Shayne deliberately added to his discomfort. "Two-hundred dollars?"

Kyle turned his back and rummaged through the kitchen cabinets. Shayne listened to Mrs. Highland a few minutes, then promised to put the boy on a return bus.

Kyle waited for him to hang up. "You can put me on the bus, but I'll get off at the first stop. I'm not going back.

Undercover Heart

They treat me like shit."

Shayne was beat and in no frame of mind to deal with a moody teenager. "Life's a bitch. Deal with it."

Stunned into momentary silence, Kyle paused before responding. "Home sucks. It's not fair the way they treat me."

Digging through the cabinets, Shayne tried to find something easy to cook that a teenager would eat. "Whoever told you life is fair lied. The way I see it, you're what, fourteen?"

"So?"

"So, you don't have much choice for the next three or four years except to put up with them. They may be jerks, but at least you have parents. No matter how unfair they seem, it's better with them than living in foster care. Nobody there gives a shit and that's a fact."

Opening the freezer, Kyle considered the dinner choices. "I don't like frozen pizza."

"Imagine a home with a hundred kids where you were served a balanced diet that came out of gallon cans. Frozen pizza is a gourmet meal."

Kyle studied the cardboard boxes. "Couldn't we go out?"

Shayne grinned. "Sure. You buying, Mr. Big Bucks?"

"Dad has more money where that came from. He'll hardly miss it."

"Your mom said he flew out early this morning, arrived at the hotel, and realized he didn't have any cash. I think it's safe to say he missed it."

Kyle shrugged. "He has a wallet full of plastic. I'm sure he didn't starve."

Shayne shut the refrigerator. "Let's grab a burger. I'm

too tired to deal with you and cooking."

Kyle continued to provoke him throughout the meal. Shayne did his best to ignore him, or at least not rise to the bait.

Three burgers later, two of which Kyle ordered, but dissected more than actually ate, Shayne headed for the station. He needed to track down his lieutenant and see about a couple of days off to drive Kyle home. No doubt the kid would hold true to his threat and get off the bus at the first stop. From what he'd seen so far, the punk would probably find a way to slip past his mother at the airport if he put him on a plane. The only other option was to make one of the Highlands come after him and Shayne didn't want any of them back in Dallas. Nor did he want to babysit the brat until they arrived.

Lieutenant Richter looked Kyle over as he shook his hand, then focused on Shayne. "Pasadena, huh?"

"Yeah." Richter knew the Houston/Pasadena area like the back of his hand, as did Shayne.

"Take a couple extra days." He handed Shayne a brown envelope. "Run this down while you're there."

Shane narrowed his eyes at his boss. Richter also knew Shayne would be ready to get the heck out of there the second he dropped the kid off. "I'll run it down, but you need to find another guy for the job."

"We'll see."

* * *

Kyle was a pain in the butt all evening. He refused to talk to his mother when Shayne called to let her know he'd drive him home the next day.

Shayne came out of the bathroom and found him lying on the weight bench, unable to budge the bar. When Kyle caught him watching, he scrambled off and shrugged.

Undercover Heart

"Weights are lame."

Shayne pitched a pillow and blanket on the sofa. "Make yourself at home."

"I might sneak out."

"I sleep with my gun. If you even get up to pee, you'd better say something so I don't accidentally blow your head off."

Kyle's eyes widened before he swallowed and rolled up in the blanket. Shayne wasn't sure how much the kid believed him, but he made sure Kyle saw he had his holster in his hand before he turned out the light. He wouldn't put anything past the kid.

Shayne wasn't overly concerned about Kyle's problems, except they were causing him to make an unscheduled trip south. The last place he wanted to go. He'd spent a large portion of his life in the Houston area and he sure as hell didn't want to go back now that he knew James Highland and family lived there.

The next morning, Shayne hit the bench for his usual workout. Kyle pretended to sleep, but Shayne was conscious of his audience as he lifted weights. After a few minutes, Kyle made an act of yawning and crawled off the couch. Mornings didn't seem to be his best time of day, if he had one. It was too early, he whined. The couch was lumpy and he was hungry. Shayne pointed him toward the shower and folded the covers. He had no desire for a kid brother and he did not want to deal with his bullshit.

Breakfast at McDonald's was the cheapest place to fill the kid up, but Kyle continued to complain. He ordered the biggest breakfast on the menu, but only ate half the food then went back for a sausage and biscuit to take on the road. Shayne wondered how much the Highlands' grocery bill ran.

About the only thing the kid approved of was the black

Mustang.

Shayne shrugged. "It's not mine. The department provides different vehicles every couple of assignments."

"Do you own anything worth having?"

"I have a new place to live and a new role to play from month to month. Stuff makes moving harder."

"Don't you make good money? I mean, if it's that dangerous, they should pay you big bucks."

"It pays all right."

"Ever kill anybody?" Kyle asked.

"No." Shayne was surprised he'd waited this long to ask.

"Did you do Dani?"

Shayne managed not to react. That one he hadn't expected. "No."

"Mom's afraid you two hooked up. She says Dani hasn't been the same since she got back. She's constantly asking Dad questions about you. Is she any good in bed?"

Shayne raised one eyebrow and glared at him. "I have no idea, but even if I knew, I sure as hell wouldn't tell you."

Why the hell did the kid have to mention Dani? In a weird sort of way, her vulnerability reminded Shayne of his first few years at the orphanage. Those days before reality had set in and he'd figured out the world stunk. He must have been somewhere around five at the time.

But no matter how many times he told himself he didn't need anyone, he still craved someone in his bed at night. His options were limited. He had no interest in a commitment and one-night stands weren't worth the risks.

Undercover Heart

Dani talked as if she cared, wanted to help. Still, she'd get over it quick enough. Everyone else always had.

The radio blasted him out of his thoughts as Kyle tuned into a heavy rock station. "Does that bother you?"

"Listen to what you like."

Shayne's phone rang before they got out of town and he had to turn around and run back by the office. Kyle sat in the corner and pouted while Shayne dug through his desk for surveillance photos. Trial was set for next week. By the time they got back on the road, Kyle was whining for lunch. Shayne forced him to wait an hour on general principle, before pulling into a taco place. By then Kyle was too hungry to complain. He ordered a bonus meal and an extra taco, but again left half the food on the tray.

He changed radio stations without ever listening to a full song for the next hundred miles, with the volume so loud Shayne was sure his eardrums would burst. Why didn't the kid have an iPod or MP3 player with ear buds?

Still, listening to the obnoxious music was preferable to arguing with Kyle for the four hour drive. Besides the music, Kyle had to stop at least once an hour for a restroom break. Without fail, he returned carrying another soda, which meant they had to stop again a short way down the road.

They ran into heavy rain north of Houston. Given that, Wednesday afternoon rush hour, and the music, Shayne's nerves were shot before he made it half way across town. He strengthened his vow to never have kids. Kyle wasn't even helpful with directions, but it wasn't a problem. Even though Shayne didn't know the exact house, he knew the neighborhood. At least the rain let up before they hit Pasadena.

By the time Shayne found the house, again with no assistance from Kyle, he was ready to throw him out on his butt and just keep driving. He glanced out the window at the ranch style house and hoped he could drop Kyle off and escape before running into James Highland, or even worse, Dani. Just the thought of her made him break out in an adolescent sweat. Thankfully she lived in Galveston.

They'd barely stepped out of the car before a woman raced down the front steps and pulled Kyle into her embrace. Shayne wondered whether she was going to hug him or strangle him.

Kyle stiffened and pulled away.

"Look young man, you have put everyone in this family through a nightmare with this stunt."

"What do you care? Afraid you won't get elected as PTA president next year?"

The woman glared at him. "That's uncalled for."

"Yeah, well, it's true. You care more about people thinking you're a great mother than being one."

A loud smack cracked through the air as Mrs. Highland slapped Kyle across the face.

Shayne lunged and grabbed Kyle from behind before he could plant his doubled up fist in the woman's face. "What the hell are you doing? Going to punch a woman? Your mother, no less?"

Mother and son stared at one another a long moment. Kyle's fist remained clenched. A little girl rushed outside, and of course, Dani was right behind her. The little girl huddled up to a stone pillar on the porch, but Dani ran to her sister's side. "Are you okay?" She stared at Kyle. "What has gotten into you?"

The kid pulled against the restraint of Shayne's arms, but he held tight. "You aren't going anywhere."

Mrs. Highland's shoulders shook and she covered her face with her hands. Dani put an arm around her waist. "It's

Undercover Heart

okay."

"No, nothing's okay!" She turned toward the house and stopped short when she spied the little girl. "Everything is a mess."

Dani led her sister onto the porch and then placed her other arm around the little girl. "Come on, Molly."

"What about Kyle?" the little girl asked.

"Shayne will handle Kyle until your daddy gets home," Dani told her.

Didn't seem that he had a choice.

"Get your hands off me!" Kyle demanded, shoving against the restraint.

"You ready to behave?" Shayne asked.

"What the hell do you care? You don't have to put up with this crap! You get to leave."

Shayne jerked a little tighter. Being here wasn't exactly a trip to Disneyland for him either. He was certain the uncomfortable situation Kyle had put everyone in with his little road trip had never entered the kid's juvenile mind or maybe that was his intent. The world revolved around Kyle.

"I can't leave until you settle down." Shayne kept his hold. "I don't care how ticked you are, you don't hit women."

Tugging harder, Kyle tried to squirm out of his grasp. "Kid, I do this stuff every day. You aren't going anyplace. I'll turn loose when you get control of yourself."

Dani came back out on the porch. "Mrs. Becker across the street just called the police."

Great! He held tight to Kyle, who at least had stopped trying to kick his shins. "This the first time the cops have been called out?"

54

She nodded. "As far as I know, yeah. James is on his way home from the airport. He should be here any minute."

"You ready to behave?" Shayne asked Kyle. "Running now will make things worse."

A cruiser pulled up to the curb and Kyle jerked again. Shayne released him, poised to regain his hold if the kid tried to bolt. Instead Kyle rubbed his arms and looked like he might throw up the tacos he'd devoured for lunch.

Two officers got out, but luckily Shayne didn't recognize either of them. He'd worked a sizeable bust here a year ago in a local college.

The older officer nodded as Mrs. Highland came out of the house and joined Dani. James pulled into the drive within seconds of the cruiser. They could have a party. Kyle at least looked subdued for the first time since he'd disrupted Shayne's life the afternoon before.

"We got a call about a disturbance," one officer said.

Kyle kept quiet, but Mrs. Highland stepped forward. "It's nothing, officer. My son ran away and my..." She seemed at a loss as to how to introduce Shayne. "Umm..."

The officer glanced at him and Shayne pulled out his badge. "DEA, but that has nothing to do with this."

The officer examined the badge and handed it back.

James looked from one person to the next. "Officers, I'm James Highland, the father of the runaway. Agent Kelley is my son from a previous relationship. Kyle, my younger son, ran away and caught a bus to Dallas to meet his half-brother. Shayne was considerate enough to drive him home. There's no need for the police here."

"Sir, we still have to file a report."

Mrs. Highland stood to the side, ringing her hands. "Could we take this inside and off the front lawn?" She

Undercover Heart

glanced across the street at the neighbor's house. "We've made a spectacle enough for one afternoon."

James held out his hand and indicated that everyone should follow his wife inside. Shayne would have gladly left, but that was no longer a viable option. At least not until the police took their report.

Once inside the oldest officer took the lead on questioning. After he'd gathered the facts and reached the part where Kyle doubled up his fist at his mother, the officer did exactly what Shayne planned to do. He lectured the kid on all the repercussions and possible charges. Shayne remained quiet, letting the officer assume the bad cop role this go round.

The Highlands remained quiet also, although Shayne wasn't sure whether they agreed with the officer and him scaring the kid a little or whether they were nervous themselves. Somebody had to get control of Kyle or he was lost.

Shayne finally got a chance and put in his two cents. "Your call Kyle, but if you don't turn yourself around, you're going to be one of the kids me or someone else hauls in. Ask your Aunt Dani how that felt and she wasn't even guilty."

Dani nodded. "He's right, kiddo. It was the most humiliating, helpless experience. You need to listen. These officers are trying to help you now, but if you continue on this path, the next time will be worse."

"You might consider getting him a counselor," the younger officer suggested.

By the time the officers left, Shayne would have liked nothing better than to follow them out, but Dani maneuvered herself between him and the door. "Thanks."

He shook his head and tried not to stare at her tight jeans and lacy pink top. Her little pink flip-flops were the exact shade as her blouse. She really was as seriously pretty as he remembered. Just as innocent too.

James wrapped an arm around his wife. "Maybe we should consider finding Kyle a counselor."

"He doesn't need a stupid counselor. He needs his father around," Mrs. Highland retorted.

"I should have known you'd turn this around and try to make it my fault. Everything is, right?" James put his hands on his hips and glared at her.

"You two set such a wonderful example for us innocent kids," Kyle scoffed.

James glared at his youngest son. "I suppose you're proud of this little escapade? You've had everybody worried sick and Shayne had to take time off to drive you home."

"Right! Wonderful big brother brings delinquent little brother home and saves the day. Figures," Kyle taunted.

"That's enough out of you, young man. I'm not listening to any of your smart mouth. I'm fed up with your shenanigans." James gripped the table. "All because you are a spoiled, self-centered brat who thinks everybody owes him something."

"Wrong! I don't want anything from you." Kyle stomped off down the hall and slammed a door so hard, Shayne flinched.

"Why don't you consider a family counselor? Or even some parenting classes?" Shayne suggested.

"I know how to parent my son!" James said.

Obviously.

Shayne held his tongue.

Mrs. Highland wiped her eyes. The woman looked beat. She was an older version of Dani. Her dark hair had a few strands of gray and was shorter, but the family

Undercover Heart

resemblance was uncanny. "I made Kyle's favorite meal. I thought that we could sit down tonight and have a nice pot roast as a family. Talk through this."

These people had no idea where this kid was headed. "Pot roast isn't going to solve this," Shayne said.

"We should ground him for life. This is the worst stunt yet," James added.

"I'm going to check on Molly." Dani headed for the hall. "She hasn't come out of her room since all this started."

"So Kyle pulls this sort of thing often?" Shayne asked the Highlands.

"Lately it's been constant. He's angry at everyone and everything." Mrs. Highland twisted her wedding band. "We need to relax and think this through. Let me put dinner on the table. Full stomachs will help."

As Mrs. Highland escaped into the kitchen, Shayne wasn't feeling the love from her anymore than he did from Kyle. Mostly the woman seemed nervous and uptight.

"Excuse me a minute," James said, then followed his wife into the next room.

Shayne closed his eyes and took a breath. He opened them and scanned the view from the living room. The floor to ceiling windows looked out over a back lawn and pool. A baseball glove was thrown in a chair by the back door as if waiting for Kyle to pick it up and head out to toss a few balls.

How many guys were pushing twenty-six the first time they set foot in their father's home? And why did it matter how his biological father lived?

Shayne walked around the den stretching his stiff joints. Most of the furniture looked like antiques, probably expensive antiques. Mrs. Highland's pot roast smelled good, but he had no intention of sticking around for a fun family dinner.

Photographs of everything from dance recitals, to little league, to formal family portraits covered one entire wall. James and Patty's wedding picture stopped him cold. Shit! He'd never known anyone he was related to. To see his features so clear in another human being felt...

He swallowed the lump in his throat and let out a breath. He did not belong in this house.

There was one of Dani in an orange cap and gown, clutching a diploma and grinning. So, she'd graduated from UT. He'd spent a semester in Austin a couple years back.

Something about her threatened to pull him in. But he didn't need a woman in his life, he just wanted one in his bed. He blinked the image away. Something told him, with Dani, the two were a package deal. And that was one complication he did not need.

Dani bolted into the room. "Kyle's gone!"

Chapter Five

*D*ammit! Shayne wasn't surprised Kyle had run away again, but he'd hoped his intuition about the kid was just his natural cynicism.

"You're kidding me." James raced from the kitchen, with Patty hot on his heels. He pointed toward the phone. "Stay at the house and call Kyle's friends. I'll comb the area."

Patty nodded, already reaching for the phone.

Shayne couldn't leave now. Kyle might be half way to Mexico before his parents figured out that whatever was bothering him was more than an adolescent tantrum. He followed James outside and headed toward the Mustang.

Dani yanked the passenger door open and jumped in beside him. "I know the area."

So did he, but he didn't enlighten her. He started the engine and backed out of the drive. "What does Kyle like besides baseball and karate?"

"How do you know what he likes?"

"Pictures in the den. Where's the nearest baseball field?"

Dani blinked. "I don't see why he'd go there. It's deserted. I'm sure he's at a friend's house by now."

Shayne cruised up and down the neighborhood streets, both he and Dani scanning the area for any sign of

Kyle. Even with the humid Houston air Dani's unique scent of peaches and coconut suntan lotion filled the tight confines of the car. Interesting blend.

"He have a girlfriend?" Shayne asked.

She tucked a strand of dark hair behind her ear. "He's only fourteen."

"Exactly. He's fourteen, pissed off and looking for sympathy. He'd look for someone he can control or overpower. Good chance if he has a girlfriend he'll want to..." He searched for an innocuous term. "hook up."

Dani's mouth dropped open. "I don't think he's old enough to think about hooking up."

"Sure you don't teach nursery school? Even if he hasn't had a girl yet, I guarantee he's working on it."

"You're jaded. He's a child." Her dark eyes flashed.

"He's no child, Dani. He already asked me how hot you are in bed." Why the hell had he allowed the conversation to go down this path?

"No way." Dani shook her head.

"No way he asked or no way we're going to end up in bed?"

Her jaw jutted out and she held his glare. "Either one."

That sounded like a challenge. His pulse pounded at the image of Dani tangled in sheets, her dark hair damp and... "He asked and he wanted details."

"That's just wrong." She tossed her hair back. "Is this your obscure attempt at a come on?"

Shayne stopped at a residential intersection and glanced in the rearview mirror to be sure nobody was behind them. Hoping to scare her away or maybe hoping not to, he leaned across the console, pulled her toward him, and kissed her like he'd been aching to do since he'd arrived.

He took a breath. "When I come on to someone, I don't play games. We've both wanted this all evening. You denying that too?" He pressed his hand against her shoulder and used his tongue to entice hers to join in the evocative skirmish.

Dani leaned into the embrace and tangled her fingers in his hair, urging him closer. "No."

Okay, so she wasn't quite as naive as his first impression. He allowed one more kiss, and then eased away from her heat. "We've got to look for Kyle."

Her eyes fluttered open, her mouth still moist from his kiss. "Right."

Shayne ran his thumb over her bottom lip. Talk about error in judgment. Her taste lingered on his lips. "You were going to show me where he plays baseball?"

"Turn right." She sat back in her seat and closed her eyes. "You're wasting your time. I'm sure Patty's already found him."

They pulled into the ballpark as the last rays of sun faded. Shayne got out. "Keep the doors locked."

"But..."

He slammed the door. Doubtful that he'd find Kyle here, but he was desperate for a few minutes of solitude to collect himself and hammer his emotions back under control. He'd thought if he kissed her, the reality wouldn't compare to his imagination. So much for that theory.

He'd assumed once he was away from Dani, he'd forget about her. That hadn't worked in his favor either. He was acting like a frustrated, hormonal teenager. Forget common sense. Get her alone in a car and his sex drive shifted into full throttle.

Shayne gave his eyes time to adjust to the dark and glanced around the field. The bleachers were deserted, as was the field, but if Kyle was anything like him at that age, he'd look for a secluded place to lick his wounds. Shayne walked around the edge of the diamond to the dugout. Stepping into the shadows, he squinted. He could sense him, more than see him. "Kyle?"

"How'd you find me?"

Shayne sat on the wooden bench and stretched his legs out in front of him. How many times had he been where Kyle was? When nobody understood. Nobody gave a shit. "Pal, you're talking to the master at running. One time, it took them three days to find me."

Kyle stood up and leaned against the rail, studying Shayne. "I'm not going back."

"Your choice. Why don't you level with me? What's eating you?"

Kyle stared at his sneakers.

Shayne felt for the kid. "I don't want your family."

"Well they want you. Dad's always loved you more. Molly stared at you like you're freakin' Superman. And Dani moons around like she'd like to jump your bones."

Shayne leaned his head back, not looking at Kyle. "Listen. Your parents have been there for you. Your father, and I emphasize *your* father because he sure as hell isn't mine, loves you. He just doesn't have a clue what's eating you. The man didn't give a damn about me for almost twenty-four years. As for Molly, I've never even spoken to her." Shayne pegged Kyle with a hard glare. "And Dani is none of your business."

"Little touchy there, Bro?" Kyle's white teeth flashed in the moonlight. "Even Mom thinks you're a hero for bringing me home."

Undercover Heart

Fat chance of that. Patty hated him. "I'm not trying to move in on your territory."

"But you'll be working here. I heard your boss."

"Not if I have any choice." Shayne resisted the urge to meet Kyle's eyes, not wanting to make him uncomfortable. "You're lucky to have parents."

Kyle dropped down on the bench next to him. "Parents suck. You don't know how much of a pain they are. They won't let me grow up or make any decisions. Everything has to be their freakin' way."

Shayne let his gaze wander across the moonlit diamond. "Take my word for it, no matter how much things suck at home, it's easier with a family than without one."

"They treat me like a kid," Kyle insisted.

"If you want people to treat you like an adult, act like one. Quit behaving like a spoiled brat and show them you can make solid decisions. Talk to them."

"They don't listen. They preach."

"Then show them. Stop running from your problems, because they don't go away. I think I was about twenty before that one slapped me in the face." Shayne stood up. "Come on. Dani's waiting in the car."

Kyle groaned. "Do I have any choice?"

"We need to get you home before your parents have a heart attack. At their age, you could do them in, you know?"

Kyle flashed a grin. "In my dreams."

At the car, Shayne held the seat forward for Kyle, then crawled behind the wheel and started the engine.

Dani turned in the seat and offered Kyle a consoling smile. "Are you okay?"

To Shayne's amazement the kid didn't come back with a smart reply. "Yeah."

Dani looked back at Shayne as if she wanted to say something. At least with Kyle in the backseat, the topic of the damn kiss was off-limits. Why the hell had he kissed her? How with one lustful look could she make him feel like the villain?

The word 'innocent' flashed across Dani's forehead like a neon sign. Dani wasn't the type for a quick roll in the sack. But those full tempting lips of hers hadn't exactly been guiltless.

Even now, if Kyle hadn't been watching, Shayne wasn't sure he wouldn't crawl on top of her and kiss her until she begged for more. He shifted into reverse and held his tongue.

At least Kyle remained blessedly quiet. Shayne didn't know whether what he'd said had sunk in or not, but he hoped so. Now if James would just keep his cool, maybe they could work this out.

"Call and let Patty know Kyle's with us. Give them time to cool down," Shayne suggested.

Dani pulled her cell phone out of her purse and pushed the power button. "Dead battery. I keep forgetting to charge it."

Shayne shoved his phone at her. "That's going to do you a hell of a lot of good if you ever really need it."

Dani ignored his comment and gave her sister a quick call. But even so, she held her breath as they pulled in front of the house. James and Patty stood waiting on the front lawn. Shayne opened the car door and Kyle crawled out as if he were facing a firing squad. If they'd just calm down and let him know that they loved him, Dani knew everything would be okay. Kyle wasn't a bad kid. He was just crying out for attention.

James grabbed him by the collar. "Get to your room. I've a good mind to..." He glanced up at Shayne and Dani. "Excuse us." Yanking Kyle along, he stomped into the house with Patty close on his heels.

Shayne leaned against the car and shoved his hands into his pockets. It didn't take a genius to sense his disapproval.

Shayne's voice was monotone. "Will he whip him?"

"I don't know. You don't think he deserves it?"

"At fourteen, it won't do any good. If James hits him, he'll just run again and again until eventually they won't find him."

She sensed that they weren't talking just about Kyle anymore. What kind of horrible childhood had Shayne experienced? How could anyone make that up to him? As much as Dani loved Kyle, at the moment Shayne was the one her heart reached out to. "That sounds suspiciously like the voice of experience."

His jaw set and he crossed his arms.

"Life was pretty rough for you growing up, wasn't it?" Dani coaxed.

He stared into the night, refusing to look at her. "I got by."

Dani didn't know what to do to reach him, to relieve his fears. Her life had been comfortable, mostly happy, at least until her parents' death. She offered him a reassuring smile. "Let's go inside."

"No."

"James has never hurt him."

Shayne rubbed his forehead. "I'll still wait out here."

Kyle's blood curdling scream broke the silence. In a split second, Shayne took off toward the front porch just as Kyle raced out the door. "I'm not staying here! I hate you," Kyle screamed over his shoulder.

Shayne tackled him in the middle of the front lawn. "Settle down."

Pinned to the grass, Kyle kicked and struggled to break free. One foot connected with Shayne's shin. "Let me go."

Shayne grunted and positioned a knee on each of Kyle's legs. Biceps bulged as he held Kyle to the ground. "Not until you calm down."

Kyle fought until he exhausted himself, but he was no match. "This is none of your damn business," he spat through gritted teeth.

Dani stood beside Patty and James, mesmerized. She was afraid for Kyle, but not because of Shayne. But because of the kid's anger and poor choices. Shayne had taken over the situation and neither James nor Patty intervened.

"You made it my business when you came to Dallas. If it hadn't been for your stunt, I wouldn't be here." Shayne's voice was quiet and succinct as he continued to restrain Kyle. The softer his tone, the more threatening he sounded "Is this your version of an adult?" He paused to give Kyle time to answer. "Let me know when you're ready to behave."

Kyle's breaths were ragged, but the fight seemed to have run its course.

"Now, I'm going to turn you loose and you're going back in the house with Dani and your mother. Got that?"

"If he touches me, I'll kick his ass," Kyle threatened.

"Your dad's staying out here with me."

Patty stepped forward and Shayne straightened, pulling Kyle with him.

Glaring at his father, Kyle shoved past. Patty followed him into the house. Thankfully, Patty had sent Molly to a friend's for the night. This turmoil with Kyle was beginning to give her nightmares.

Dani kept her stance by the front porch. Patty didn't need her inside. And she might learn something out here to help her nephew.

Shayne stepped in front of James and blocked his route to the steps. "Slow down and listen a minute."

"This isn't your fight."

"It is tonight."

Dani exchanged worried glances with James. He looked done in. She shrugged at Shayne. "You're being a little too tough on Kyle. He's not a bad kid."

Shayne glared at Dani, then turned to James..

"You don't know him. Don't understand," James added.

Shayne folded his arms. "You're the one who doesn't understand."

"Really? How's that?" James' voice oozed sarcasm.

"Kyle's running full tilt down a rocky path and you're chasing him."

James sighed. "I just don't want him making the same mistakes I made."

Dani sucked in her breath and watched Shayne's face for a reaction. Was James talking about getting his girlfriend pregnant when he was only a year or so older than Kyle?

Shayne gritted his teeth. "I talked him into coming home and talking to you. Your role is to listen. How the hell are you going to deal with his problems if you don't understand what they are?"

"So if I listen to him, everything will be just peachy?"

"No." Shayne paused. "But if you don't, he'll be out of here before daybreak."

James rested his hands on his hips and stared up at the stars. "You're right about that." Closing his eyes for a second, he turned and faced Shayne. "I'm not sure what to say to him."

"Just listen. Stay calm. Tell yourself you aren't going to let him piss you off, no matter how hard he tries. Because, he will try."

"Oh yeah. That's one thing he's mastered."

"He knows which buttons to push to make you react. Throw him off guard, don't."

As James passed under the harsh porch light, the exhaustion was etched in the lines across his brow. She squeezed his arm. "Everything will work out. How about just give him a hug tonight and talk tomorrow after you both calm down."

"Maybe." James raised an eyebrow and shrugged, before turning back to Shayne. "I owe you an apology."

"You owe Kyle one."

Shayne waited until James went inside and then headed for his car.

Dani didn't know if James was in any shape to pull it off, but Shayne's advice made sense.

She walked down the drive to Shayne. He stood immobile against the Mustang, eyes closed, jaw set. "Are you okay?"

Turning his back, he braced his palms on the Mustang hood. "I've been the kid running and I've had the crap beat out of me by a foster father who thought he could straighten me out. It doesn't work. Kyle's already pissed and all James is doing is alienating him."

That innocent little blond boy in the picture on James' shelf surfaced for a second, then the wall went back up. The system hadn't protected Shayne. He'd had no recourse. Nowhere to turn.

Taking a risk, she eased up beside him and wrapped an arm around his waist. He straightened and held her against him, but she wasn't sure he was conscious she was there. Dani increased the pressure, simply held him, marveling at the fact he didn't pull away. She wasn't sure of all the demons he was fighting, but whatever they were the simple human contact had to help.

She nodded toward the house. "Come on inside. They aren't screaming. I think what you said to James may have gotten through to him. You're smart with kids."

"Usually the ones I see are already so screwed up there isn't much you can do to help. Occasionally you get a shot at one before he's too far gone."

"Kyle will be fine."

Shayne stared off into the distance and seemed to be talking to himself. He gritted his teeth. "I did not want to get involved with this family."

"Sometimes things happen for a reason, you know."

She wanted to soothe all the raging emotions churning inside him. People needed people. Human beings weren't meant to be alone. She kissed the corner of his mouth, rubbing her nose against his.

Dani sensed he wanted to pull away, but he didn't.

This man drew her like an opposite magnetic pole. She'd never met anyone who intrigued her like Shayne Kelley. All those idiosyncrasies. All those protective walls. Around people, he put up a cold, distant front, yet she felt the emotion in the tenseness of his embrace. Tough and vulnerable.

His hands were on her waist, but he held her slightly away. There were levels to Shayne she'd bet even he wasn't aware of.

She nuzzled into his neck and inhaled a hint of aftershave. His arms tightened and his breath stirred her hair. She slid her hand beneath the hem of his shirt and spread her palm flat against his tight back. Closing her eyes, she enjoyed the sensation of the smooth warmth of his skin beneath her fingertips. One minute he pushed her away and the next.

Her hand slid further up his back and her lips touched his. His mouth descended on hers and took control with a desperation that threatened to drive her insane.

He lifted her up, and then allowed her to slide slowly down his body until her toes touched the grass. "Do you know what you're doing to me?"

His intense heat scorched through her clothes and his lips crushed against hers, his tongue invading the secret recesses of her mouth.

He tugged her blouse out of her slacks, unbuttoned a couple of buttons, ran his hands beneath the front of her shirt, and spread them flat over her stomach. He closed his hands around her waist and bent his head to meet the kiss.

Dani wanted to hold him and comfort him, but she hadn't planned to turn it into this. She placed her hands on his shoulders and pushed back. "Slow down."

He released her and narrowed his eyes. "You started this."

Undercover Heart

She stepped back like she'd been burned. "I didn't plan to be undressed on the front lawn."

"I didn't plan..." His hands came up as if he might grab her, then his fingers curled into fists. "Lady, just...What the hell am I doing?"

Chapter Six

*D*ani stood transfixed as the Mustang disappeared, her body on fire from Shayne's touch. The hot flames spread to her cheeks. She smoothed her blouse and touched the tip of her tongue to her swollen lip. Geez. What had just happened? She couldn't get involved with Shayne Kelley! She hated complicated relationships and this one had emotional rollercoaster written all over it.

But if he were to turn around right now and come back, she might just hop in and see where they ended up.

This was crazy! She took a deep breath and stomped up the steps into the house, running smack into Patty. Dani stepped back to go around, but Patty moved to block her path.

"Where have you been?"

She was so not in the mood for one of Patty's lectures. "Patty, don't start." She tried to move the other direction, but her sister didn't budge.

Patty placed her hand on her shoulder. "Look at me."

Dani met her eyes, challenging her to say something.

"You're a mess. What did he do to you?"

"Nothing," Dani snapped. Whatever had happened, it wasn't any of Patty's business.

"Don't lie to me. Haven't I got enough to deal with?"

Undercover Heart

Dani shoved her hands into her pockets. "Shayne left. We're all upset and now isn't a good time to get into anything. How's Kyle?"

Glancing over her shoulder, Patty answered. "They're still talking. I haven't heard anything, so maybe they're getting somewhere. Who knows?"

Dani softened and hugged her big sister. "Don't worry about me. I'm fine. We just sort of argued."

"Shayne isn't like us," Patty pointed out. "Don't get involved."

Dani flinched, but held her tongue. Of course he wasn't like them. How could he be?

James came back into the room and glanced from Patty to Dani. "Where's Shayne?"

"Probably headed back to Dallas," Dani said.

"He left?" James glanced out the window and doubled up his fist as if he might bury it in the wall. "Why the hell didn't you stop him?"

"What was I supposed to do, drag him back inside?" Again it was her responsibility to keep the guy from leaving?

Closing his eyes, James let out a long breath. "So he's gone. I'm right back where I was two years ago."

"Not really," Kyle said from behind him. One shoulder propped nonchalantly against the doorframe, he wore a smug grin.

Dani found his arrogant stance annoying.

James turned. "Kyle, go back to your room."

"I can't be part of this family discussion?" Kyle held his position and raised a challenging eyebrow. "I'm sure you'll find your beloved son again, Daddy."

Dani wondered whether James had enough self-control left to follow Shayne's advice about how to handle Kyle. *Keep your cool. Don't react.*

"Go to bed. Now." James glared at him, but at least his tone remained monotone. "Next time you decide to leave, I may decide to change the locks."

Dani pulled the pillow over her ears and tried to tune out her sister and brother-in-law arguing in the next room. She wasn't fond of sleeping at Patty and James' house to begin with, but there'd been enough chaos for one night without going head to head with Patty regarding the wisdom of a single female driving to Galveston alone after dark.

Evidently the chaos wasn't over. Kyle and Molly's rooms were down a separate hallway, but Kyle had to be aware also.

"Are you planning to come to bed? I haven't slept in days worrying about Kyle," Patty demanded.

"Oh, and you don't think I've been worried too? I've got two sons to consider here," James countered.

Bed springs squeaked. "Might I point out that one happens to be a grown man who is quite capable of taking care of himself? You need to focus on doing something about our son before it's too late."

"What have I been doing all evening if not dealing with Kyle?" James snapped.

Dani winced as the bedroom door slammed, but she wasn't sure who'd stomped out, Patty or James.

Dani agreed with Patty. James should spend more time with Kyle. Take a father son weekend to the beach. He was a mixed-up teenager who needed his father. James and Patty had given Kyle everything he ever wanted, spoiled him to the point that he thought the world owed him, but now wasn't the time to reverse that. Not when Kyle felt that Shayne threatened what little attention he had from his father.

Shayne on the other hand, didn't want anything from anyone. Not his father and not Dani. The opposite of his half-brother, Shayne didn't expect love or for anyone to spoil or care about him.

How could anyone penetrate Shayne's defenses? James had no pull whatsoever. And it wasn't Dani's place. Yet in a weird way she felt responsible. She was the one who'd first made contact.

What was she thinking? Whether it was her place to help or not was irrelevant. They might not even get another chance to try. Shayne didn't want to be part of their family.

James obviously admired what Shayne had accomplished with his life. She too respected what Shayne had done, and all on his own. But why had he chosen such a dangerous profession? One that put his life at risk on a regular basis. She couldn't forget what his boss had said about Shayne not being afraid to die. The whole concept was completely foreign.

She understood the hostility toward his father. Understood that he'd spent twenty-four loveless years letting it fester. But if he didn't deal with the anger, it was going to destroy him. What Shayne failed to understand was that time wasn't an infinite commodity.

She rubbed the tears trickling down her face. She'd give anything to be able to go back in time and erase the final angry words she'd spoken to her father. She'd rewritten the conversation in her mind, perfected it until she could recite it without thought.

But she'd never get the chance to right that wrong.

* * *

"Why Houston?" Shayne paced in front of his lieutenant's desk. "Send someone else."

Richter didn't waiver. "You're the best man for the job."

"You damn well know why I can't work in Houston," Shayne pointed out.

"And you damn well know why you need to be in Houston." Richter kicked back in his chair. "In seven years, I've never known you to run from anything. You meet every challenge head on."

Shayne braced both hands on the dusty windowsill and stared out at Dallas rush hour traffic. "This is different."

"Kelley, deal with your father, then you'll be better equipped to move on. I need you a hundred percent and what's going on in your life right now would distract anybody."

He turned to glare at his boss. "Since when did you become my shrink?"

Richter set his jaw and crossed his arms.

Shayne took a deep breath, but turned back to stare out the window. James was an annoyance. He wouldn't have to know Shayne was living in the area and even if he found out, Shayne could avoid him for the few months he'd be there.

Dani was a different complication. It pissed him off that he couldn't get her out of his mind. And it scared the hell out of him. Enjoying women was a pastime, no more. As soon as they showed the first sign of developing any sort of attachment, Shayne moved on. The plan had always worked before.

He turned and met Richter's determined black eyes. "You aren't going to budge on this, are you?"

Undercover Heart

* * *

Monday morning, Dani arrived at school primed for her summer challenge. The school district, in conjunction with the Galveston police department, had been almost too jubilant when she'd agreed to tutor a group of troubled teens for six weeks in summer school.

Understandably, none of the other teachers were eager to spend their summer babysitting a bunch of teenagers who resented being stuck in a classroom in the first place. But to Dani, helping kids was the most rewarding aspect of teaching.

These kids were in trouble and needed a little one on one to help them catch up academically. On a more personal level, they just needed to know someone cared.

Dani took a calming breath, put on her most welcoming smile, and stepped into the classroom. She found six students, all occupying the back row of desks in a classroom arranged for thirty kids.

They were older, considerably bigger than her junior high kids. "Good morning."

Belligerent stares. Nobody spoke or made the slightest effort to return her greeting. She reminded herself that this wasn't going to be easy.

"How about if we start out by introducing ourselves?" She kept her smile in place and wrote her name on the board. "I'm really excited to be here. My name is Ms. Cochran and I teach seventh and eighth grade math. I've been teaching in the school district for two years." She nodded toward one of the two girls in the group, a tall, gangly blonde dressed in black from neck to ankle. "Would you like to go next?"

No answer. The girl slumped down in her chair and continued to doodle on the lavender pad in front of her.

"Calvin," the lanky black boy in the corner interjected. "I'll be a senior, if I can get through Algebra, then I'm outta this hell hole."

Before Dani could call Calvin down for language, the younger, white boy next to him jumped in. "You really think you'll graduate? You're dreamin'." He wove the pencil he was holding between his fingers, popped his hand on the desk, and snapped the pencil in half. "We're all stuck here for life."

"Not me. I ain't spending a minute more in this crappy sandbox than I have to. I get that piece of paper in my hand, the judge releases me, and I'm history. I don't need nothing from this island," Calvin said.

The girl snarled her pierced lip. "You don't need a piece of paper to be history, Calvin. We're like freakin' yesterday's news. They spread us out on the floor, the dog takes a crap, and then they throw us out with the garbage. I don't need no more paper for them to shit on."

Dani held up her hand. "It may seem like nobody is there for you, but I wouldn't be here if I didn't care."

"Shut up, Amber. If he wants an education, ain't none of your business." Ignoring Dani, Calvin's Hispanic co-conspirator nailed the blonde with a glare.

"Well I ain't wasting my energy on that crap. Freddie's gonna take care of me as soon as that damn judge releases me."

"Freddie's got to get out of prison first," Calvin said. "And I wouldn't hold my breath. They take statutory rape pretty serious, I hear."

Amber flashed Calvin a go to hell look. "Weren't rape. I was willing. I'll be seventeen in October and then they can't do anything to stop us." As she crossed her legs, Dani noted that the girl had a ring of flowers tattooed around her left ankle.

Undercover Heart

"You're still a minor for another year and he's already in his twenties," the redheaded boy in the center chimed in.

"You think you're an expert on everything, Tad." Amber started digging in her purse, tossing the contents haphazardly on the desk as if she was searching for answers. "Just because your name's always at the top of the honor roll doesn't mean you know shit about the streets."

Tad shrugged. "Don't have to live on the streets to know a tramp when I see one."

Dani clapped her hands. "That's enough!"

Amber added a tampon to the growing pile on her desk. "Just because no girl'll let you in her pants don't mean I'm a tramp because I know how to satisfy my guy."

"Quiet!" Dani interrupted. "This is a classroom and we will respect each other." She picked up a marker and started writing below her name on the dry erase board.

"No vulgarity." She printed the rules clearly in red marker. "Respect each other. Address each other by your given names."

Her hand shook. What had she signed up for? "Do not interrupt when others are speaking." She clicked the top back on the plastic marker and placed it on the rack. "That's a start. Now, if everyone will move to the front."

Groans echoed through the room like a haunted house on Halloween, but nobody moved.

"Would you like me to draw up a seating chart for tomorrow?" She grinned. "I'm lonely up here all by myself."

"That sucks," Calvin replied. "I mean, stinks," he clarified with a toothy, kiss-my-butt smile. Dani figured the tiny diamond stud twinkling in his right ear probably sent out the same belligerent message to every authority figure in his life.

"You could move to the front on your own," she suggested.

Slowly they all gathered their belongings and took seats in the front row.

"Much better. If you'll come up as I call your name, I'll assign everyone the books required for this session."

By noon when the class finally broke for lunch Dani was mentally exhausted and about to drop. Definitely a bigger challenge than she'd expected. The kids ranged in age from fourteen to seventeen. Their educational needs were as varied as their personalities. They all had specific academic goals to accomplish. Except for Tad, the youngest of the group and a straight A student who had just 'checked out' as he put it the last two months of school. Could she handle six weeks of this?

Was Kyle destined to end up like these kids? Was that what Shayne was trying to get across to James?

At least the class only met Monday thru Thursday. She'd still have long weekends to work on fixing up her house. Organizing it would be an outlet to relieve stress if today was any indication. She'd been in it a year and still had a few boxes sitting around. Now she was finally emotionally ready to unpack some of her parents' things from storage. Her bedroom was half painted, but she hadn't even picked colors for the others.

The next day the class showed a slight improvement. Everyone balked, but at least they sat in the front. She gave each student basic skills tests in the areas they were lacking and spent a half hour with each determining where to focus. However after they broke for a forty-five minute lunch, things went downhill. When the counselor arrived for his twice a week session and it was time to resume class, Dani could only locate four students.

Leaving Mr. Smith with the class, she went in search

of Amber and Mario. She'd about decided they'd skipped out when she caught a glimpse of movement down one of the deserted hallways. Silently she headed in that direction. She was almost beside them before she realized they were plastered together between two locker banks.

Mario's back was to her and Amber was the first to notice they had company. She jerked her hand out of the back waistband of Mario's baggy jeans and pushed him away. Mario straightened and Dani saw a flash of Amber's bare midriff before the girl yanked her gray T-shirt back into place.

Mario moved to the side and pulled his shirt together, but not quick enough to hide a large snake tattoo on his shoulder. Amber stepped around him and tucked a strand of dirty blond hair behind her ear. "We were just getting to know each other. You told us to get along."

If Dani let them get away with this she'd never be able to maintain control. But if she reported the incident to their probation officers, they were done for. "I'm going to let this slide, but I will report the next incident, no matter how insignificant."

"You ain't reporting us?" Amber asked.

"I'm not here for sex education," Dani said.

Mario looked sheepish, but Amber gave her a half smile before she ambled off down the hall. "I'm not having any problems in that class anyway."

Dani followed them back to class. She was not impressed with Mr. Smith and neither were the students. The counselor talked down to them as if they were preschoolers. The students chatted while he lectured. They tittered and giggled behind his back. They said anything they could to shock him. Maybe if he'd wear something a little less conservative than a brown suit and tie.

She winced, thinking about how she must have

looked to Shayne the first time they met. Her coordinated slacks and blouse weren't exactly what the kids wore these days.

Wanting to give the counselor a reasonable shot, Dani kept quiet. She listened to the kids avoid Mr. Smith's attempts to draw them out and wondered how to diplomatically get someone with a little more experience with this age group. Who was she fooling? Mr. Smith was probably the only counselor willing to spend his summer with a group of belligerent teens.

Mario glanced across at Calvin and smirked. "Think he wants to hear about how the bed thumps the wall and my mama moans and cries when my step-daddy comes home drunk and drags her to the bedroom?"

Calvin shrugged. "At least you got a home. My foster family walks around like they're afraid they're going to do something to set me off."

Tad sat silently at his desk, his feet stretched out in front of him, and stared at an open novel.

Foster home? Dani hadn't realized Calvin lived in a foster home. She recalled his remark yesterday about not needing anything anybody in this town had to offer. Images of Shayne ran through her mind. It was just wrong the things some kids were subjected to.

Shayne had been one of those kids. After seeing the way he dealt with Kyle, she figured if anyone could get through to Calvin and the other kids, it was Shayne. Not only did he know the law, he could relate to what it was like to feel unwanted and alone.

Dani tried to focus her energy on her class, but Shayne's face kept flashing into her mind. She'd never met anyone who was so incredibly intriguing or who was so impossible to get close to. Still, he was everything but what she was looking for in a relationship. Shayne was wild,

Undercover Heart

calloused and lived like a nomad. If she was smart, she'd forget Shayne Kelley.

Chapter Seven

Shayne grabbed his cell phone, keeping an eye on the guys in the park. He'd been about to join them when the phone rang.

"What? Marijuana? How much did he have?" Lt. Richter's words distracted him and he forgot about what was going down across the parking lot. "No, I'll go. Got a number?"

He hung up, dialed the detective's number, and identified himself. Not that this surprised him, but he'd hoped Kyle had straightened out some. He listened while the guy filled him in. "No, don't pull any punches. Put them through the drill." It was time somebody straightened Kyle out, and his parents were clueless. "Don't hurt them, just scare the hell out of them. I want them in tears. And stall the parents."

Shayne clicked the phone off. What Kyle lacked in judgment, he made up for with balls. Let him simmer in jail for the afternoon and maybe he'd be in the mood to talk by the time Shayne got there.

He pitched the phone into the seat of the Mustang, locked the door, and strolled across the park to join the party. He wasn't in any particular hurry and he might as well see if anything was going to actually happen here before he had to face the Highlands. If Kyle had to squirm an extra hour or two, so much the better.

Undercover Heart

Two hours later when Shayne walked into the Houston police station, James did a double take. First he looked surprised, then changed to confused. "Shayne. What--?"

"Kyle had the officer call me. Said his big brother, the DEA agent, would get him off. Actually threatened the guy."

James stood up, ran his hands down the front of his Dockers, and narrowed one eye. "Kyle knew you were in Houston?"

Shayne nodded. "He overheard Richter talking about a Houston assignment."

Another couple stood up. James massaged his temples with his thumb and forefinger. "This is my son, Shayne. He's with the DEA."

"We're Cody's parents. They won't even let us see him. Can you tell us what's going on?"

Shayne shook the guy's hand. They were all staring at him like they expected him to wave a get-out-of-jail-free wand and solve all their problems. "Let me handle them." Not that the parents had any choice in the matter. The boys were in police custody.

James frowned. "What are you going to do?"

"Scare them a little. Make them consider the consequences."

James shook his head. "I don't like the sound of that. You just get them out and let us take care of our boys. There are some rough characters in here."

"No shit, and these guys are angels compared to the juveniles in reform school," Shayne assured him.

"But they're just kids," James countered.

Shayne met his gaze. "They're kids on a self-destruction kick. If there aren't any consequences, they'll only get worse."

Cody's dad slid one arm around his wife. "I agree. Scare the hell out of Cody."

James reached for Shayne's arm. "Just get him out. I'll take care of it."

Flinching out of James' grasp, Shayne shook his head. "You don't listen to me any better than you listen to Kyle. That kid has problems, and if you don't shut up and figure out what they are, he's going to be so far down the effin' road you'll never be able to straighten him out!"

"I know what's best for my son."

"Do you?" Shayne shook his head in exasperation and stepped back. "Let me see what's going on."

They all sat silently, looking at him like he'd convict Kyle and his pal and toss them in a cell for twenty years. Typical reaction for parents to want to shift the blame away from themselves. Couldn't be their fault that they'd raised juvenile delinquents. Maybe he shouldn't have lost his temper, but it was past time for James to wise up or Kyle was doomed.

Shayne showed his badge at the front desk and went to the break room in search of the officer who'd called. "Are you Terrell?"

The guy stood and extended his hand. "Yeah. Thanks for coming."

Shayne shook his hand. "What's going on?"

"I ran them through the drill." He grinned. "They took offense to being strip searched."

Shayne raised one eyebrow. "They won't forget that for awhile."

Undercover Heart

"We separated them on arrival. They've been handcuffed, fingerprinted, searched, interrogated, and are currently wearing jail issue and sitting in separate cells with the dregs of last night's round up."

"How are they holding up?"

"Cody Dunlap broke easy. No offense, but your brother is an arrogant little punk. He tried the belligerent act and assured me that I was a lowly cop and his big brother, the important DEA agent, would get him out and if I touched him, you'd have my badge."

"And?"

"I touched him. Sorry, but he's an irritating little prick."

Shayne could relate to what Kyle had probably put the guy through. "No kidding. He opens his mouth and I want to plant my fist in it."

"The strip search had him in tears." Terrell smirked. "Probably didn't help when I told him the guys in reform school were going to love his cute little white ass and if they ever found out his brother was a narc, he might as well write it off."

Shayne smiled at how Terrell must have looked from Kyle's perspective. He was black, weighed in at well over two-hundred, and had hands the size of a football player. But he could have been a lot harder on them. "How long have they been in the cells?"

"Not more than a half hour. We're keeping an eye on things."

Shayne glanced at the rap sheet. "Probably the longest half hour of their lives. Mind if I handle them?"

Terrell shook his head. "Be my guest."

"Let's leave Kyle a while longer. Tell him nobody's shown up yet."

Terrell grinned and shuffled off in the general direction of the cells.

Shayne studied the security cameras. Cody was easy to spot. The kid sat huddled on the corner of a bunk, looking scared enough that Shayne figured he wouldn't be back in here any time soon.

Switching to Kyle, he was amazed to find him in almost the same shape.

He had Cody brought to an interrogation room. The boy slinked into the room, glancing behind the door. Shayne was the only one there. Cody's parents sat hidden behind a one-way mirror. Shayne motioned toward a chair. "I'm Shayne Kelley, Kyle's half-brother."

Cody's voice broke. "Are you going to get us out of here? This place gives me the creeps."

Shayne sat down on the edge of the table and studied Cody. He was trembling. "Look, Cody. This is your first offense and that's in your favor. You'll have to go to court. If you behave, you will probably get off with probation and some community service time. This is the easy one. You show up here again, things get nasty."

Cody nodded. "There won't be a next time. This was my first. Kyle said we wouldn't get caught. You have to believe me. I'd never even seen weed before he pulled it out of his pocket. I knew we shouldn't."

"If I were you, I'd trust my own judgment. Guys like Kyle can get you into serious trouble before you realize what hit you. You can do more damage in ten minutes than you can unscramble the rest of your life. You don't want to end up in reform school."

"I just want to go home." Cody didn't even attempt to look tough.

"Your folks are posting bail. Between you and me,

Undercover Heart

they seem like decent people."

Cody wiped his nose on the back of his hand. "They're going to be so pissed."

"What'll they do?"

"Probably ground me for life, or longer."

Cody would be okay. "Just talk to them. They'll understand. You've got some papers to sign and then they'll bring you your clothes. Don't let me see you in here again."

"You won't. I swear."

Shayne saw Cody and his parents off and asked James to come back to the break room. The longer Kyle had to squirm, the better.

James paced back and forth across the scuffed tile floor. "You're wasting time while your little brother is still in that cell."

"Coffee?" Shayne asked, pouring himself a cup.

James started back across the room, shaking his head. "I understand what you're doing, but enough is enough. It's time to get him out."

Shayne propped one hip on the side of the avocado green Formica table and watched Highland pace. "You're making me dizzy. Sit down."

James dropped into a chair. "I know he screwed up, and he will be punished. He's a teenage boy. You know how that is. They have to try their wings. Test their parents. It's typical teenage antics."

"I don't think so."

"I do."

"Then you aren't paying attention. You have to find a

way to communicate."

James gritted his teeth. "He doesn't listen."

"Neither do you." Shayne leaned forward. "Kyle's screaming at the top of his lungs for attention and you're just screaming back. Neither one of you has enough sense to shut up and actually hear what the other one's saying."

"You aren't going to release him until I hear you out, are you?"

Shayne waited silently.

"All right. I'm listening," James said.

Shayne placed the untouched cup of coffee in front of James and walked over to pour another one. "This is more serious than just teenage rebellion."

James took a drink of the coffee, staring into space. "I got a promotion last October which means I have to work out of town most weeks. I haven't been spending enough time with him. I'll plan a weekend, take him out on the gulf fishing."

"One weekend on a boat isn't going to cut it. There's more to this than a kid craving his father's attention."

"Like what? You seem to have all the answers. What do you think I should do?"

Shayne turned a chair around and straddled it. He understood James was upset and that it probably galled him to be forced to listen to advice from him. "I don't know what Kyle's problem is. But this is what he's told me."

James looked up. "What?"

"The other night he said he was tired of being treated like a kid. I suggested he try acting like an adult."

James grinned. "So he doesn't take your advice any better than he does mine. This is not exactly adult behavior."

Undercover Heart

"He wants to grow up, but he doesn't know how. Maybe if you gave him responsibility, let him prove himself."

"He has. He's proven that we can't trust him not to run away. Patty can't sleep because she's afraid he won't be there the next morning. Do you know what that's doing to our family?"

Shayne took a drink of coffee. "He's threatened by me. He thinks I'm trying to move in on his territory."

"That's ridiculous. You're grown. You aren't exactly under foot. You've been to the house once."

"Yeah, well he didn't hop a bus all the way to Dallas just to say hello. He was primed for a fight."

"I hadn't thought about it that way." James closed his eyes and took a deep breath. "I probably have been obsessed lately with finding you." He stared Shayne in the eye. "It took so long and..."

"I suggest you get Kyle talking and concentrate on what he's not telling you. Sometimes people will talk to a counselor when they can't talk to their family."

James stood up. "I'll give it a shot. Can I take him home now?"

"Let me be the bad guy on this one." Shayne nodded toward the door. "You go home."

James held up his hands. "So what happens now? What do we do?"

"I'll have him home tonight." Shayne filled him in on the process. "Get a lawyer. You'll have to go to court with him, but he'll probably get probation and community service. First offense."

Shayne watched Kyle through the security camera as

a drunk stumbled over and flopped down on the lumpy bunk next to him. Kyle moved as far away as he could. The drunk scooted closer causing Kyle to bolt for the front of the ten by ten cell where two younger guys leaned against the bars. Shayne figured the kid had had enough to shake him up and asked the guard to bring him into the interrogation room.

Kyle looked almost as frightened as Cody until he recognized Shayne. Straightening his back, he put on a tough front. "So where were you?" he demanded. "I've been in here, like, forever."

Shayne watched Kyle flop down in the seat across the table from him. It'd only been about three hours. "You aren't my first priority."

"Some brother. What, you leave me to rot in jail while you finish screwing your girlfriend?"

Shayne had decided to let Kyle determine the direction of the conversation. It hadn't taken him long. "Let's dispense with the brotherly shit. Fact one, you've never given me the slightest reason to feel brotherly toward you, or made any attempt to hide your hatred. Fact two, you're under arrest for possession and I'm a D.E.A. agent. If you want me to help you, then first you help me. Who sold you the weed?"

Kyle's mouth dropped open. "What?"

"I want names and addresses, and anything else you know. If, and I repeat, if you cooperate and we catch the dealers, then we might consider a deal. If you don't, then you and I have nothing else to discuss."

Kyle's eyes widened. "Are you serious? Where are Mom and Dad?"

"I sent your dad home. He can't help you out of this. I can, but only if you cooperate."

"They wouldn't just leave me here like this," Kyle

rushed to assure Shayne, or maybe himself.

"Not their call. Names, Kyle."

"I don't know the guy's name."

Shayne looked disgusted, jotted a note on his clipboard, and stood up. "Guard, I'm done here."

"Shayne! Just get me out of here and I'll help," Kyle pleaded.

Shayne stopped at the door, but didn't turn.

"Please."

Hiding a smile, Shayne turned, but didn't bother to sit. "Talk."

Kyle started spilling his guts. The dealer was about ten years older than the kids he supplied and lived in an apartment a few blocks from the school. All the kids knew him. Whatever they wanted, he could get.

Shayne listened to every word. Kyle pressed his legs together like he might wet his pants. His eyes were wide and bloodshot and his knees were knocking.

"I want the apartment number and you'll have to identify him."

Kyle had given up all pretense of acting cool. "No problem. Can we go home?"

Shayne continued to glare. "If we catch this guy, you might get off with probation and community service, but that's only because this is your first offense. You get caught holding again, you'll end up in reform school. And as you get older, the consequences quadruple."

"That other officer explained all that and about reform school. I won't do it again." Kyle pressed his knees together.

"Have you ever done anything harder than

marijuana?" Shayne remained rigid, jotting down notes.

Kyle stared uncomfortably at his disposable shoes. "I only started with grass during Spring Break."

"Who got you started?"

"There's this girl I liked. Her sister gave us some. Everybody does it."

"Was she worth it?"

Kyle shook his head, miserably. "She never put out."

Shayne hid a grin. "Those kind are trouble. They'll talk you into doing things just to see how far you'll go and they seldom deliver."

Kyle nodded his agreement. "She got crazy when I just tried to feel her up. Go figure."

Shayne almost felt sorry for him. It didn't sound like he was having much success in the romance department. "Think the old man'll stand behind you?"

"What do you mean?"

Shayne figured he could use the past to his advantage. It had to be worth something. "When the going got a little tough, he sold me down the river. If I'd have gotten into a jam, he sure as hell wouldn't have been there for me."

"He'll help, if he can." Kyle hesitated. "Don't you think?"

Shayne raised his eyebrows. "Beats me. I hardly know the guy. I'll get your clothes and then you're going to show me where this dealer lives."

The kid was virtually dancing when he stood up. Shayne started to suggest he stop by the restroom, but decided a little discomfort could work in his favor.

Undercover Heart

"Just get me out of here."

Kyle was quiet on the drive home. They cruised by the apartment building and Kyle pointed out the guy's truck. As they were pulling away, he had Shayne slow down. "That's him over by the dumpster. See the guy in the blue and white striped shirt?"

Shayne pulled out his phone and took a picture of the license plate and the guy. "Maybe we can keep some other kids from going through this."

Kyle squirmed in the seat. "Can we go home now? I need to take a piss."

"Why didn't you go before we left?"

"In there? No way." Kyle shook his head. "Those guys are weird."

"You piss in my car and you're dead." Shayne covered the couple of blocks to the Highlands. Kyle bolted out of the car and into the house. He didn't even stop to speak in his rush.

James stared at Shayne for an explanation. "What's wrong with him?"

"Afraid to drop his pants for the past four hours," Shayne whispered.

"Is he all right?" Patty looked from Shayne to James.

James hugged her. "He will be."

Shayne filled them in on what had gone down and tried to ignore Dani standing beside her sister.

"Do you think he learned anything from this?" James asked.

"Who knows? He was pretty freaked. I wouldn't downplay it. It's serious. I probably made it sound worse than it is."

James extended his hand. "Shayne, thanks. I am going to try and listen to him."

Shayne gripped his hand. "He'll push your buttons."

"I know."

Shayne started toward the door. "I've got to get going. I left some things unfinished."

"How can I get in touch with you?" James asked.

"Call the police station. They seem to be pretty good at tracking me down."

Dani followed him out to the Mustang. "Thanks for helping Kyle."

"Doing my job."

She stepped in front of the car door. "I'm impressed with the way you handled Kyle and Cody, which is why I need to ask you a favor. I'm teaching a special detention class."

Shayne closed his eyes. He did not like the sound of the word detention. "What the hell's that?"

"It's six kids who've had a little trouble and need to catch up on their studies and get back on track."

"Trouble with the law?"

She nodded. "It could really help if you'd talk to them. We meet at Galveston High. Counseling sessions are Tuesday and Thursday afternoons, if you have any free time."

"What I've got to say, they don't want to hear."

"But they need to," Dani coaxed.

Shayne shook his head. "Call a DARE officer. They'll send a counselor."

Undercover Heart

She grimaced. "The counselor who's been assigned talks to them like first graders. They make fun of him and he's doing more harm than good."

"Report him. Get him replaced." He let his gaze make a quick trip from her pretty, pixie face, down to her shoes and back up again. "You have no business dealing with six juvenile delinquents. They need someone older, less attractive, and preferably male."

"I knew you could be a hard ass, but didn't take you for a sexist!" she snapped. "Never mind. It's not your problem." She spun toward the house.

He grabbed her arm. "Let me guess. You think you can love their problems away?" He shook his head, released her arm, and glanced at his car door. "You know what, you're right. It's not my problem if you want to risk your life with a bunch of juvenile delinquents."

She leaned against the car door, preventing his escape. "You always have to have the last word, you couldn't let me storm off."

"I make a point not to waste my time arguing with people bent on making stupid mistakes."

"I am going to help these kids." Her pretty little jaw jutted out. "You could make a difference in their lives and you know it. Take Calvin for instance. He's in a foster home and feels like nobody cares."

"Nobody does!"

"Wrong!" Dani's dark eyes snapped. "I care."

"Maybe you should focus on your own safety before you get hurt. You can't save the world, Dani."

She stepped closer. "We have to try."

Shayne closed his eyes and his nostrils filled with the scent of peaches. He opened them and almost drowned in her warm brown orbs. The tip of her tongue moistened her lips and he tried not to think about how incredibly sexy that one innocent gesture was. "Cut to the chase. What do you want from me?"

"I want you to be honest about your feelings. Why do you keep glancing at your car like it's a lifeline? You aren't running from your father, or Kyle, or the family. You handle them like you'd handle your job. Why do I make you so nervous?"

He gulped then slid a hand down her cheek. "I'm not a relationship guy, Dani. And you aren't a one-night stand sort of girl."

She covered his hand and held it against her face. "I think the attraction between us is too strong to just walk away. I think we owe it to ourselves to see where it leads."

He was drowning in those incredible brown eyes. "And I think you are way too innocent for your own good."

She leaned forward and covered his lips, her mouth warm and inviting. Her breasts pressed against his chest. "I'm not nearly as innocent as you think."

He gripped her shoulders and set her away. "Find someone else, Dani."

Undercover Heart

Chapter Eight

"Mario, your seat is over there," Dani said.

Mario slid his book off the desk, exchanged glances with Calvin, and dragged his feet across the room to his seat.

By Wednesday the kids were beginning to ease into Dani's routine. She couldn't allow Calvin and Mario, buddies and the oldest kids in the class, to sit together or she'd never maintain control.

Dani walked around the room giving individual assignments and trying to help each student when they had problems. Since they were in various grades and working on different subjects, there was no formal lecture.

She smiled at Amber and handed back the assignment she'd completed the day before. "Nice job."

Since she hadn't heard a word from Shayne since he'd left the Highlands' house two days earlier, Dani decided to give Mr. Smith one more session before voicing her concerns. Maybe the kids were just testing him and making him nervous. She could relate to that. However, Thursday's session was even worse than Tuesday's. Calvin, Mario, and Amber seemed to have devised a contest to see who could make the man blush.

Calvin was in the lead for the afternoon. "Yeah, if my old man knew how to keep it in his pants that damn ho wouldn't have yelled rape, he wouldn't be serving five years, and I wouldn't be hanging with an uptight foster family."

"Okay, Calvin. Thanks for sharing." Dani stepped to the front of the class, reluctantly jumping in to rescue Mr. Smith. "Maybe we could focus on the future."

In all fairness, the counselor might have been able to handle a normal class. He reminded Dani of a Sunday school teacher she'd had as a child.

Each week she was required to brief the probation officer who'd been assigned to keep four of her six students under control. Officer Monroe was supposed to stop by for the last half hour of class, but he was running late and poked his head in just as Mr. Smith left. The kids picked up their books and started toward the door.

Calvin pasted an obviously fake smile on his face as he passed. "Nice to see you, sir. See you tomorrow, Ms. Cochran."

Dani had to admire the kid's guts.

Amber flashed a seductive grin at the probation officer and sauntered out the door as if she were the star of a Broadway play, exiting a stage.

Dani acknowledged Officer Monroe, but waited for the kids to leave before initiating a conversation.

"You look like you have something on your mind," Officer Monroe said as soon as all the students were out of earshot.

Dani erased the board, except for her class rules. "The studies are going okay. Maybe a little slower than I'd like, but this is the first week." She took a deep breath and turned to face him. "I don't think the counseling sessions are helping. The man talks to them in this monotone voice like they're little kids. He says things like, 'What do you think your parents would say about that? Do they approve of your language?' Every single one of them is laughing at him."

Undercover Heart

"He's all we've got."

"What if you talked to them? Took a little tougher approach?" she suggested.

Monroe shrugged. "I'm not a counselor. Frankly, I doubt anybody could do much for them anyway. You do what you can, but kids like these just go from bad to worse."

She flattened both hands on her desk. "They certainly don't have a chance if people give up on them."

"You're absolutely right." He rubbed his eyes. Do you have a better idea?"

Dani shoved her papers into her satchel. She knew when she was being placated. "I've asked a friend of mine to come talk to them. He's a DEA agent who works undercover with high school and college kids. He hasn't agreed yet, but we'll see."

"Have you mentioned the idea to Mr. Smith?"

"I broached the subject during break. He wasn't exactly enthusiastic."

"I'm sure he wasn't. Still, I have no objection if your friend wants to talk to them."

"Good." Dani ended the conversation. She knew police departments and probation officers were spread thin and had more important things to do than counsel her little class twice a week, but if somebody didn't take an interest, these kids were lost.

As she drove home, she couldn't quit thinking about how much Shayne had to offer, especially for Calvin. She opened the sunroof on her yellow VW beetle and wondered if there was a chance Shayne might actually show up. Very slight, if any. Still, if he expected her to come begging, then he was going to be disappointed.

She was still worried when she pulled into the carport

of her white frame beach house. She looked out at the sunbathers basking in the afternoon sun and grinned. Taking a deep breath of salt air, she willed all the nagging thoughts away. After almost a year of living on the beach, she still couldn't believe the little stilt house actually belonged to her. Or it would in twenty-nine years.

There had to be a way she could get through to the class. She just had to keep thinking. Retrieving her satchel full of papers to grade, she headed up the stairs. She hit the top step of her balcony and noted the back door was wide open. Who was here today? She inhaled the scent of fried chicken. Had to be Pearl, bless her heart.

Her elderly neighbor turned from the stove as Dani came through the door. "I figured you could use some good home cooking after a day in the classroom."

Dani kicked her shoes off, dropped her satchel on top of two plastic bins stacked in the corner, and inhaled, grinning at Pearl. "Tell me you dropped by to adopt me."

"Women have to take care of each other. Men sure aren't much good at it." Pearl dusted flour off the front of her bright floral blouse and tugged her shirttail over her ample hips.

Dani scooped one finger in the bowl of mashed potatoes and licked her finger. "You're not fooling me. You hate to cook for one."

A wistful look crossed the older woman's tanned, sun-aged face. "You'd think after three years, I'd be used to it."

"I know." Dani gave her a hug. "But I'm sure not complaining about the company." She washed her hands, and squeezed by Pearl in the narrow galley kitchen to grab two plates from the cabinet. "Not going to be able to keep the house open much longer. It hit ninety-four today, but I am so dreading turning on the air conditioner."

Pearl stopped what she was doing, looked out the

kitchen window, and inhaled. "You enjoy the sounds and smell of the sea like I do. That's why Buster and I retired down here."

Dani stepped beside her and glanced out at the beach, watching two guys tossing a football. "Listen to the gulls. You don't hear that with the windows closed."

Pearl nodded. She placed a platter of fried chicken on the table, followed by the bowl of mashed potatoes and another of fresh green beans. "Let me get the rolls and dinner is served."

Shayne walked into the off-campus pool hall and scanned the crowd for his mark. He spotted him sitting at a small table in the back of the room, hitting on a little blonde. The girl blushed as the guy led her onto the dance floor and rubbed against her chest. He wondered if she'd even guessed that in addition to sex, this guy wanted to land a new customer. The sad thing was that he'd probably succeed with both before she realized he was trouble.

Every time Shayne looked at the kids he was working, he thought about what Dani was doing. A young, pretty female trying to control oversexed juvenile delinquents. She had no business teaching that class. You'd think if she was too damn naïve to understand the risk, the school board or somebody would have enough sense to put someone older in the job.

He watched the scumbag run his hand up the girl's blouse as she smiled up into his face like he was some hero. Were all women that blind?

He shook his head. Dani was an adult. Protecting her wasn't his responsibility. So why was he seeing her when he looked at this girl?

* * *

Tuesday when Mr. Smith arrived for the afternoon session, he glanced around the room then cocked an arrogant salt and pepper eyebrow at Dani. "No big, important DEA agent here to solve everybody's problems?"

She bit her tongue and managed not to frown. "Evidently not." She should never have mentioned the possibility to him.

Mr. Smith placed his neat, leather briefcase on the desk and nodded to the class. Everything about the man from his tidy navy blue suit to his powder blue shirt looked uptight. "Are we ready to contribute to the conversation today?"

Tad snapped another pencil into two pieces. Amber reached for her purse and started digging. Even Tung and Beth, her two quiet students, joined in the chorus of groans.

Calvin rolled his eyes. "Who the f--, hell cares? I'm sure you have enough to say for all of us. Why don't you let us slip on out for the afternoon and you can talk to yourself?"

Mario stood and high-fived Calvin. "We get the afternoon off and he can give himself a lecture. Works for me."

"Now, we're not going to have any of that language today, are we?"

Amber mouthed something to the guys and all three burst out laughing.

Tad flipped the book on his desk closed with a resounding clap and glared at Mr. Smith. "Well, gee, you're already limiting the conversation. Last time you said you wanted us to feel free to say what was on our minds."

Mr. Smith cleared his throat, but before he could answer, Calvin piped in. "He wants us to talk. We're just supposed to hold off until he passes out the scripts."

"Class," Mr. Smith said.

Undercover Heart

    Amber put one psychedelic blue fingernail in her mouth. It matched the blue rhinestone lip piercing. "Gee, Mr. Smith. Weez just dumb kids. We don't know how to talk without them kinds of words."

    "Wait till he changes into his slippers and slips into his yellow cardigan," Tad interjected. "That always helped Mr. Rogers get a handle on the day."

    "Yeah, well this neighborhood is all out of beautiful days." Amber tossed her blonde hair back, folded up a stick of gum, stuck out her tongue, and evocatively rolled the gum into her mouth.

    Too bad these kids didn't put some of that sharp witted brainpower to a more positive use. Out of six students, she had two introverts and four extroverts. The same kids entertained every day while the other two hardly uttered a whisper.

    "Class!" Mr. Smith took a deep breath and crossed his arms.

    Mario leveled his pointed stare on Mr. Smith. "It's a beautiful enough day. The company just sucks."

    "Come on, Mario. Don't you want to lay all your sordid little problems out for Mr. Rogers?" Calvin sneered.

    Amber suddenly sat up straight in her chair, swallowed her gum, and flashed a seductive grin toward the door. Dani turned and found Shayne leaning against the door jamb. How long had he been standing there? From the scowl on his face, long enough to realize the class was out of control.

    Mr. Smith had noticed him too. He squared his shoulders and straightened his already straight jacket. "Well, who have we here?"

    Dani stepped up beside Mr. Smith, edging her way into the center of the room. "I'd like to introduce our guest.

Agent Kelley is an agent with the DEA and he's agreed to talk to us today."

Calvin looked Shayne up and down. "He doesn't look like a narc."

"No shit!" Amber agreed, her big brown eyes feasting on Shayne like a stray dog stalking the corner butcher shop.

Shayne walked across to stand beside Dani. "Some cops don't look like cops." He slowly appraised the students. "Could be one of the students in this room is an undercover officer."

All six students glanced at their classmates as if considering the possibility.

Mario stretched his legs out in front of him and adjusted his hips in the wooden chair. "Kids ain't cops."

Mr. Smith moved to the corner of the room, took a stance, and watched Shayne as if he was just waiting for him to screw up. Dani sat in her chair and gave Shayne the floor.

He took off his sunglasses and pushed his hair back out of his eyes. "You're not sure, are you? I'd be willing to bet, every time you go out in a crowd you pass at least one undercover officer."

"I could smell him," Calvin answered.

Shayne leaned against the desk and crossed his ankles. God, he looked good dressed in faded jeans, sneakers, and a black T-shirt. Dani couldn't decide whether she was more mesmerized by his appearance or how he'd captured the kids' attention.

He focused on Calvin. "What'd you get busted for?"

"Truancy and possession," Calvin answered.

"And did the officer who arrested you have on a uniform?"

Undercover Heart

"No, but I knew he was a cop."

Shayne tilted his head. "Then why'd you get caught?"

Mario wadded up a piece of paper and squeezed like it was someone's neck. "Because the son of a bitch set us up. We were just sitting on the beach, minding our own business. He said he had some good stuff."

"And you bought it?"

Calvin looked out the window. "Mario bought it. I just tagged along."

"Let me get this straight. You knew this guy was a cop and you just tagged along with your friend so you could both get busted?" Shayne asked.

Mario and Calvin exchanged glances and Calvin shrugged.

"Somebody's always watching," Shayne said.

"You can watch me any time," Amber offered, drawing Shayne's attention.

Dani studied Shayne, wondering how he would handle Amber. The girl craved attention from every male in the room, well, except Mr. Smith. She'd dismissed him as a nonperson.

Shayne didn't blink an eye. "You in for drugs too?"

She shook her head and flipped her hair over her right shoulder. "My boyfriend got nabbed for statutory rape and some other stuff. We had a little blow. Now, my stupid probation officer says I have to stay in school and keep my grades up or they'll throw me in juvie. But, they can't do that."

Mario scoffed. "Sure they can. They're the effing pigs. They can do anything they damn well want to."

"He's right. And a word to the wise, you might want to

cut the crap and stay on their good side," Shayne suggested. "Some of us get our kicks out of making your life miserable just because we don't like the slogan on the front of your shirt."

Amber folded her arms across the hot pink words, 'I really am that good!' on the front of her black, skin tight shirt and slumped down in her chair.

Dani didn't understand why Shayne was so determined to put them on edge. There needed to be a balance. Yes, they needed to wise up, but also know they could trust adults and the police.

"You aren't old enough to be a cop," Tad commented.

Shayne grinned. "How old do you think I am?"

"Pretty old. Twenty-one," Amber guessed.

"Nineteen maybe," Mario said.

Calvin shook his head. "I'd know you were too old to be in high school."

"Wouldn't matter to me, even if I knew you were a cop," Amber straightened and flashed a smile that was too hard for her sixteen years. "Want to demonstrate how to do a full body search? I'll be your subject."

"I could call your probation officer and arrange for one, if you'd like," Shayne offered.

"So how old are you?"

"Old enough." Shayne ignored the question and turned to Tad. "How about you? Why are you here?"

Tad straightened the two books on his desk. "Just got bored with school. Who needs this shit? I could pass my GED tomorrow. I'm going to join the Air Force when I turn eighteen anyway."

"Then you need this shit." Shayne paced across the

front of the room. "Do you know that today, the Army is the only branch of the military that will accept a GED? All the others require a diploma. They all require drug tests. Usually involves a background check. Might want to rethink your plan."

Amber stuck out her chest and graced Tad with a smile. "I just love a man in uniform."

Calvin stretched his long legs out in front of him. "Girls like you just want to get laid. You don't love anybody."

Dani saw Shayne's eyebrow rise, but he let the comment pass. Instead, he turned to Calvin. "So, do you want to share your plan for the rest of your life?"

"Get the hell off this sandbox."

"Then what?" Shayne asked. "Gotta be somewhere."

Calvin studied his sneakers. "Then I'll see what happens. One of my friends will put me up and help me find a job or something."

"You're never going to make it just waiting to see what happens or relying on friends. Take care of yourself. Nobody else has any skin in the game. Nobody else gives a shit." Shayne stood back and surveyed all six students. "Here's your thought for the day. Only one person is with you from birth to death. Yourself. Don't expect anybody to solve your problems or be there to bail you out. You make choices, good or bad, and you're the one who lives with the consequences. Not your parents. Not your friends. Not your teachers."

Dani bristled. These kids needed to know that adults cared. They needed to know they weren't in this alone and that there were adults out there they could count on, people willing to help. They already felt rejected, alone, and let down. How could Shayne tell them nobody would be there for them? For some reason her eyes were drawn to Beth, the shy girl who always stayed to herself. "I think what

Special Agent Kelley is trying to say is that it all starts with you. You make good choices and parents and teachers will help see that you get what you need to succeed."

Shayne narrowed one eye at her and turned back to the students. "Make your own choices. I'll see you around."

"Are you coming back?" Tad asked.

Dani watched Shayne's face. She was wondering the same thing. However, if he did agree to come back, she had a few things to get straight with him first.

Shayne shrugged. "Would you like me to?"

"Sure, you're a lot better than Mr. Smith," Mario pointed out.

"Ditto on that," Calvin agreed.

Amber dropped her purse back on the floor and smirked at the older counselor. "Obviously."

Tung, the Vietnamese boy in the corner, looked Shayne up and down, but didn't comment.

Beth didn't look like she cared one way or the other. Dani wondered what such a quiet girl could have done to end up on probation.

Dani got to her feet and moved in front of the desk. "Agent Kelley, thank you for taking time out of your busy schedule to talk to us. Hopefully you can come back again, if it's convenient."

He turned to her but didn't respond.

She smiled at the class. "Good job today. Class dismissed. See everyone tomorrow." She turned to Shayne. "Agent Kelley, do you have a minute?"

Undercover Heart

Chapter Nine

Shayne put his sunglasses on and waited by the door while the six students filed out and Dani stacked her papers neatly. He wasn't thrilled with being held after class.

Mr. Smith picked up his briefcase and narrowed his eyes at both Dani and Shayne. "Ms. Cochran, I presume you'll let me know whether my services will be needed going forward." With that he marched stoically past Shayne and out the door.

Dani slipped the papers into her satchel and snapped it closed. "Today I finally saw a chink in their armor. You made an impression." She picked up the satchel and stopped beside him, flashing him a glare. "But we have a small difference of methodology."

He felt his jaw stiffen. "You asked me to help."

"Yes, but not to tell them that nobody cared. What kind of message is that to send out? I don't want them to think they're out there alone."

"They are."

"No, they're not. There are teachers and parents who care about them. Probation Officer Monroe might help."

"If there are so many people just lining up to help, why'd you track me down?" He looked around the empty room. "Why am I here?"

"You're here to help educate and lead them. You

speak their language."

"You didn't specify any rules. The best lesson I can offer is to teach them to help themselves. I'll be damned if I'll tell them the world loves them and all they have to do is reach out and be surrounded by supportive adults. That's bullshit and the sooner they understand that, the better chance they'll have."

Dani's eyes flashed and she stretched to her full height and stared him down. "People care."

"Bull—shit!" Shayne pulled his sunglasses off.

Her shoulders went back and her mouth became a thin line. "Maybe I was wrong. I don't think you're the best person to help them."

Shayne gripped the door jam. How could a grown woman be this naïve? "Fine. Coddle them and assure them how much everybody cares. Be sure to send flowers to their funerals." He turned and started down the hall.

"If that's the way you feel, then don't come back!"

Shayne stopped and turned. Dani stood in the center of the hall like a lioness fighting for her cubs. Her velvet brown eyes glistened in challenge. She was amazing. Misplaced or not, those kids weren't worthy of her passion.

He turned and stormed down the hall. He slapped his palms against the glass door and stalked out of the school.

Shayne revved the engine on the car and told himself to calm down. He didn't listen. Nobody but Dani would think a hug and a little personal attention could solve these type problems. He slammed the car into first and pulled out of the lot. These kids were going to roll over Dani like a fleet of Mack trucks. But she couldn't see it. She had some storybook scene in her mind of them all joining hands in a circle around a campfire and singing 'Kum Ba Yah'.

He gritted his teeth, grabbed his cell phone, and

dialed his lieutenant. "I need a favor."

* * *

Dani scrubbed her house until there wasn't a grain of sand, but she was still furious. She tried to unpack and organize, but couldn't concentrate. Opening the top on a box of her mother's dishes, she peeked inside and sucked in a breath. It still didn't seem real that her parents were never coming back. They'd never see her little house. They hadn't even gotten to see her walk across the stage at graduation. Of course, Patty and James had been there, but it wasn't the same. There was this huge emptiness in her heart.

She took out a bright blue onyx bowl and set it in the center of the coffee table. Maybe if she had more of her mother's things around it would be like having a part of them here. She trailed one finger around the rim of the bowl. Her dad had bought it one weekend when the family made a trip to Nuevo Laredo. It used to sit on the end of the breakfast bar and her parents pitched restaurant matchbooks in it. Strange habit since neither of them smoked.

What would it have been like growing up with no parents? Did Shayne really believe what he'd told the class? Surely along the way at least a few people had helped him out, been there for him.

She closed the lid on the box. So what if she didn't finish unpacking this weekend? Another few days wouldn't make much difference. The goal was to have the house organized and clean by the end of summer. No more boxes.

She grabbed her satchel off the top of two plastic bins stacked next to the front door and pulled out the folder of homework she needed to grade for Monday. These kids mattered more than some boxes piled in the corner. Besides, without the boxes, what would she set her satchel on?

Might as well grade Tad's algebra paper first. Perfect

score, as expected. The kid was so bright. Why had he decided to stop going to class at the end of last semester? She didn't know much about any of the kids other than they were on probation and catching up with schoolwork was part of the deal.

For their junior composition, she'd had both Amber and Mario write a theme on where they saw themselves in five years.

Amber's paper was one endless, five page paragraph. All the sentences ran together, with minimal punctuation, and every other word misspelled. The sixteen-year old saw herself in California living with some older guy named Freddie. She planned to dance in whatever club Freddie found a job bartending. The tips would be 'fenomenul' if they'd let her wear the leopard demi bra and thong Freddie had bought her.

Dani wondered if she'd added that tidbit for shock value. No kids in this girl's future. She wanted to be Freddie's baby. And he'd take care of her and buy her sexy clothes and a red convertible. Dani crossed her arms, pushed back from the table, and sighed.

Mario took a more serious approach. His paper was surprisingly well written. He aspired to be an artist and live in Greenwich Village or maybe San Francisco. He'd have his own flat where nobody bothered him. He saw himself painting pictures of nude starlets. Dani grinned. Typical fantasy for a sixteen-year old male. She wondered if he had any talent.

Beth had turned in a book report on Little Women. The paper reflected perfect grammar and a natural talent for writing, even though she didn't show much enthusiasm for the subject matter. Dani wasn't sure what to do to draw the girl out. She and Amber were in the same grade, but they never exchanged words, not to say hello, argue, or even discuss the class. Dani wondered if it was because Amber was white and Beth black, but Amber seemed perfectly at

Undercover Heart

ease with Mario and Calvin who were both minorities. Beth didn't socialize with anyone.

* * *

Monday morning Dani found Officer Monroe waiting by her classroom door. Seemed like a strange time for him to visit when the kids weren't due to arrive for another half hour.

He smiled as she approached. "Good morning."

Dani shifted her satchel to the other arm and slipped her key into the lock. "What're you doing here so early? Is there a problem?"

"No, not a problem. Just a change in agenda."

"What sort of change?" She flipped on the light and placed her satchel on the desk.

"I had a visit Thursday afternoon from your friend, the DEA agent."

Dani spun around to face him. "Shayne Kelley?"

He nodded. "Special Agent Kelley said you had a productive session. He made some interesting points."

This didn't sound good. Shayne had no business going to Officer Monroe without her consent. "Like?"

His gaze scanned the rules she'd printed on the side board. "I'm concerned about your safety."

"My safety? I'm in a public school and there are other summer classes going on at the same time. I don't see a safety issue."

"I do." He looked her straight in the eye. "Agent Kelley will be replacing Mr. Smith for the Tuesday and Thursday afternoon counseling sessions."

"No!" Dani closed her eyes and forced her voice to

calm down. "What if I disagree with your decision?"

"Well, if you're not happy with the change, I can talk to the school board and suggest someone else take over the class."

"You can't do that two weeks into the summer session." Dani was furious that Officer Monroe and Shayne had seen fit to make this kind of decision without even consulting her. "I do not agree with Agent Kelley's methodology."

"He suggested that you might have some reservations about his involvement." Officer Monroe shrugged. "But I am concerned for your safety. The agent's presence twice a week will help remind the kids to watch their step."

Dani gripped the edge of her desk. "So I have two choices. Either work with Shayne the rest of the summer or let someone else step in and take over the class? I'm not giving up on these kids."

Officer Monroe grinned. "I'm sure you and Agent Kelley can work something out."

* * *

Dani watched her students at lunch Tuesday and silently rehearsed her speech for Shayne's arrival. She was still trying to figure out why he was willing to drive an hour each direction, twice a week to fill in as counselor. Still, she had a couple of things to get straight before letting him talk to the class again.

Tung and Beth had remained frustratingly quiet all morning. Even the other four seemed to have calmed down slightly over the weekend and were adjusting to the class routine.

She watched Tung in the lunchroom talking to a couple of younger boys from one of the other classes. She didn't like the looks of the meeting, but couldn't put her finger

Undercover Heart

on why. Beth sat alone and silently nibbled a sandwich, while Calvin, Mario, Amber, and Tad cut up and laughed at the next table. They weren't a great influence, but she'd feel better if Beth was laughing with them rather than sitting by herself. The girl even walked behind the other students on the way back to the classroom.

Since Tuesday and Thursday were cut short academically by the counseling, Dani took up the papers and gave everyone a short homework assignment.

She saw Shayne at the door and turned to the class. "Everyone get the books you'll need for your homework together so you don't forget. I'll be right back."

Shayne waited at the door, wondering what Dani was going to say. No doubt she wasn't happy with him going over her head. He looked her up and down, enjoying the way her black slacks cupped her ass before she turned toward the door.

The slacks were nice, but her blouse made him dizzy. Bright primary colors swirled across a black background. She'd even used a neon blue scarf to tie her hair back.

He kept quiet and waited for her to make the first move.

She led the way out into the hall and closed the door behind her. "You had no business going to Officer Monroe behind my back."

He shrugged. "I had as much business doing what I did as you do teaching this class."

Those warm brown eyes glowed with fire. "No, you did not. This is my job, not yours."

"It is now. I've been officially assigned."

Her eyes closed and she flexed her fingers and took a

couple deep breaths. "Okay, here are the rules. Tough love is one thing, but you will not tell them that nobody cares and undo what I'm working to accomplish. We'll talk after class."

She turned, opened the door, and led the way back into the classroom. "Special Agent Kelley has replaced Mr. Smith, so everyone please give him your undivided attention."

Shayne took a stance beside her desk.

"All right!" Amber gushed. "What are we going to talk about today?"

He glanced from one face to the other. "That's up to you. What would you like to talk about?"

Mario flipped a book closed and dropped it into the metal rack beneath his desk with a clang. "Do you really give a shit or are you just here because of a paycheck?"

Shayne thought about Dani's rule. "That depends. If you really want to pull yourself out and put all this behind you, I can help. If you don't, I become your worst enemy."

Calvin crossed one ankle over the other. "You think we're all habitual criminals."

"Jury's still out. You could go either way."

Amber pulled a strand of blonde hair over her shoulder and twisted it. "I ain't done anything criminal."

Shayne considered her rap sheet. She was sixteen years old and had been taken into custody with a twenty-three year old male when he held up a local convenience store at gunpoint. "Want to talk about Freddie Smith?"

She sat up straight and glared. "You yanked my jacket."

He leaned back against the desk and gave that little piece of information time to sink in with everyone. Tung didn't blink an eye. Tad looked out the window. Beth stared at her desk.

Dani snapped her mouth closed and studied him.

Calvin exchanged a worried glance with Mario and set his jaw. "You can't talk about all that in here."

"Sure I can, you've already been convicted. Public record. Anybody who's interested can read it. Colleges, military, potential employers."

"So we're screwed?" Mario asked.

"This is one time that being under age pays off. They seal juvenile records after seven years. That's not the case with adults."

"So all we have to do is keep our record clean for seven years and we're home free?" Amber asked.

"Think you can pull that off?" Shayne asked.

Mario didn't wait for Amber to answer. "You don't know shit about what we're up against here. How the hell are we supposed to survive?"

"My message is the same as before. Always boils down to the choices *you* make and the consequences."

"I don't choose for my old man to beat the shit out of me," Mario growled.

"No, but you choose how to handle it."

"I'm not responsible for him being a terminal alcoholic asshole. There's no choice I can make to change that."

"His choice is to be a terminal alcoholic asshole and he lives with the consequences. But you can't blame him if you stay and let it keep happening. You can't even blame him if you decide to kill the terminal alcoholic asshole."

"So where does my choice come into play? I didn't

ask to be born to him."

"You look at your options, weigh the consequences, good and bad, and make your best choice. Stay or leave? Put up with it or turn him into the authorities."

Dani stepped up beside Shayne. "See, there are always people there if you just reach out for help. All you have to do is ask."

Two hours later, Shayne stood to the side while Dani dismissed the class. He'd been about as tame as he knew how to be today. If she had a problem with his approach, they were in for a rough summer.

The last kid walked out and Dani started loading her satchel with papers. "If we're going to make this work and do what's best for the kids, we need to be in sync."

He raised one eyebrow. "What do you have in mind?"

He wasn't sure why he accepted Dani's invitation, other than the obvious, that he wanted to see how she lived. Was she as reckless in her personal life as she was in her professional world?

He followed her yellow Volkswagen a couple miles down Seawall Boulevard, past where the actual seawall ended, until she made a left down a sandy road into a community of beach houses. She pulled her little car in under a small weathered stilt house. He parked behind her and looked out at the water. Could be a pretty cool place to live until a hurricane decided to blow this direction.

Crawling out of the car, he glanced up at the white house with weathered green shutters. A flock of seagulls squawked overhead. "Do you own this place or rent?" he asked as Dani bumped the door to the VW shut with her hip.

"Well, me and the mortgage company own it." Dani grabbed her school stuff. "Come on up."

Undercover Heart

He dodged as two boys darted by, tossing a Frisbee.

"Hey, Dani!" one yelled.

She dropped her purse and caught the flying purple disk just before it careened into the side of her head. "Watch where you're tossing that thing." She sailed it back to the smaller of the two.

Shayne nearly tripped over a calico cat and followed Dani up the stairs onto a large, crowded deck. He stopped. The back door to the house was standing wide open, except for the screen.

Before he could reach for his gun and grab her, Dani swung the screen open and stepped inside.

Chapter Ten

A little red headed girl sat cross legged in front of the TV and a lady with the same shade ponytail was busy folding laundry on the couch.

Shayne sucked air into his lungs and waited for his heart to start beating again. How the hell did this lady get in when Dani wasn't even home?

He didn't want to know.

"My washer flooded the kitchen again and Phil says we can't afford to fix it until payday. Hope you don't mind," the woman explained.

Dani ruffled the child's hair and grinned at the woman. "No problem. Shayne, this is my friend Felicia and her daughter Chastity."

"Oh." For the first time Felicia actually turned from her laundry. She looked up at Shayne and started piling the stacks of clothes into her basket at lightning speed. "I didn't realize you had company. I'll be out of your way in a minute. I can come back for the last load later, tomorrow even. Chastity, pick up your dolls and turn off Ms. Dani's TV."

"No rush."

"I don't want to interrupt." Felicia propped the bright pink laundry basket on one hip, piled her daughter's dolls on top, and bolted for the door.

As Felicia made her hasty exit, the calico cat slipped

through the door and strolled nonchalantly toward the kitchen.

Was it Shayne's presence that made the redhead so nervous or was she just being polite?

Dani dropped her satchel on the overstuffed sofa and her purse on the matching yellow chair. The house seemed pleasant and relaxed, much like Dani. Sort of a hodgepodge of styles all held together by plastic storage bins.

Shayne stuffed his hands in his pockets and tried to get control. He probably didn't make the redhead half as nervous as being alone with Dani made him.

The mouth-watering smell of roasting beef wafted out of the narrow galley kitchen. Glossy magazines and a blue bowl filled with bright paint samples littered a glass coffee table. There was a stack of boxes in the back corner behind a butcher block table and chairs. Everything was just jumbled enough that the house seemed comfortable, homey.

But if Felicia could just walk in any time, what was stopping a less welcome guest? "How many people have keys to your house?"

Dani grabbed a bright yellow bag of cat food and headed toward the door with the cat rubbing between her ankles. "Only Patty."

"So how did Felicia get in?" He dreaded the answer even before she opened her mouth.

He heard pellets hitting a metal bowl on the deck, then Dani came back inside. She flashed him a look that said, 'duh!'

"Please tell me you don't leave your doors unlocked."

"Of course not." She brushed past to deposit the cat food bag under the kitchen counter.

He followed her into the kitchen. "So how did they get

in?"

Her eyes widened innocently. "She probably used the key I keep--" She paused. "Oops, if I told you, then you'd know how to get in too."

"That has got to be the dumbest, most irresponsible, lame brained—"

"Don't call me stupid." She turned and crossed her arms, her mouth set in a mutinous line. "Your cop radar is working over-time. I know my neighbors."

"Lady!" Shayne's stomach growled and he remembered he hadn't eaten since breakfast. He closed his eyes. They were getting nowhere. "Let me take you to dinner. No reason we can't eat while we argue."

Dani rubbed her hand across her forehead and down her nose. "That's ridiculous. There's a roast in the crock pot." She started toward the hall, unbuttoning her blouse and revealing a black, lace trimmed tank top. "Try not to arrest the cat while I change into some shorts."

He took a deep breath as she disappeared down the short hall, trying to erase the image of her breasts outlined against the thin cotton. He paced across the living room. A humid ocean breeze through the open windows stirred the newspaper on the kitchen table. The deck wrapped around three sides of the house.

Anybody could get in, if not through the door, they could pop one of the screens off and climb through. Judging from the cheap window locks, it wouldn't offer much protection to lock them anyway. Dani had no concept of security.

She reappeared still wearing the black tank top, but she'd traded her trim slacks for a pair of tight white shorts. Her feet were bare and her dark hair loose. "Have a seat. Kick your shoes off. Argue with me while I get dinner on the table."

Undercover Heart

Dani pulled a bag of fresh zucchini from the fridge as Shayne took a seat at the table. "Is your air conditioning out?"

A wave of hair fell across one eye as Dani looked up. "Oh, no, are you hot? I could turn it on. It cools down after dark."

"I'm fine. Just wondering." He nodded at the open windows. "You don't lock those either?"

She straightened and tossed a head of lettuce in the sink. "Get off my case, Shayne. I've been here a year with not a single incident."

He held up both hands in surrender and swallowed his next argument. None of his business. "How's Kyle?"

"Grounded for life, to hear him tell it. He has chores around the house and his court date is next week." She squatted and retrieved a glass bowl from a bottom cabinet.

Don't stare at her ass. "Good. Is James out of town?"

"Yeah." Dani straightened and placed the bowl on the counter. "He doesn't have much choice. He has to earn a living and the promotion they offered him last year was too good to pass up. He'll be back for court though."

"If something doesn't come up." Shayne rolled the corner of a royal blue placemat between his fingers and tried not to stare at Dani's long, tanned legs.

"Look, I know what you're thinking."

Shayne was jarred out of his thoughts. "What?"

Dani started slicing the zucchini into the bowl. "You're worried about Kyle, but he has the support of a family. He'll be fine."

A voice boomed through the back door. "Anybody home?"

Shayne looked up as a heavy, elderly lady, dressed in lime green pants and a hot pink blouse shuffled in.

Dani peeped around the corner of the kitchen. "In here."

The woman extended her chubby hand to Shayne. "Hello. You the new mister?"

Shayne had no idea how to respond as she pumped his hand. "New mister?"

"Pearl Montgomery, from next door. That's my house right through there. The peacock blue one." She pointed through the screen door then dropped another stack of paint samples on the table. "Picked these up for you at the hardware store. Take a look at the sunflower yellow for the living room."

She turned back to Shayne. "This was a nice place till the last owners ran it in the ground, then just up and left. Put a new roof on it the spring before. Probably getting it ready to sell. Dani and I are trying to decide what colors to paint."

Dani stepped into the room. "This is Shayne. He's helping counsel my summer school kids."

"Ms. Montgomery." He took a closer look at Pearl. Her thin gray hair looked like it had been chopped off with a dull knife and she had it pinned back from her face with tiny orange and black ladybug clips.

She wrapped one arm around his waist and gave him a hug. "Pearl. Everybody calls me Pearl."

Pearl focused on Shayne a minute, then ambled across the room. "You have good hair. We don't have too many men with hair anymore since the Anderson boys grew up and took off. We got a few kids running around, but the only men we got are old and bald."

Dani put a hand over her mouth and stifled her laughter.

Undercover Heart

    Shayne frowned at Dani, but there were no words to describe Pearl.

    Pearl held a paint strip up to the living room wall. "When the first folks lived here, they had this room the color of sunshine. She always had us over for iced tea. Nice folks. That was back when my Buster was around. Imagine me and Buster sipping afternoon tea?" She chuckled. "Oh well, he's gone. They're gone. Everything changes. You still haven't come over and dug up any of my plants. Buster never saw the use in plants, but he's not here now, so I figure if I like plants, it's none of his concern."

    "Oh, do you have any hibiscus?" Dani asked. "I love the dark pink ones."

    Shayne looked at Dani, but she didn't seem the least bit thrown by this woman's chatter.

    Pearl sort of talked her way to the door. "I got to be getting back. If I was you, I'd have this room painted that sunflower yellow. It looked real good that color."

    "Looks like it's going to be me doing the painting. I had two different estimates, but they're outrageous."

    Pearl looked around. "We'll get it done. I'll help. Come on over and see if I have any hibiscus that suit you." She waved toward the windows. "Nice meeting you, Sean."

    The screen door swung shut behind her and Dani burst out laughing. "Oh man, you should have seen the look on your face." She bent over double. "What I'd have given for a camera."

    Shayne stared at the door in disbelief. "None of these people even knock."

    Dani sobered. "Why would they? The door was open."

    "What happened to Buster? She talk until she drove him insane?"

"I never met him. He died three years ago." Dani sighed. "Some days she talks about how lonely she is and how much she misses him. The next she can't say anything nice about him, after almost fifty years together."

Shayne tilted his head. "That lady left most of her groceries at the market."

"I like her. She's a character." Dani wandered back into the kitchen. "Maybe I'll paint each room a different color. All different pastels. The kitchen could be moss green."

"I don't know. I'd consult Pearl before I bought the paint," he suggested. "She might have different ideas."

When they walked out to the deck, Dani smiled at the bouquet of bright pink hibiscus blooms now in the center of the table. "Leave it to Pearl. I have the greatest neighbors."

Dani added a couple of floral placemats and pointed Shayne toward a chair as she placed a big bowl of salad and their plates on the table. "Take off your shoes and try not to look so uptight. You're at the beach. Relax."

He kicked his shoes and socks in the corner of the deck and took a seat. "I'm relaxed."

Dani joined him at the table and picked up her fork. "I hope you like dinner. My mom loved to cook. This is her recipe."

"Smells good." He looked out at the ocean where the crowd was beginning to thin out for the evening.

"Are we going to talk about the kids or not?" Dani took a sip of iced tea. "You've been here an hour and so far all we've discussed is my lack of security."

He arched one eyebrow.

She forked a bite of salad. "I want the class to know that at least one person is really there for them. At least one person cares what happens."

Undercover Heart

"You're setting false expectations. What happens when they get in trouble again and decide to take your advice and go to their parents? But instead of all this wonderful support you preach about, they get the crap beat out of them? You plan to take them all in? They have to learn to make good choices and depend on themselves."

"I have nothing against good choices. Shayne, I know you had it rough, but I won't let you tell them that nobody cares about them."

"Nobody does." Shayne looked her straight in the eye. "You're temporary. You can care all you want, but the fact is that in a few months when summer school is over and they're hanging with their friends on the beach and the temptation to smoke a joint or shoot up presents itself, you won't be there. Or when life sucks and they decide to swallow a bottle of sleeping pills in the middle of the night, Ms. Cochran won't be there to talk them out of it."

"What're you talking about?" Dani asked. "Suicide?"

"Did you even bother to check their records?" He popped a bite of roast into his mouth and chewed.

"No, I didn't. I won't hold juvenile mistakes against them." She paused, bothered by his last remark. Maybe she'd made a tactical error in not checking. "You're avoiding my question. Did one of these kids try to commit suicide?"

"Beth took a bottle of sleeping pills. Would have died if her father hadn't come home from work early and found her unconscious."

Dani shivered. "Do they know why?"

As the breeze kicked up, Shayne caught his napkin and stuffed it under the edge of his plate. "Dunno. She didn't deny the attempt, but all she said was that she didn't see any reason to live. From what I can tell, she hasn't changed her mind."

"I should talk to her."

"And say what? What can you say that her new therapist hasn't already said? Beth's not talking." Shayne dropped his fork. "Want to cover the girls first? Let's take little miss wise-to-the-world Amber. Amber and her twenty-three year old boyfriend held up a 7-11 on their way out of town. They didn't make it out of the parking lot. Cocaine stashed under the front seat, a box of condoms in the glove box, and a loaded Magnum to keep the money coming in. Armed robbery, statutory rape, possession. Freddie's up for serious time. The only thing that saved Amber was that it all took place on her sixteenth birthday. Pays to be a minor."

Dani stood and moved to lean against the rail. Suicide, cocaine, armed robbery. And that was the girls. She closed her eyes. What kind of world had these kids grown up in? What could she possibly do to help? "I don't want to hear anymore."

Shayne came up behind her and rested a hand on her shoulder. "The only thing that can save them is to learn to rely on themselves. Decide to put themselves first and make a better life."

Voice of experience? Dani turned and wrapped her arms around his waist, burying her face in his shoulder. "I wish I could have been there for you."

He eased her away and pushed the hair out of her eyes. "Believe it or not, sometimes life with a family sucks more than being a ward of the state. There was nobody there to lean on, but for the most part we were protected from abusive situations. And we learned to be self-sufficient."

She looked up into his azure eyes and her knees almost buckled at the loneliness there. Placing a hand against the side of his cheek, she tilted her head. "We all need someone. That's what makes us human. I miss my parents so much sometimes I can't sleep, but I know they loved me. As a child, there was always a safe home and people to take care of me. It would've never entered my mind to commit suicide."

"What happened to them?"

Dani fought back tears. She hadn't intended to think about her parents tonight. "Dad owned a small piper cub. One beautiful Saturday morning, the end of my junior year at UT, they flew to Austin to have lunch with me. I took my boyfriend along to meet them and we told them our plan to take a year off from college. Go to New York. Get jobs. Have fun."

"And they didn't buy into the plan?"

"They flipped out. Patty was always the model daughter. Me, well, I was the free spirited problem child who always acted before thinking things through. Patty got through college in three years. Three years into it I still lacked a few credits being a senior. Instead of enrolling in summer school to catch up, I wanted to play."

He ran a hand down her cheek. "And?"

"And we all said some things. Things I should never have said. They went back to the airport. The plane never made it home to Pasadena. Mechanical failure, the report says."

"It wasn't your fault."

Dani winced. "But I'll never get the chance to apologize. To take back those hateful words. They just wanted what was best for me."

"Yeah, but you had no way of knowing what was going to happen."

Dani sniffed and reached for a tissue. "I guess that instead of feeling sorry for myself, I should just be thankful for having them as long as I did." She wiped the back of her hand across her eyes. "Pretty selfish, huh?"

Taking her face between his hands, he stared into her eyes. "No. There are a lot of things you are, but selfish isn't one of them."

Her gaze locked with his. Her body ached, drawn to his buried vulnerability. She could only stare as he bent his head and covered her lips. "Careless," he said. "Reckless," he added with another kiss. "Opinionated." She closed her eyes. "Quirky." Another kiss. He was slowing down. Did he need her to provide more words in order to keep kissing her? "Warm," he growled. His hand cradled the back of her head tilting it for a better angle. "Sexy."

Don't stop. Please don't stop. She tasted his tongue and touched the tip of hers to it. She didn't dare open her eyes. His hands slid beneath her shirt and roamed up her sides. If she was dreaming, she didn't want to wake up. She slid one hand up the back of his t-shirt and her fingers curled into his hot skin. His lips trembled against hers. The summer breeze tossed her hair across her face, but it felt cool compared to the warmth of his lips.

"Oh, I'm sorry." A feminine voice penetrated the hot haze that engulfed Dani.

She opened one eye. Sorry? Who was sorry?

Undercover Heart

Chapter Eleven

*D*ani wasn't sure what to expect when Shayne arrived on Thursday. She couldn't stop thinking about that kiss. He'd used Pearl's interruption Tuesday night as an excuse for another of his hasty departures.

The morning had been productive and the students went outside for a short break after lunch. Dani stopped by the ladies room, then headed out to make sure they heard the bell to start class.

Shayne should be here any minute. How would he react to her? How would *she* react to him?

Shouldering her purse, Dani pushed the outside door open just as Shayne spun Tung around and twisted one arm behind him. She blinked. Handcuffs clinked shut around the kid's wrists as Shayne read him his rights.

What was happening here? The other kids had backed to the edge of the school lawn and Mr. Matthews, the seventh grade summer school teacher, held onto two younger kids.

Dani watched in shock as Shayne and Mr. Matthews escorted all three boys toward her. Shayne shook his head as he approached. "You might want to make other plans for the afternoon class. Doubt I'll make it back today."

"What did he do?"

He led Tung past. "Just take the other kids back to

class."

Dani wanted to question him further, but Shayne was all business. She motioned for everyone to go inside and followed them to the room. They were all whispering and glancing back toward the office.

Calvin flopped down in his chair. "Tung's history."

Mario nodded. "He's screwed."

"What kind of moron brings drugs on campus?" Tad asked. "He was asking to get busted."

Amber shook her head. "You guys don't get it. When you need money, you do what you have to. His customers are here."

"Well, then he should have arranged to meet the little dipshits someplace else," Tad said.

Beth didn't utter a sound.

Dani held up her hand. "Enough speculation. I'm sure Agent Kelley will do what's right."

"Kelley will make sure he goes down. Like he said, it's all about choices and Tung chose to screw up." Mario smirked.

"And you don't think Tung should pay a price for his action?" Dani asked.

Mario shrugged off the question.

She had the class spend the afternoon writing a paper about choices. From all accounts, Tung had been selling cocaine to two eighth grade boys when Shayne arrived on the scene.

She waited all evening to hear from Shayne. She finally gave up. He didn't even have the decency to call and let her know what was going on with Tung. She'd have called Shayne, except he evidently still didn't trust her with his cell

Undercover Heart

number. The only way she knew to contact him was to call the Houston PD. Mario was probably right. She wouldn't take bets that Shayne pulled any strings to help the boy out.

Saturday was Molly's eighth birthday and Dani had volunteered to help Patty with a girl's lunch at a frilly tea room in Houston. The little girls would love dressing up in fancy clothes and eating off pretty dishes.

Dani studied the group of giggling, innocent little girls and wondered how kids progressed from this to the hard-edged, troubled teens in her class.

Patty watched the girls dressing up in lacy hats and pearls, then turned to Dani. "You don't seem too into this."

Dani placed a floppy white hat covered with lavender and white flowers on her head and adjusted the angle. "I'm sort of distracted by my summer class."

"Oh, I don't even want you to think about them today. I can't believe you volunteered for that class in the first place. Not smart." Patty tied the lavender ribbon under Dani's chin. "Put them out of your mind."

Dani needed to talk about what had happened Thursday, but she hesitated to tell Patty about Shayne's involvement. "How's Kyle?"

"He has to serve eighty hours of community service, picking up trash in city parks. A big thanks to Mr. Kelley for not helping him out."

"Shayne wasn't the one who broke the law," Dani pointed out. "Maybe this will make Kyle think the next time he wants to smoke pot."

* * *

Tuesday when Shayne arrived, the class was uncharacteristically quiet, as if they were waiting for a lecture. It didn't come. Shayne just watched them watching him.

Mario finally broke the silence. "So where's Tung?"

"Behind bars, waiting for a hearing."

Amber dropped her purse in front of her chair. "What about the two kids he was selling to?"

Shayne glanced around the room. "Also facing charges. But they were released into their parents' custody."

Calvin set his jaw. "Did you even try to help Tung?"

Dani held her breath, as anxious for Shayne's answer as the rest of the class.

"If you mean, did I try to get him out of the charges, no, I didn't." Shayne looked from face to face, pausing a second on each. "What I see when I look around this room is five intelligent adolescents on the verge of adulthood. You're smart enough to understand consequences, which is why I won't give an inch if you break the law. Tung knew what he was doing."

"But he's a minor," Calvin pointed out.

Shayne raised one dark eyebrow. "He's seventeen. He was already on probation. My guess is that they'll try him as an adult."

Mario shook his head. "But he's not."

Amber squirmed. "Will he go to prison?"

"He's habitual. Let me ask you something. If he was selling to your kid brother, how would you feel? Would you want Tung off the street? He wasn't just selling pot."

Calvin glanced out the window. "He was selling coke."

Beth looked at Shayne. "If Tung wasn't selling drugs, they'd find someone else to buy from. There's nothing anybody can do to stop it."

Dani's head jerked up. She couldn't believe Beth had

entered into the conversation willingly, even if she did have a defeatist attitude.

"Where would we be if nobody even tried?" Shayne asked.

"Same place. Some things are just the way they are. You learn to live with it," Beth said.

Dani exchanged glances with Shayne, but she wasn't a trained counselor. She wasn't sure what to say to the girl. She took a shot. "People can't help unless they understand what the real problem is."

Amber grabbed her purse again and started digging. "Adults don't understand nothing. They think they're helping, but they just make things worse."

"Can you give us an example?" Dani asked.

"Sure." Amber pulled a stick of pink striped gum out of her purse and popped it into her mouth. "When the CPS lady dragged me back to my parents after Freddie and me tried to skip town, she said I should talk to them. Think they were interested in what I had to say? The old man beat the crap out of me. I still have bruises from the red welts his belt left on my bare ass."

"Report it to CPS," Dani suggested. Geez, she was beginning to sound like Shayne.

"Yeah right? They don't believe anything I say."

Shayne shoved his hands in his pockets. "Show them the welts. I guarantee they'll get you the hell out of there."

"Right, straight into a freakin' foster home," Calvin chimed in. "You haven't lived until you take that trip."

Shayne turned and walked across the room. "I was a ward of the state of Texas for sixteen years. There are good foster homes and there are not so good ones, but before I'd put up with an abusive father, I'd give it a shot."

Amber shrugged. "I'd probably get raped the first night."

Dani watched Beth as Shayne talked to the class. The girl sat stoically in her chair, staring down at her desk. Why had she tried to kill herself?

The bell rang and Dani pushed her hair back. "Class dismissed. Be on time tomorrow. Three tardies equal an absence."

Mario and Calvin gathered up their books and stopped in front of her desk. Mario slung an old denim backpack over his shoulder and looked at Dani. "So when do you want us to start?"

"Friday. We can at least get it washed down and scrape the loose paint. I'll borrow a couple ladders."

She ignored the storm cloud that darkened Shayne's face. It wasn't his business.

He followed the kids to the door and closed it behind them, turning to glare at her. "What the hell was that all about?"

"Calvin and Mario need something to keep them off the streets. I need my house painted. Amber may help too. Perfect plan for everyone."

"Are you certifiable? Those kids are looking for trouble and you're inviting them into your home." Shayne slammed his palms on her desk. "Dammit, Dani. Open your freakin' eyes."

"It's my house!" She turned away from him and erased the board.

"And you run it like a damn community hangout for misfits!"

She slammed the eraser back in the tray. Why was he so upset? "I'd rather them hang out at my house than some pool hall. I'll get my house painted, they'll have something constructive to do with their time, and they'll earn a little spending money."

"Yeah, money they'll spend on drugs."

Dani placed the day's papers in her satchel and clicked it shut. "Then you can arrest them!"

"You're going to regret letting them know where you live."

"I'll be fine." Dani recognized the tension in the creases around his tight lips. He was truly frightened for her safety. "How about taking me to dinner tonight? You look like you could use a break."

Shayne shoved the hair out of his eyes and looked at her like he wasn't sure whether to hit her or accept the invitation. "You don't have enough sense to realize the danger with these kids. Don't expect me to protect you."

"Protect me from what? They're kids."

"Kids with juvenile records."

"I'm hungry, Shayne. Dinner or not?"

He started to answer, but closed his mouth without saying a word. He headed toward the door, then turned. "Why the hell not. I don't know whether to admire your idealism or detest your blind gullibility."

"You worry too much." She picked up her purse and satchel. "Why don't you just come by the house and we'll go from there?"

By the time Shayne followed her to the house, Dani had changed her mind about going out to dinner. Once home, she was too tired to leave again. She wanted to relax and she wasn't thrilled about the possibility of arguing with

Shayne in a restaurant. She needed to diffuse his anger and make him realize that her plan made sense.

At least the house was empty today. The big round thermometer on the deck showed the temperature pushing 100. She held her sweaty hair off her neck. "What do you say we take a swim and then order a pizza?"

"Works for me."

Dani grinned and headed toward her room. "I think James left a swimsuit here you could wear."

"I have clothes in the car."

Dani turned half way down the hall and studied him. "You keep clothes in your car?"

Shayne raised one eyebrow. "I'm a college kid. Never know when I'll meet a hot lady and get lucky."

Dani wondered how close that was to the truth. At least the grin on his face was teasing.

She shook her head and headed for her room to change. The royal blue bikini was too revealing. The black one-piece was too harsh. Tugging on the strap of her daisy floral one-piece and untangling it from the mass, she decided it was the least alluring. Until she made up her mind just how far she wanted this relationship to go, best to dress with caution.

By the time she came out, Shayne was waiting on the deck, staring out at the surf. Nice shoulders, narrow waist, baggy black and red swim trunks. "You're quick."

As he turned Dani sucked in her breath. No kid physique here. Still, he could use a bit of sun. She grabbed the sunscreen off the patio table, squirted a dollop into her hand, and pitched the bottle to him. "Help yourself."

She tried to ignore the bulging biceps as he lathered the lotion across his arms and chest, even rubbing the back

Undercover Heart

of his neck. Enough of this. She couldn't just stand here and ogle him like some sex-starved teenager. "Grab a boogie board." She took the top one off the pile in the corner of the deck and raced down the steps toward the surf.

The water felt fantastic. Exactly what she needed to wind down. However, it didn't have its usual calming effect. The sensation of brushing against Shayne as he swam next to her kept her on edge, even though every time they touched, he drew away. Dani couldn't decide if it was her in particular that made him uncomfortable or if he was so defensive with everyone.

After catching a few waves, Dani paddled out past the surf and hoisted herself up on her board, lying on her stomach facing Shayne, enjoying the way the water glistened off his skin. "I'm just going to lie here and if a wave decides to take me in, fine. If not, no big deal."

Shayne crawled on his board and grabbed the rope handle on hers so they wouldn't drift apart. "Nice afternoon."

His eyes were striking, reflecting the water. Tiny green flecks transformed his predominantly blue irises into the most incredible azure. "Very."

They floated in peace a few minutes, just rocking with the waves. Dani nibbled at her bottom lip. "Mind if I ask you a question?"

"What?"

"First, I'm happy you're here." She glanced at him and waited until he smiled before continuing. "I'm not exactly sure why, given our differences, but I want us to spend time together and get to know each other." She hesitated. "I guess I'm just a little confused about what you want."

"Somehow, I knew you'd get around to that." He seemed to put a great deal of consideration into his response. "I wish I could give you a straight answer."

"So, give it a shot."

"I told myself that it was wrong to come here, to spend time with you. This is a mistake, but I can't seem to stay away."

"Mmm, I like that second part."

"I'm trying to be honest, Dani. Don't let your emotions get involved. I don't want to hurt you, but the most this can lead to is an affair, a brief affair."

Dani registered his words, but she wasn't convinced that there might not be more than an affair in their future. Unless she found a way to break through his defenses, she'd never know. She tugged the rope, pulling his raft close to hers. Gently, she touched her lips to his. He tasted deliciously of salt and Shayne.

He pulled her closer, then slid off his raft and dumped her off hers into his arms, crushing her against him. "You can do better than that," he said, taking control of the kiss.

One hand cupped her bottom while the other slid her swimsuit strap aside to fondle her breast. He pinched her nipple, then lifted her up until his mouth could take possession.

Her head was spinning. He avoided casual touching. No welcome hugs, no hand holding gestures. Yet when they were alone together, he didn't seem to have any more self-control than she did.

She tilted her head back. His lips kissed their way up her chest and neck. Her body slid full length against his. Oh yeah, the man was hot.

Strange the way he said he shouldn't be around her, yet admitted that he couldn't stay away. She could see the two objectives battling through his mood swings. One minute he shied away and the next he kissed her as if he never wanted to stop.

Undercover Heart

His tongue traced the shape of her lips, then teased them apart and began a thorough exploration of the interior. She tilted her head to one side and deepened the kiss.

Shayne wrapped his arms around her waist, his lips lingering on hers. "You taste salty."

Dani rubbed her nose against his. "All we need is Tequila and we'd have Margaritas."

"Now there's an idea."

"I have some mix in the freezer."

Shayne hoisted her up on her float and positioned himself on his to catch the next wave. "Race you to shore."

By the time Dani showered, Shayne was waiting with a margarita, complete with salt rimmed glass.

She took her glass. "Still want a pizza?"

"Whatever sounds good to you." Giving her a quick kiss, he went to clean up.

Dani wasn't in the mood for hot, heavy food. She pulled out a bag of tortilla chips and dumped hot sauce into a bowl. Hearing the shower running, she tingled at the idea of Shayne in her shower, nude. The same shower she'd just been in, nude. "Whoa."

Shayne came out dressed in gray plaid shorts and a white shirt. It was hard to concentrate when he was so close. Did she make him uncomfortable at all? If so, he hid it well.

They took their feast out to the deck and sat across the patio table from one another. She laughed at his funny tales of some of the busts he'd been involved in. She loved seeing him at ease. He loaded a chip with hot sauce and popped it in his mouth. "This is great."

Dani raised one eyebrow. "Everything is better at the

beach."

Famished from the swim, Dani wolfed down as much of the chips and salsa as Shayne did. She picked up her Margarita and followed him to the edge of the balcony to relax in the glider and watch the surf. Neither one had bothered with shoes. Dani propped her feet on the rail and wiggled her toes. "Warm, wet sand is therapeutic. My feet always feel so good when I get back from the beach."

Shayne studied her feet. "You paint your toenails."

Dani tilted her head sideways and grinned. "So?"

"I just never understood girls who took the time to do that," he commented. "They look pretty."

Dani wiggled her rosy toenails. "Maybe next week I'll splurge on fire engine red. What do you think?"

"Could be pretty hot."

She couldn't restrain a giggle.

"What's so funny?"

Dani shook her head. "I knock myself out trying to impress you and all it took was pink toenails?"

His gaze touched every inch of her body like a warm caress then returned to her face. "Oh, I noticed other things, believe me."

Dani grinned.

Shayne stretched his feet out in front of him and stared past Dani, across the sand. She granted him his silence. Sipping her Margarita, she noted his almost empty glass. "Would you like another one?"

"Not right now."

This seemed to be one of those times Shayne needed quiet. As Dani sat in silence, she wondered what she could do to bring him out of his shell. As soon as she glimpsed the tiniest nick in his armor, the slightest vulnerability, he quickly closed off. Like coming here when he knew he shouldn't.

Methodically, she sipped her Margarita. Maybe if she didn't crowd him and gave him space, in time he'd open up more and let her inside.

She stood and grabbed the chips and empty salsa bowl from the table. It only took a minute to clean up and put the bowl in the dishwasher. She wiped off the table, and glanced over at Shayne. He hadn't moved. Taking her time, she straightened the kitchen and living room.

The salty breeze was hot and sticky tonight. Shayne rubbed the sweat off his neck, leaned back in the glider, and propped his feet on the wooden rail. The moon was just shy of full and illuminated the Gulf like a floodlight.

The cat stretched and sharpened its claws on the deck, then crouched down and stalked toward the colorful windsock that popped in the breeze. The cat hunkered down then pounced, catching the windsock half way up, flipped backwards off the deck, and darted under the house.

Dani dropped down in the glider beside him and rested her arms on the rail. "Sometimes I think the sound of the surf is all that keeps me sane."

He listened to the waves crashing into shore and almost sighed in contentment at the smell of salt spray. "Yeah, except tomorrow is another school day. And one of the guys I'm working has a party Saturday night."

Dani steepled her fingers and widened her eyes. "I guess that means you won't be asking me out for Saturday night?"

He was tempted to ditch the party and do just that, no

matter how stupid. "Wouldn't want to wear out my welcome."

"Shayne, you're always welcome."

He'd known more peace the couple evenings he'd spent here than any other time in his life. Dani might credit that to the surf, but it was a hell of a lot more than that. She'd created a haven with her home. An atmosphere that encouraged people to relax and feel like they belonged. He watched the cat climb up on the deck rail and stretch. Animals too, it seemed.

The breeze stirred Dani's hair and Shayne reached over and twisted a tendril between his fingers. She had no idea how extraordinary she was. Not one in a thousand had the genuine compassion for other people that this woman did.

She turned and laid her head on his shoulder. "You seem absorbed in thought tonight."

"God, you're beautiful."

"A compliment from Shayne Kelley? Let me grab my recorder." She leaned back and snuggled against his side, tugging his arm around her shoulder and threading her fingers through his.

He let his feet drop to the deck and pulled her across his lap for a kiss. Her hair smelled like coconut suntan lotion and her full lips were bare of cosmetics as his mouth covered hers. He was losing himself. But he couldn't walk away. Not yet. He closed his eyes and drifted with the kiss. Warm, sexy, seductive, comfortable.

Her fingers buried in his hair and she shifted and straddled his lap, deepening the kiss. He cupped her hips in his hands and squeezed. She was so damn sexy. Just one more aspect of the situation he was going to have hell walking away from. Her breasts pushed against his chest and she wiggled her hips and adjusted her position to fit him.

From a distance, someone cleared their throat. "Oh shit. Sorry, teach. I should have called."

Dani tensed and scooted off his lap. Her cheeks flushed the dusky rose of a summer sunset. Dammit, twice in a row. Shayne followed the direction of the voice to find Amber standing at the top of the stairs.

They'd have more privacy in Grand Central Station.

Chapter Twelve

Dani scrambled to her feet and smoothed her hands down her hips. "No, don't be silly."

Amber held her stance.

"You okay?" Dani rushed across the deck and wrapped an arm around the girl's shoulder. "You've been crying."

Shayne finger-combed his hair back, but kept quiet.

"I feel so stupid." Amber started shaking and stuffed a piece of paper into Dani's hand. "I trusted him. I promised to wait forever for him to get released from prison. And the son of a bitch sends me a stupid letter. He didn't even call."

Dani stepped back and straightened the wadded up note.

Shayne leaned against the rail. "This guy isn't worth your time."

"But he promised." Amber cut her eyes at Shayne and rubbed her drippy nose with the back of her hand.

Shayne went inside and returned with a glass of water and a couple tissues. He handed them to Amber.

"Thanks." She took a giant gulp, then handed it back to him and turned to Dani. "I loved Freddie. He said we were going to disappear together. Vegas or California. He was going to take care of me."

Dani moved to sit sideways in the glider and focused on the young girl. "You need to figure out how to take care of yourself."

"How?" she wailed. "I don't want to be alone. I want Freddie."

"I'm going to shove off." Shayne pulled out his keys and focused on Amber. "Ms. Cochran knows what she's talking about. Listen to her."

That was a first. Dani smiled her appreciation at Shayne, warmed by his vote of confidence. She waved goodbye and focused on Amber. "Why don't you tell me about Freddie?"

The girl flashed a knowing gaze toward Shayne's departing figure. "Why don't you tell me about you and the hot cop?"

Amber could cause trouble in class Tuesday after finding Shayne here, but at the moment the girl needed help. "This isn't about Agent Kelley and me."

"Well, Ms. Cochran, you were straddling the guy's crotch when I showed up. Something sure as hell is about you two. You'd have to be nuts not to go for him, even if he is a narc."

"Agent Kelley has some issues he has to deal with before he's ready for a relationship." Dani paused. That was the first time she'd admitted Shayne wasn't at the same place in life she was. He wasn't ready for commitment. Possibly never would be.

She shook herself. Okay, there were other things that needed her attention right now. She rubbed her eyes and tried to figure out the best way to turn the conversation away from her and focus it on Amber. "Everyone has things in their life to overcome."

Amber groaned. "Something tells me you're trying to

make some brilliant all-knowing point here."

"Just that before you can find success in a relationship, you have to first be comfortable with who you are. Agent Kelley isn't there yet and obviously neither is Freddie."

"And neither am I? That's what you're saying."

"If you give yourself time to grow up and concentrate on taking care of yourself, instead of looking to Freddie to solve your problems, you might be amazed at the outcome."

"I'm totally ready for a relationship. I want a guy. My own guy who loves me." Amber rolled Freddie's note around her finger. "Living at home sucks. And I don't know how to be alone."

This wasn't working and Dani struggled for the right words. The best approach. "If there were two guys. One was a nice guy and really cute. But he lived with his parents and when he wanted to buy you something he had to ask them for money. The other maybe wasn't quite as good looking, but had his own apartment, a job, and a car. Which one would you be more attracted to?"

"Well, duh. Why do you think I'm with Freddie? Or, was with Freddie. He can take care of me." Amber stopped and narrowed her eyes at Dani. "Was that a trick question?"

"Sort of." Dani watched the calico cat bound haphazardly across the deck chasing a bug. "Guys aren't any different. They'd choose the girl who had her act together. Someone who could take care of herself, make her own decisions, pay her own bills."

Considering Amber's minuscule cutoffs, crop top, and lack of a bra, Dani wasn't sure she was being entirely honest with the girl, but she had to get her point across. There were guys all up and down the island who'd be more than happy to jump in the girl's bed. "When that right guy comes along, you want him to be with you for the right reasons. Sure they

151

like to sleep with hot girls, but they don't typically settle down with them."

Amber frowned at Dani's house and reached down to rub the cat's head. "You've got a fancy degree and have your own place. So sex wasn't why the cop had his tongue down your throat instead of mine?"

Dani flinched at Amber's crass conclusion and forced her fingers to uncoil. "If you'd put all that energy you waste trying to find a boyfriend into trying to find Amber, figure out who she is and what she really wants, the guys will be lining up."

"But that'll take years." Amber sat back and let the cat crawl into her lap.

"You're sixteen. There's no rush. Graduate. Get a job. Go to college." Dani reached over and rubbed the cat's head. "Show Freddie what he gave up."

A grin slowly spread across Amber's face. "That could be pretty cool. He gets sprung and I'm all educated and classy and don't need him. Got my own apartment. And I might not even let him move in right away. Make him sweat."

Dani resisted the urge to point out that in the five years until Freddie got sprung, Amber would have forgotten what it was she saw in him in the first place. "You might even have another, better guy by then."

Scratching the cat behind the ears until it purred, Amber giggled. "Oh, wouldn't that just piss him off good? He'd have a shit fit."

* * *

Dani spent the weekend organizing the painting project she'd hired Calvin and Mario for. The boys worked their butts off scraping paint off the exterior of the house Friday afternoon until dark and were back bright and early Saturday morning to continue the job. Dani made sure she had plenty of water and soft drinks for them and was amazed how diligently they worked. She'd bought three kinds of lunch meat and assorted snacks for lunch and invited them to stay for a cookout Saturday night. About twenty of her neighbors showed up with food in hand to accompany the burgers she was grilling.

The boys were so exhausted they wolfed down three burgers each and devoured almost the entire plate of chocolate chip cookies Pearl brought, then headed for home. Dani was beat from going up and down the stairs all day supervising Calvin and Mario while at the same time trying to move everything out of the dining room so she could start painting the interior. By the end of summer, this place might not be worthy of Better Homes and Gardens, but at least it would look like a home.

By ten, all Dani could think about was a long, hot soak in a bubble bath. She didn't look for Shayne to show up. Probably for the best anyway.

How dangerous was that party he'd mentioned?

* * *

Monday after class, Dani pulled out her folder and dialed the cell number listed for Beth's mother. Missing one day of summer school was equivalent to a week or more during a regular semester and it wasn't like Beth to miss.

"Hello," a woman's voice answered.

"Mrs. Stevens, this is Dani Cochran, Beth's teacher."

No answer, but a voice over an intercom called, "Code Blue." Oh no. Dread filled Dani's mind. "Is everything okay?"

"Ms. Cochran, she's in ICU." Mrs. Stevens' voice trembled.

Dani clasped her hand over her mouth then sucked in a breath. "I...I'm so sorry." The room swayed. "What happened?"

"Sometime during the night Beth slit her wrists."

"Oh my gosh. Is there anything I can do for you? For Beth?" Dani's offer sounded shallow, even to her, but she felt so helpless.

"We're just waiting," Mrs. Stevens' voice cracked.

"May I come wait with you?" Dani asked. She might not be able to help Beth, but she could pick up dinner for the parents or something. Lend a shoulder.

Mrs. Stevens cleared her throat. "If you want. Just don't expect much. She lost a lot of blood before I found her."

"Okay." Dani hung up and frantically stuffed the days' homework into her satchel. She grabbed her purse and started toward the door only to find the probation officer blocking her exit. "I have to go. I'll have to get you a report tomorrow."

"What's wrong?" Officer Monroe asked.

"One of my students tried to kill herself. She's in ICU." Dani scrubbed the tears from her cheeks. "I have to be there."

He waited while she locked her classroom. "You're shaking. Let me drive you."

"I'm fine. I'll need my car." Dani shook her head. "I really don't have anything new on the other kids. They're all showing up. Completing their work."

Without giving him a chance to respond, she sprinted down the hall toward the exit. She had to get to Beth.

* * *

Dani approached the hospital information desk and followed their directions to ICU. Mr. and Mrs. Stevens were easy to spot. They were leaning against the wall outside their daughter's room. Dani's heart reached out to them. Mrs. Stevens wasn't crying, but not exactly dry-eyed either. Mr. Stevens clutched his wife's hand.

Dani realized now that she was here, suddenly she didn't know what to say to Beth's mother.

The woman narrowed her dark eyes at Dani as if trying to place her.

Dani extended her hand. "Mrs. Stevens, I'm Dani Cochran, Beth's teacher."

Beth's mother was tall, slender, and wore a navy pantsuit, as if she'd been dressed for work when she found her daughter. She squeezed Dani's hand. "Thanks for coming. This is my husband, Mike."

Dani shook his hand. He was a nice looking black male, although not quite as professionally dressed as his wife, wearing khakis and an olive green shirt. He dropped Dani's hand and slipped his arm around his wife.

"Any change?" Dani asked.

Mrs. Stevens closed her eyes. Mr. Stevens hugged his wife close and tilted his head. "She lost a lot of blood, but they tell us she'll pull through. It's her emotional condition that has everyone most concerned."

Dani tucked her hair behind her ear. "Could I see her?"

The couple exchanged looks and Mrs. Stevens nodded. "Don't expect her to acknowledge you. She just stares straight through us as if we aren't even there." Her eyes filled with tears and she turned into her husband's arms.

Steeling herself for what she might face, Dani eased the door open and took a deep breath. She pasted a pleasant look on her face and approached the bed. Beth lay perfectly still, an IV in her arm and a blank expression on her face. Dani touched her hand. "Hi, Beth."

Nothing, not even a blink or a twitch.

"We missed you in class today." The words sounded lame, but Dani couldn't come up with anything better. "Maybe you'll be back in a few days."

Still no response.

Dani held her hand for a few minutes, but felt helpless. "Beth, I just want you to know that I care and I'm here if I can do anything for you. If you need to talk."

As she walked out of the stark hospital room, Dani fought tears, at least until she could go down to the waiting room or someplace away from Beth's parents. But when she looked up, Shayne was talking with Mr. and Mrs. Stevens. Why was Shayne here?

Another man stood to the side holding a clipboard. Dani hadn't heard the conversation, but she could feel the tension.

Dani searched Shayne's face and found that impassive façade he was so good at hiding behind. She swallowed the lump in her throat. Was Shayne here because he cared about Beth or was it strictly professional?

Mrs. Stevens stiffened her shoulders, crossed her arms over her waist, and then went into Beth's room without a word to anyone.

Mike Stevens looked between Shayne and the man with the clipboard. Judging by his blue coat, Dani assumed he was a doctor or therapist.

"It's our fault. We let this happen to our daughter," Mike Stevens said.

The doctor met Mr. Stevens' frustration with calm. "Do you have a theory on who might be doing this?"

Dani looked at Shayne, but he didn't give her any answers.

Mr. Stevens held up both hands. "I don't know. She's not close to any kids that we know of. She doesn't bring anyone around. We don't have all of her passwords to know any more than what I saw."

"She hasn't mentioned anyone bullying her?" Shayne asked.

"Nobody. She stays to herself." He turned toward the door, but stayed in the hall. "We had no clue until this morning. Still wouldn't if Beth hadn't left the computer logged in and up. I have no idea how to handle this."

Shayne touched his arm. "First step is to file a police report. There are laws against cyber bullying similar to other types of bullying and the police will have access to a computer forensics team. Hire an attorney. There are some good ones out there. If you want, I can check around and come up with a few names. They'll confiscate all the electronics Beth had access to, but it's necessary to track whoever is doing this."

Mr. Stevens handed Shayne a business card. "I'd appreciate your help. From the few things I read before the ambulance arrived, looks like someone by the name of Spider."

"If they're doing it to Beth, good chance they're targeting other kids too," Shayne said.

The doctor thumbed through a couple pages on his clipboard. "I don't see anything here that indicates a bullying issue."

Mr. Stevens turned on him. "You've been counseling her since she slit her wrists the first time. Almost two months. This time she almost succeeded in taking her life. How come you didn't catch this?"

Undercover Heart

The doctor's head jerked up. "Beth refuses to talk about anything beyond day to day events. School. Grades."

"You're supposed to be trained to pull these things out of patients. Keep them safe!" Mr. Stevens accused.

"We do the best we can, but if a patient is determined not to open up, there isn't a lot we can do," the doctor explained.

Mr. Stevens jaw set. "If you'll excuse me, I need to check on my daughter and wife."

Dani grabbed Shayne's arm before he could follow Mr. Steven into Beth's room. "What are you doing here?"

He shrugged. "Monroe called me. He was worried about you."

Dani started shaking. She couldn't stop. "How can kids be so cruel? Life is hard enough. They should stick together. Support one another." Her stomach lurched. She darted for the exit, hoping maybe if she distanced herself it wouldn't be true. That innocent girl could be lying in the morgue right now and her blood was most likely on the hands of other kids! At least she didn't think it was any of the summer school kids. They didn't talk to Beth at all.

Not wasting time on the elevator, Dani pushed through the stairwell door and bolted down the flight of stairs and out the front door of the hospital. The humid coastal heat smacked her in the face almost taking her breath, but it was fresh and blessedly free of antiseptic. She closed her eyes and filled her lungs.

She heard the hospital door swish and opened her eyes just as Shayne grabbed her shoulders. "You all right?"

He pulled her close, but she couldn't stop trembling. "Whatever kids did this are like rabid dogs. They attack the weak and feed off their vulnerabilities." Her words came out as a whimper. "What kind of world do we live in?"

Shayne smoothed her hair and cradled her face against his shoulder. "I don't know, baby. I don't know."

Shayne wanted to make it all go away for her, for that fifteen-year old girl upstairs. He wished the world didn't stink, but it did. As much as he'd like to protect Dani from reality, he couldn't. It was just a fluke she'd managed to avoid it this long.

"Come on. Let me buy you a drink somewhere. It'll help you calm down."

Dani wrapped both arms around his waist and squeezed. He didn't want to even think about how holding her, comforting her made him feel. She was always so together on the outside, but so vulnerable inside.

She leaned back and swiped at her eyes, smearing her makeup. "I don't want to be around people."

Shayne curled an arm around her shoulders and led her toward the parking lot. "Leave your car. I'll drive you home."

Shayne sat on the overstuffed sofa with his feet propped on the coffee table and cradled Dani in his lap. He'd managed to heat up some leftover soup while she took a bath and changed into a pair of loose gray workout shorts and tank top. The soup was a waste of time. She hadn't taken three bites, nor was she her typical chattering self.

He'd found a half-full bottle of White Zinfandel in the fridge, and she'd managed a glass before curling up on the sofa. At least the air conditioning was on and the windows were closed. He wasn't in the mood to sweat tonight and he sure as hell liked the idea of the windows being locked for a change.

Dani scooted down to a horizontal position and slid

one arm behind his back, resting her head in his lap.

"Want to talk about it?" he asked.

"No."

"You can't worry yourself sick over everyone else's problems. Gotta distance yourself or you'll go insane."

They hadn't bothered to turn any lights on before they sat down and the house was dark. It was getting late, but he wasn't sure he should leave her. It just wasn't like Dani not to talk things out. He yawned. It'd been a long, grueling day, and that was before Monroe had called about Beth Stevens. The damn pool hall hadn't closed until 1:00 this morning and then he and a couple other guys had ended up at the apartment of the guy he was targeting. The three hours sleep he'd managed to snag had run out. He stretched and arched his stiff back. "Scoot over."

Dani sat up and shoved her hair back, allowing him to stretch out on the sofa. She lay down and pressed her slender back against his chest.

He closed his eyes. "We'll get up early and I'll run you back by the hospital to get your car on my way to work."

"Okay." She tugged his arm across her waist and pressed his hand to her stomach.

He slid it beneath the hem of her short T-shirt and rubbed her bare midriff. Her body fit his too perfectly. Within minutes her breathing became rhythmic. Didn't take her long to fall asleep. Guess that didn't say much for him sexually, but tonight he was too wiped to worry about it.

Dani awoke the next morning flat on her back. The sun was just coming up and the room glowed pink through the blinds. She shifted from an unaccustomed weight across her stomach. Her T-shirt was up to her right armpit and Shayne's hand covered her bare breast. He was lying on his side, sandwiched between her and the back of the sofa.

She reached over with her free hand and gently tugged on a strand of straw colored hair. "Copping a feel, Special Agent Kelley?"

Shayne opened his eyes and yawned, then noticed where his hand was. He kneaded her breast then rubbed his thumb over her nipple. "Complaining, teach?"

Dani rolled over to face him. Was there even a chance for this relationship to work? He was here now. She scooted up on the cushion and covered his mouth with hers.

He shifted positions so she was lying on top of him. Commitment phobic or not, she wasn't about to make it easy for him to walk away. He still might dump her, but he'd know what he was missing when he left. She tugged at the bottom of his T-shirt and yanked it over his head. He returned the favor.

Oh man, she couldn't get enough. In seconds flames consumed her. His hands roamed over her bare back and down to cup her knit covered bottom. She ran her palms across his chest and down his six-pack to slip beneath his waist while she allowed her breasts to brush against his. His fascination with her breasts gave her power. His hands cupped her bottom and held her tight against his heat. Shayne wasn't anywhere close to control. She nuzzled into the curve of his neck and nibbled the tight muscle, causing him to jolt.

The alarm buzzed far off in her bedroom, but she pretended not to hear it, unwilling to break away from Shayne. He sat up, bringing her with him and out of her daze. "Better turn that off. I'm going to be late for class if we don't get moving."

"Late for class?" She pressed against him for another kiss. "It'll add to your cover."

He eased out of her arms, stood, and snatched his

shirt off the back of the sofa where she'd tossed it. Not the warm response she'd hoped for. "Get the alarm, Dani."

She clutched her shirt in front of her and shuffled to the bedroom to silence the obnoxious sound. By the time she pulled the shirt over her head and returned to the living room, he was tying his sneakers.

"I can cook breakfast."

He shook his head and looked around, grabbing his sunglasses off the kitchen table. "We need to get moving."

She let out a sigh and blew the hair out of her face. "Just like that?"

"I've got to get on the road."

Fine, she wasn't about to plead with him. He'd held and comforted her overnight and was ready to run for the hills come morning. At least they hadn't had sex. She went to the bedroom and pulled on a pair of jeans and an oversized sweatshirt.

When she came out, he was sitting on one of the barstools, elbows on the bar, and his head resting in his hands. He looked up and even given the grim line of his mouth, she glimpsed the emotion. "Look, Dani. This isn't going to work. I don't make much of a long-term anything. You know?"

Consoling. Steamy passion. Ice cold. Vulnerable. Her emotions were raw from trying to keep up with his abrupt mood swings. "It doesn't have to be that way. That's a choice you're making."

He stared at her a long second, then grabbed his keys off the bar. "If you want me to drop you off to pick up your car, we gotta go."

Chapter Thirteen

*A*lone. Friday night and Dani was alone. Felicia's husband had sailed into port and Dani couldn't intrude on what little time they had together. Pearl's grandkids were on the island for the weekend. And Dani wasn't in the mood to spend time with Patty and James.

But she'd spent other Friday nights alone. Why did this one feel so...lonely?

Okay, so she could at least get something done. She sat cross-legged on the living room floor and opened a box of her mother's china, but handling her mother's things only awakened old memories. She hadn't felt this depressed since the weeks after their deaths.

Shayne hadn't hung around after class or mentioned stopping by her place. He'd put up another wall, taller and harder to overcome than the last.

Every time she thought about the night they'd spent together, she felt flushed and weak-kneed. Just thinking about his hands on her body made her skin burn. She'd lost all inhibitions that morning in his arms. How could he not believe in love? He just needed to open his mind, if not to love, at least to caring.

She'd stocked the fridge with a six-pack of his favorite beer. All she lacked was the man himself. Give him time and he'd be back. What was between them was too strong to ignore.

Undercover Heart

The doorbell chimed and Dani jumped. It was only eight. It could be him. Her neighbors seldom knocked.

She yanked the door open, ready to give him a hard time or kiss him senseless. She wasn't sure. She found Felicia and Phil instead. They rented a tiny beach house on the opposite side of the stilt neighborhood.

Phil held up a bottle of wine. "We thought we'd walk down to the clubhouse and celebrate my homecoming in the hot tub. Want to come?"

Dani covered her disappointment behind a smile. "I have plastic wine glasses. I'll meet you down there."

The steamy water bubbled and massaged Dani's aching muscles and the wine started to knock the edge off her gloomy mood. She hadn't slept much all week. Between worrying about Beth and the added stress over her and Shayne's strange relationship, her nerves were tied in knots.

Felicia covered one of the jets with her big toe, causing a gurgling hiss. "Still working with Shayne?"

Dani looked down. "That's about all we're doing."

"He hasn't asked you out?"

Dani shrugged and let one hand float on top of the bubbles.

"So he's not coming around?" Felicia asked.

Dani came down here to relax, not be grilled. "He hasn't even called."

"So call him," Felicia suggested.

She hadn't told Felicia all the details, especially about him working undercover. "No. That would just irritate him. You have to understand Shayne. He's sort of distant."

Felicia exchanged a knowing glance with Phil. He flashed a cunning grin. "So tell me about this guy."

Dani bit her tongue. "Felicia hasn't filled you in?"

"She just said he was your brother-in-law's illegitimate son."

"Shayne was conceived when James and his girlfriend were in high school. They gave him up as a toddler." Dani stood and reached for her towel. She really wasn't up to this tonight. She ran her hands down her arms wiping the water off and shivered in the soft evening breeze. "I'm tired. Think I'll head back."

She trudged back to the beach house and stopped short when she recognized Shayne's Mustang parked beside her little Beetle.

Her heart pounded as the climbed the stairs. The front door was open, but Shayne sat in the glider. "I didn't expect you."

"Didn't expect to be here." He scrutinized her swimsuit then held up her house key. "Under the doormat? Seriously?"

Dani shrugged. The royal blue bikini that had seemed like such a good idea in the store last spring suddenly made her feel nude under his heated stare. "Haven't you ever heard of hide in plain sight?"

He narrowed one eye as she approached, but didn't pursue the argument regarding her lack of security.

"What are you doing here?" She moved in closer to test her power.

"Beats the hell out of me. I told myself not to come, but I still kept driving."

Oh wow. She took Shayne's hand. "I'm shriveled. Let's go inside."

She could feel his eyes boring through her as she walked into the house. The door lock clicked behind her.

Undercover Heart

Shayne grasped her shoulders and spun her to face him. He grabbed both ends of her towel and pulled her against his chest. His hungry lips crushed hers.

Dani wrapped her arms around him, and tilted her head back, returning his kiss. "I missed you."

Shayne backed her against the wall and deepened the kiss. "I can relate."

"I'm getting you all wet," she pointed out between kisses.

"I'll dry." He ran his hand under her swimsuit strap and eased it down. His lips traced a path down her neck and took full possession of her left breast.

"What is it about you-" He sucked her taut nipple into the damp warmth of his mouth and gently bit the soft flesh. "-that makes it impossible for me to stay away?"

"Umm," Dani moaned, cupping his face between her hands. "Does it really matter?"

He dropped her soggy bikini top on the floor and ran his tongue around her right nipple. His hands explored her back, slipped lower and kneaded her bottom, pushing her into his hard length. The skimpy excuse for a swimsuit didn't offer much protection against his zippered jeans. His lips returned to hers and his tongue thrust deep into her mouth, forceful and insistent.

He pulled back and rested his forehead against hers, heaving. "I want you."

She grabbed the hem of his t-shirt and pulled it up.

As her palms explored his hard chest, he untied the tiny bows on each side of her swimsuit bottom and it dropped to the floor. She moaned as Shayne ran his hands over her bare buttocks and up the insides of her thighs. His finger slipped inside her and Dani's breathing stopped. Fear and excitement warred with sharp-edged swords within her heart.

He wasn't in love with her.

She ached for him.

She should stop him.

She didn't want him to stop.

Her body closed around his finger like a glove as he pushed deeper and moved inside her. A strange whimper came from deep in her throat.

"Open your legs." He slid his finger in and out working her into a frenzy.

Her muscles turned to rubber and she sagged against him as his hand continued to probe and pump, sending the most exquisite vibrations through her. She clung to him to keep from melting into a puddle as her body moistened.

Shayne pushed himself into her hand. "Touch me."

Rough denim chafed her thighs and reminded her he was completely dressed while she was not only nude, but had allowed him to caress her intimately. Dani flushed but didn't unzip his jeans.

He let out a deep groan, and then stepped back. "I'm too old for these games." Turning her toward the bedroom, he gave her a gentle shove. "Just get dressed."

Dazed, Dani stumbled into her bedroom and closed the door.

Turning on the light, she stared at her nude reflection in awe. Her heart hammered inside her chest. He'd come back. But for how long?

She tugged on a pair of panties and a long sundress, brushed her wet hair back from her face, and left the bedroom. It had never occurred to her that he might think she was playing games. Even if she'd wanted to, she didn't

Undercover Heart

know what kind of games other women played.

She stopped by the kitchen, grabbed a beer out of the fridge and poured herself a glass of wine. She needed it whether he did or not. She found him on the deck. Her swimsuit draped neatly on the rail to dry. Handing him the beer, she tried to form the right words.

"I wasn't playing games. I want you. I just--" She closed her eyes and shrugged. "I'm not casual about sex."

Shayne looked her up and down and pierced her with his blue eyes. "Casual! You think this is casual?"

Dani shivered. "Are you going to tell me it isn't?"

He guzzled his beer in one swallow. "You're driving me insane. I had no intention of coming here when I got in the car tonight, but before I realized it, I was pulling into your carport. Why is that?"

"How am I driving you insane?"

"First you weren't here, then you showed up in that bikini."

"You like my suit?" Dani tried unsuccessfully to hide a grin. Trying to loosen him up.

"I'd like to get you out of my mind. I'd like to not come here every weekend. I'd like to not get hard every time I'm within ten miles of you."

Warmth flowed through her blood in a hot rush. "You have a similar effect on me."

"You don't get it, do you?" Shayne reached for her hand and pressed it against his fly. "Every damn time."

Moving her palm over his hard length, Dani met his eyes. She eased her hand away as the full magnitude of her feelings registered.

She sucked air into her lungs. "I just want everything

to be perfect."

"Life isn't perfect. I'm not perfect." He swallowed the rest of his beer. "Just go to bed, Dani. I can't take any more tonight."

"You aren't leaving?"

He set the empty bottle on the rail. "I don't know. Just leave me alone. Please."

She'd never been so turned on and at the same time so frightened of someone before. What was he feeling? What was she? One thing she had figured out was that Shayne Kelley needed solitude. At least he felt comfortable enough to know he could get that here. If he didn't, he'd have stayed in his apartment tonight.

She kissed him on the cheek, made her way back into the house, and closed herself inside her bedroom. Remembering he had no linens, she gathered up what he'd need and took them out to the sofa.

He was still standing at the rail of the deck, staring out into the night. She wanted to go to him, comfort him, and soothe the tight lines from around his mouth. She took one last look, dropped the linens, and retreated back to her bedroom.

Dani tossed and turned in the sheets. The two other times she'd been in serious relationships she'd thought she was in love. She hadn't had a clue.

Shayne was sleeping in the next room. On her sofa. In her house. Or maybe he lay awake wrestling with their strange relationship too.

Staying in bed was senseless. Dani wasn't any closer to sleep than she had been two hours ago. She got up and tiptoed into the living room to check on her guest.

Shayne slept, relaxed and still. He'd locked the patio door but left the drapes open. The whir of the air conditioner

Undercover Heart

and the ticking kitchen clock were the only sounds. Dani eased closer and knelt in front of the sofa. The moonlight illuminated his fair hair and accented his face. Dark eyelashes rested against his cheek. She wanted to touch the lock of blond hair that had fallen across his forehead, but was afraid of waking him.

How could he believe love was bullshit? Love was the most powerful, magical force in Dani's life. Shayne could deny it all he wanted, but the fact remained that he kept coming back, even against his own judgment. Even if he labeled what was happening between them as simple lust, there were certainly any number of girls in Pasadena who could have appeased that problem.

Dani poured Shayne a cup of coffee as he joined her in the kitchen the next morning, dressed in the jeans from the night before and no shirt. "So, we're painting the house today?"

Hiding her astonishment, Dani turned to put bacon on to fry. Anything to keep from staring at his perfect six-pack. "You don't have to work today?"

"Taking a day off." He sipped the steaming coffee and let his gaze wander down her body. "What's on the agenda?"

Dani noted his raised eyebrow appraisal of her khaki shorts and red tank top. The way he kept staring at her legs warmed her more than the steaming coffee. "Trip to the hardware store for paint and supplies. This house is going to be worthy of a spread in Coastal Living magazine when I'm done. You're going to love it."

"Sounds like a lot to accomplish with everything else. Summer school's a full time job."

Dani popped open a can of cinnamon rolls and started placing them in a pan. "I haven't had a real home since my folks were killed. I've got to make this place mine, you know? Don't you want your own house? A place to come home to every night?"

He shrugged. "Never thought much about it."

"You'll understand when you see the finished project." She plopped the pan in the oven and dropped down on the stool next to him. "I've been thinking about getting a puppy."

"A cat and a puppy?"

"I don't have a cat. It just sort of hangs around."

"Yeah, I wonder why. You feed it and give it fresh water. And what's that string with the ball tied on it hanging from the rail? You have a cat, Dani."

"Okay, so I have a cat." She took a bite of crisp bacon and grabbed the notepad off the bar. "We have to make a list for the hardware store." Stain for the hardwood floor in the dining room, more paint samples.

Shayne took the pen out of her hand. "Locks."

Dani tilted her head toward the side deck. "I can just see a porch swing out there."

"Where are your helpers today?"

"Mario and Calvin? They've got the outside ready to paint as soon as I decide on a color."

Shayne hauled in the last load from the car and grabbed a drumstick out of the bucket of chicken they'd picked up on the way home from the hardware store. If he installed the locks today, he could stop worrying about her. Of course, locks were useless if she continued to leave the front door wide open.

Dani spent the afternoon scrubbing out cabinets and getting the kitchen ready to paint. Shayne let her do her thing while he read instructions and tried to figure out how to install locks. His experience with domestic chores was severely limited.

Pearl dropped by with a lemon pie and a pitcher of iced tea. Dani had at least a couple neighbors who didn't appear threatening. The woman could cook, even if she was color blind.

Dani grabbed the paint samples and she and Pearl spent the next hour picking out colors for every room.

After Pearl left, Dani took Shayne's hand. "Let me show you what we've decided."

The living room would be yellow, although Pearl wanted a brighter shade than Dani chose. The kitchen and dining area had to be green. No, not green, pistachio. Dani had decided to paint her bedroom some sort of French cream, even though it was already half blue. The spare bedroom was destined to be violet whimsy and the bath just called for shrimp ice, whatever the hell color that was.

For the life of him, Shayne couldn't visualize what she had in mind. "Sounds like a box of crayons. Are you sure you want a lady who wears lime green pants to decorate your house?"

Her mouth turned up in a wide grin. "Yeah, I guess I do. But I like what we've come up with. I'm going to wallpaper one wall in the dining room with a palm tree mural and maybe add a sea shell border in the front bedroom. I still have to pick that out."

In spite of his nagging doubts about Dani's safety, Shayne couldn't help getting a little into the remodel.

"I can't wait to get started." Dani rubbed her hands together.

He glanced at his watch. "I'm hungry. Let's clean up and I'll spring for dinner."

She tilted her face up for a kiss. "Now that's the best offer I've had all day."

Shayne took the first shower while Dani put things away around the house. When he came out of the bathroom, she stuck a cold beer in his hand and took her turn in the bath. He'd enjoyed the day with Dani. Even installing locks, this house relaxed him.

Just as he popped the top on the beer, somebody knocked on the door. Glad he'd installed the lock.

"I'll get it," Shayne yelled down the hall. He opened the door and found James, Patty, and the kids waiting on the front deck. James' and Patty's mouths dropped open. He wasn't too thrilled with their presence either.

James focused his unnerving stare on Shayne's bare chest. "What's going on here?"

Shayne set his jaw. "None of your business."

Kyle stood back with a smug grin, while Molly fidgeted and chewed a fingernail. James took a step forward and glared. "I have a right to be concerned."

"Not really," Shayne said.

Patty placed a restraining hand on James' arm. "Calm down."

Dani stuck her towel wrapped head out of the bathroom. "What's going on?"

"That's what I want to know," James returned, glancing at her then glaring at Shayne. He looked at Patty and pointed at Kyle and Molly. "Get them out of here."

Before Shayne could answer, Dani, wrapped in only a huge white towel, stomped out of the bathroom and stepped between him and James. "Shayne was invited. What are you doing here?"

Patty turned Kyle by his shoulders. "Take your sister to the car."

Kyle rolled his eyes and grinned, leading Molly down the stairs. "Like we're too young to figure out what's going on."

Patty moved up beside James. "We thought we'd come down and take you to dinner. Maybe spend tomorrow on the beach."

"Obviously she already has company," James pointed out, turning his attention to Shayne and staring at his beer bottle. "You know you're only going to hurt her."

Shayne took a long swig of beer, leaned back against the wall, and leveled his gaze on James.

Dani sighed and glanced at Shayne's belligerent expression, but he didn't acknowledge her. She turned to her brother-in-law. "You should've called."

"We called your cell around lunch. It rolled to voicemail," Patty said.

"That or they just weren't answering." James narrowed his eyes. "Shayne, nothing good can come of this."

"How dare you come into my home and insult my guest." Dani poked James in the shoulder with one finger, clutching her towel with the other hand. "We're adults and what does or does not happen between us is our business! You should go now."

Patty took one look at Shayne, stepped back, and tugged James' arm. "Come on."

James shook off her hold and jabbed a finger at Shayne. "You're not the right man for her."

"You're out of line," Shayne answered succinctly.

Patty squeezed James' arm. "James, let it go."

Enraged, Dani shoved her brother-in-law out the door, bolted it, and turned to Shayne. He had a death grip on his amber beer bottle as he pushed away from the wall. His mouth was set in a grim line, but there was something else she couldn't decipher. He took another swig of beer, and walked out onto the back deck.

Dani let him go. If he was upset, the best thing to do was leave him alone and let him work through it on his own.

She clicked the bathroom door closed and dried her hair. She didn't rush dressing, peeping out to check on him occasionally, but giving him ample time to cool down.

When she joined him on the deck, Shayne was standing against the rail, staring straight ahead. "James is just overprotective. I think I mentioned that he sort of assumed the parental role after my parents' accident."

"Now there's a role he's obviously good at," Shayne commented.

"He didn't mean what he said."

"The hell he didn't! People are always suspicious. My whole damn life. I'm a freakin' nobody, an orphan."

"You're not an orphan now."

"I have no parents. I grew up as a ward of the state." Shayne set the bottle on the rail.

"You have a father."

"No, Dani, I don't. You had a father." Shayne looked her straight in the eye, his voice dead calm. "There's a huge difference."

"Why didn't you defend yourself to him?"

"He's not worth the breath."

Undercover Heart

"I can't believe he's acting like such a jerk and I hate that he keeps disappointing you."

"Hard to be disappointed when I had no expectations to begin with."

"Don't be so pessimistic. He'll come around," she whispered, not wanting him to give up on his father. Family was so important and she wanted Shayne to experience what it was like to fit in and be part of that. She slipped her arms around his waist. "But if he doesn't, you've grown up pretty fantastic without him."

Shayne flinched away from her touch. "Don't."

"Just let me hold you."

"No."

"Please."

He backed farther away. His back stiffened and his eyes turned to ice blue slits. He shrugged back from her touch. "What the hell do you want from me?"

"I think I love you."

"Love? God, I hate that word!" Shayne looked more confused than Dani was. "You don't know what you want. You say you may love me and want to be with me, yet..."

"Yet what?"

"One minute you're in my arms and coming on like-- like you want to have--have sex. I mean, you act like you want an affair. Then I respond and you push away. I didn't have this much trouble getting a girl into bed at fifteen. How could you have survived twenty-four years and still be this naive?"

Dani studied his face. "I guess you're right, I don't know what I want. You keep me confused. You act like you don't care if I exist, yet you kiss me like you can't get enough. You leave and swear you'll never come back, but you always do."

"I sure as hell know the difference between lust and that fairytale called love. Believe me I've got a stiff case of lust. I don't believe in freakin' fairytales."

"Maybe it's old fashioned to want the man I sleep with to admit that he cares about more than just getting in my pants. I have morals. I won't go to bed with someone just because they turn me on beyond the point of reasoning."

"If I didn't have morals, you and I would already be lovers and you damn well know it."

She gulped.

Shayne's eyes narrowed and his voice became dead calm. "Dani, I'm a grown man. I don't like your childish games."

The air cracked with electricity as Shayne stared at her a couple seconds, turned, dug his keys out of his pocket, and stormed down the stairs.

Undercover Heart

Chapter Fourteen

Dani's fingernails dug into the weathered wood deck railing and she watched the Mustang tear down the road in a cloud of flying sand. The engine screamed when it hit the pavement on Seawall Boulevard.

Her body vibrated with a mixture of confusion and blue flamed anger. She bit her lip. This time Shayne might not come back. The repetitive clash between father and son made her furious at James, but him being a jerk to his son was no excuse for Shayne being a jerk to her.

Pushing her hair back, she paced inside. Shayne's black leather duffel gaped open beside the sofa where he'd pulled clean clothes out. His dirty sneakers lay under the glass coffee table and his sunglasses were on the bar where he'd left them. How could she penetrate his protective walls? Their relationship didn't stand a chance if he wouldn't even stay and fight.

She stormed back outside, slamming the door behind her. If she spent another minute in this house, she'd self-combust. She'd never met anyone so hard to help.

The gritty sand on the wooden stairs stuck to her bare feet as she darted for the beach. Maybe the tranquility of a long walk would restore a thread of sanity.

The surf tugged against her calves and the sand sucked at her feet as she trudged knee deep in the lapping waves. A bright orange ball set on the far side of the island. Squawking gulls soared around the few straggling beachcombers squeezing that last ray of sunlight from the day.

She was still furious, but the more she thought about it, she knew Shayne wasn't angry with her. It had felt like a personal attack, but he'd been reacting to the scene with James. If his own father automatically jumped to the worst possible conclusion that left little doubt how others thought of him. Her heart ached.

But Shayne had thrown her sympathy back in her face. He'd raised that unscaleable wall to keep her and everyone else out.

The hot breeze tossed her hair and she flinched as a fish rubbed against her leg in search of an evening meal.

What was she going to do about Shayne? He'd closed off any part of himself that dealt with feelings.

And love? Forget it.

Coming to a sudden stop, she closed her eyes as a realization penetrated her anger. Her love for Shayne was no longer dependent on whether or not he loved her.

As the sun disappeared and the beach faded into muted shades of beige, Dani sat and buried her feet in the sand, listening to the ceaseless rolling surf. Shayne's power over her frightened her. Yet, at the same time, she was relieved to finally admit how much he meant to her.

He was right. She had to quit playing games and either accept what he had to offer or turn him loose. But he hadn't yet come to grips with his own emotions. How could her love penetrate defenses he'd spent twenty plus years building?

Tonight he'd added another layer of bricks to the wall he'd built between them. He'd made her angry on purpose because she was too close. Well, Mr. Shayne hard-assed Kelley was in for a battle this time if he expected her to run.

Undercover Heart

Even if she knew where to look, going after him would be a deadly mistake. He had to work through this for himself. And it wasn't like she could call him. He still hadn't trusted her enough to give her his cell number.

The one thing she knew beyond a doubt was that whether or not he returned tonight, they weren't done. She dusted sand off the seat of her jeans and picked up a few shells as she made her way back to the house. She studied a small Conch. So beautiful, and yet so empty of life.

Rinsing the sand off her legs and the shells, she fought not to dwell on the endless night ahead. She fed the cat and made herself a salad for dinner, but her mind was spinning too fast to settle into a television show or the novel that usually kept her up reading until late. Might as well accomplish something constructive.

Unpacking a box of kitchen gadgets, she stopped dead at the familiar deep growl of the Mustang. She tiptoed through the dimly lit house to the front door and waited, sensing Shayne was just outside, praying he wouldn't turn and leave. Why didn't he knock or come in? What conclusions had he come to while he was gone?

Dani waited silently watching the door until he walked in. The door clicked shut behind him. She stared into his glistening blue eyes, exercising all her willpower not to wrap him in her arms.

His stormy blue gaze locked with hers, and he slowly reached out one hand.

Staring deep into the liquid blue depths, Dani tentatively touched her fingertips to his. She curled her fingers, urging him closer. Feeling him reciprocate, she hooked her fingers with his and gently urged him toward her. She slipped her hands inside his open shirt, folded her arms around his waist, and rested her cheek against his bare chest. He didn't utter a word, just held her against him.

With one hand, Dani swiped at the tears running down her cheeks. She couldn't tell whose heart pounded the loudest or who trembled more. Dani closed her eyes and reminded herself to breathe. Tonight was about making love with Shayne.

Tonight was about having sex with Dani. Shayne needed sex. And as much as it scared him to admit it, it had to be Dani--the only woman on the face of the earth who could satisfy him. He wouldn't think about why right now. Tomorrow he'd deal with that.

He crushed her to him, running his hands up and down her smooth back. When he couldn't stand it another second, he bent his head and covered her velvet soft lips. They quivered beneath his and he almost lost his nerve. He forced himself not to detach from the immense passion that flowed from Dani's warmth into his soul. She terrified him, yet he couldn't walk away.

His psyche was screaming, "Run!" yet his body refused to be denied. He felt exposed and vulnerable, like jumping off a cliff knowing that jagged rocks waited below. There was nothing left but to make the best of the incredible fall. If she just wouldn't mention love, maybe he could survive.

His hands shook as he fumbled with the buttons on her blouse. He spread his fingers across her flat stomach in a futile effort to make them be still. Her skin felt like satin beneath his touch. Sliding his hands inside the neckline of the blouse, he let it slip off her shoulders and slide down her back to fall around her feet.

Somehow he managed to get free of his shirt as he kissed his way down to nuzzle the underside of her breast. She smelled like the peach body wash she kept by the tub. Her fingers threaded through his hair and cupped the back of his head, holding him close. Chills raced down his arms.

Undercover Heart

He was drowning in her sweetness.

He didn't want to rush, wanted tonight to be special for her. He dropped to one knee, kissing his way down her belly to the waistband of her shorts. She still had her hands on either side of his face, but she made no effort to stop him. He slid her shorts down and kissed the tiny triangle of white satin beneath, cupping her hips and holding her still for his assault. She whimpered and his lips delved lower, kissing the inside of her thighs until her legs quivered. Fighting the urge to rush things, he slipped her panties off.

Dani sank to her knees in front of him and sucked his lower lip into her mouth. Shayne let his hands roam upward, drawing circles around her dark nipples with his thumbs. She let out a little kitten sigh and leaned back, pulling him on top of her. He didn't want to crush her against the wood floor. But she felt so right beneath him. Those huge brown eyes so vulnerable, so full of compassion, beckoned him to continue.

He shucked his jeans and thought about moving to the bedroom, but he was so hard, he didn't think he could wait. He held back as long as he could, plundering the deep recesses of her mouth with his tongue, tasting and testing her for a reaction. He saw no fear, only intense curiosity as his erect penis touched her center. He couldn't think about what might happen after tonight. Just concentrate on now. He ripped the top off a condom package and prayed he could make it through the night without losing his sanity.

Shayne's gaze never left Dani's face as he pushed into her softness. She stared at him with such trust. Her eyes were like an open door, inviting him inside her soul.

His body wanted fast. His mind argued to take it slow. No words were spoken as he gave and received, caressing and enjoying the pleasure of sex. This union had been inevitable from the instant they'd met.

She began to move beneath him like a lithe feline, arching her back to meet each thrust. Her breath tickled his neck as her fingernails bit into his shoulders, clinging and grinding her hips against him, opening and taking him fully inside her.

He'd never in his life wanted to make sex special for a woman like he wanted to for Dani. His hands and lips roamed freely, savoring her body. Dani's body fit his, custom designed for that purpose.

Her body tightened around his, but it was his heart that took the brunt of the assault. They came together as if they'd rehearsed it a thousand times. He moved inside her and closed his eyes. Passion surged through his body, beyond the physical to his heart and soul. She made love to him not with just her incredible body, but with her entire being.

Dani couldn't seem to get enough of him either. Even after they stumbled their way to the bedroom, she was insatiable. She touched, kissed, and seemed to savor every inch, exploring his body with the fascination of a child with a new toy. There was no shyness. He felt like a god the way she moaned and cradled him as if he were the last man on earth. He didn't speak, but let his body communicate. Touching her swept him away until he was drowning in a tidal wave of ecstasy.

"Shayne, I lo..."

Covering her mouth with his, he cut her off before she could finish. That, he couldn't deal with tonight. Anything else, but not that. Sex, this is just sex, he reminded himself. Sex he could deal with. Somehow he'd have to make Dani understand. Tomorrow.

As the sun peeped over the horizon, Shayne slipped out of bed and headed toward the shower. His growling stomach reminded him he hadn't eaten since lunch the day before. He thought about last night and smiled. Of all the

Undercover Heart

women he'd been with, he'd never experienced anyone like Dani. He wanted her again, today, tonight, and tomorrow. But her delusion she was in love with him added a layer of complication he couldn't afford.

By the time Dani made her appearance, he'd managed to locate the pot and make coffee. Which was a task, since she'd unloaded all the cabinets the day before and nothing was put away.

He shoved a cup of coffee across the bar toward her. "Good morning."

"Great morning." She beamed from ear to ear, never taking her eyes off him. She practically glowed and he felt like shit.

Dani joined him in the kitchen, dug a skillet out of a box and placed it on the burner. "I'll have omelets ready in a flash."

Shayne watched silently while she added cheese and bits of ham. She even pulled a bowl of chunked cantaloupe out of the fridge and put some on each plate before setting the omelets on the bar.

He couldn't eat. "Dani, I'm not good at this sort of thing. Relationships." She started to speak, but he shook his head. "Let me finish. Nobody ever stood up for me like you did last night. I appreciate it, but I'm coming between you and your family."

"If my sister and brother-in-law never come back, that's their choice." Dani placed a finger to his lips. "Let's get one thing straight. My love for you is more important than my love for them."

"I don't want you to love me like that," Shayne said. "James is right. I don't know how not to hurt you."

Turning sideways on the bar stool, she forced him to look at her. "I'll take my chances. I'm not asking you to love me or make any kind of commitment. Just see where this goes. I don't regret one second I've spent with you." She flashed an enigmatic little grin. "That includes going to jail."

The words 'unconditional love' flashed through his mind. "You think you can handle having an affair, no emotional ties? Because, that's all I want," he explained, hoping she'd run like hell and save him having to push her away.

Her head tilted to the side and she arched one dark, seductive eyebrow. "Tell you what. You just enjoy the affair and let me worry about my emotions."

"I know what you're trying to do. The tactic won't work. You can't love my demons away with sex. I tried that when I was sixteen."

She climbed off her stool and straddled his legs, wrapping her arms around his neck. "Well, I don't know with whom you tried to disprove that theory, but it wasn't me. I'm gonna blow your mind."

"You are so damn innocent." He closed his eyes. "I'll hate myself for destroying that."

She rubbed her body against his crotch. "Just relax and let things happen."

Panic threatened to consume him. She was way too close. "You want a family and a home. You're looking for long term. All I want is a fling, a brief affair before I move on."

"Okay."

Shayne tilted his head and studied her. "Don't count on me sticking around."

"One day at a time." She covered his face with kisses.

Shayne didn't want to admit how much he'd enjoyed their intimacy. Yet, he hated himself. Loving Dani was too much responsibility. "Don't love me so much."

Her brow wrinkled, but she didn't slow down. "Okay, I'll just love you a little." She kissed the tip of his nose. "And, we'll see where we end up."

"Think about what you're doing. Now's a good time to tell me to get lost."

Tracing the shape of his mouth with the tip of her tongue, she slipped it between his parted lips. "Don't deny me this. If an affair's all it turns out to be, I'll deal with it." She began to move seductively against his crotch and he conceded the battle. "Kiss me, Shayne, like we're lovers."

Chapter Fifteen

After Shayne left for work, Dani tried to come to grips with her raging emotions. She was hopelessly in love with Shayne Kelley.

In spite of Shayne's insistence that he didn't believe in love, making love with him told a different story. The intensity, the gentleness, the passion. No man that made love the way he did could possibly be void of emotion.

The more she thought about the things James had said to him the night before, the more determined she became to do something about their relationship. If James really wanted to get to know his oldest son, shouldn't he be more understanding, at least hear him out? She was beginning to realize from the way James acted with Shayne that he was probably adding to Kyle's problems as well.

Breaking down Shayne's walls was difficult enough without James pulling stupid stunts. He might not agree with her, but he was going to hear her opinion.

Picking up her phone, she punched in the Highlands' number, and then couldn't push the call button. What she had to say needed to be said face-to-face.

She threw on a pair of shorts and shirt, ran a brush through her hair, and headed for Pasadena. Dani planned to take a cool approach and hoped her sister and brother-in-law had calmed down enough to reciprocate.

Being Saturday, both cars were home when she

pulled into the driveway forty minutes later. Letting herself in the back door, she glanced around. "Anybody home?"

"Hi." Patty turned from the sink, wiping her hands on a dishtowel. "Wasn't sure we'd see you for awhile."

Dani offered a smile. "Is James home?"

Patty nodded. "He's in the study. First, can we talk a minute?"

"About what?" Dani knew her sister well enough to have a pretty good idea what was coming next.

Patty sat down at the kitchen table and reluctantly Dani took the opposite seat.

"Just tell me what was going on when we arrived last night?"

"Nothing was going on." Dani took a deep, cleansing breath. "This isn't about me, it's about James and Shayne. I didn't come here to discuss my relationship."

"I'd hoped after our talk there wouldn't be a relationship." Patty fidgeted with the corner of the placemat, swiping away an invisible crumb. "I'm worried about you, Dani. Shayne isn't the right man for you."

"I'll decide who's right for me."

"He's not that innocent little boy James remembers. I honestly don't think you realize the type man he is. Look at how he handled Kyle. By the book, no emotion."

Dani heard James come into the room. "He seems that way because nobody's ever taught him any different. He doesn't believe in love because he's never experienced it, or for that matter even witnessed it."

James pulled out a chair and joined them. "Don't you think there might have been love in some of the foster homes?"

So much for calm. Did the guy honestly take no responsibility for what Shayne had been through? Dani glowered at her brother-in-law. "People have always jumped to conclusions without giving him a chance, just like you did last night. You didn't even let him explain before you were all over him. He has a difficult time trusting people and you just reinforced that with your unfounded accusations."

"I just don't want him to hurt you. You've always been protected and regardless of how you see Shayne, he's lived a rough life. He's hardened and bitter." James reached for Dani's hand, but she moved it out of his reach.

"And how do you think he got that way?" She pushed her chair back and took a deep breath, but it didn't have the calming effect she was hoping for. "First his own parents deserted him, then he spent the next sixteen years as a statistic, lost in the system. Every time he dared to trust, people destroyed it."

James stood to face her attack. "Hey, hey! Wait a minute here."

"James." It took all her effort to keep her voice calm. "I'm going to convince Shayne I can be trusted. He's put up with people looking down on him all his life. I can at least make sure he doesn't have to put up with it from you two."

James clenched his fists. "I love him and I promise I'll apologize. But I want you to open your eyes. Don't idealize him. I accept some of the responsibility, but it's taken twenty-six years for him to become what he is. You aren't going to change him in a day."

"I know that. But I won't put up with you destroying what little bit of trust I gain."

James scrubbed his hands over his eyes.

Patty stared. "Are you lovers?"

She was tired of defending their relationship. "The

point is that it isn't your place to judge him."

James put his hand on Patty's arm and shook his head to keep her from replying. "I said I made a mistake. I'll apologize."

"If you ever get the chance." Exhausted from lack of sleep and emotionally drained from the past twenty-four hours, Dani picked up her purse and walked out the door.

Patty followed her to the car. "Please listen."

"Listen to what? More about how you think Shayne's not right for me?" Dani yanked the car door open. "I know you care, but you have to let me make my own decisions. At least I give Shayne the benefit of the doubt."

"Listen to me a minute before you go storming off on your high and mighty little self-righteous trip. I am trying to protect you. And you don't understand."

"What, Patty? What don't I understand?"

Patty leaned against the fender of Dani's little yellow beetle. "Do you think my life with James has been a fairytale? Do you think it's easy to be married to a guy with those blond haired, blue-eyed, good looks?"

Until Patty's last sentence, Dani had been about to just jump in the car and leave. "What are you saying?"

Rubbing both hands over her face, Patty was quiet for a good thirty seconds before she spoke. "I don't want you to marry a man like James. A man who has women making themselves available everywhere he goes. A man who, hard as he might try, can't resist temptation."

The fight swooshed out of Dani. For the first time she saw her sister as a vulnerable, not totally together woman. She wrapped her arms around her big sister and held her tight. "Oh my God. He has another woman?"

Patty let out a breath.

"Is it serious?"

"I doubt it. She isn't the first." Patty straightened, but although her eyes were moist, no tears fell. "Sometimes we get a rash of hang-up calls, always at night. After awhile, they stop. Once I found a note in his pocket from a woman. She threatened to blow the whistle on their affair unless he agreed to divorce me." Patty stared up at the sky. "I ignored it and it went away."

"So he doesn't know you know?"

"Oh he knows. We've even split up twice, but never longer than a day or two. Mom would always take the kids and give us time to work it out. She wanted us to stay together for Kyle and Molly. The sad truth is that I stayed because I love him. He's a good man in so many ways. He's just too weak to resist the women his looks attract."

"That's bullshit. He could learn to resist." Dani gritted her teeth. "That's why James is so quick to accuse Shayne. He's judging him by his own morals, or lack thereof."

Patty backed away and squeezed Dani's hand. "I don't think men like that can help how they are."

* * *

Shayne didn't come by her house all week. Something had gone wrong with his assignment in Houston and he didn't have time to stop by for dinner either Tuesday or Thursday after his sessions. And he'd had other plans for the weekend, something to do with his college kids. She believed his story, didn't she?

Still, hearing how James treated Patty, Dani had to fight her insecurities.

Saturday morning, she got up as the first rays of sun filtered through the blinds, pulled out the copy she'd made of the papers from the private investigator, and looked up the name of the orphanage where Shayne grew up. Not knowing how late she'd be out, she packed an overnight bag and headed to Houston. There were bound to be records that might offer some insight. The drive gave her time to think through the events of the last month.

Shayne wasn't like his father. She knew it in her gut, yet she needed to understand him. And learning about his history would help. Her heart was so exposed right now. If this backfired, would she survive?

If Shayne found out she was digging into his past, he'd be furious. Yet he wasn't likely to tell her himself and she couldn't figure out how to get through to him without knowing.

The first woman she talked to at the orphanage was sympathetic, but had only worked there three years. The next remembered Shayne, but rolled her eyes and didn't seem interested in helping.

"Aren't there some records or files I can take a look at?"

The woman shook her head. "No."

Dani studied her face and tried to figure out if she was saying more than the obvious. "Not on any of the kids, or Shayne Kelley in particular?"

"Look, Miss Cochran. There are right to privacy laws. I can't allow you to rifle through someone's files and I'm not at liberty to discuss residents."

A beanpole of a woman walked into the office. Her dark eyes scrutinized Dani, but she didn't enter the conversation.

"I understand, but Shayne has issues tied to his life here." Dani's instinct screamed that if she left here without learning something, she might never reach him. "Please. The smallest clue might help. Something about what he went through."

The bird-like woman picked up a file folder and left the office, her simple black pumps clicking on the tile.

"I'm sorry, but I can't help you. Like I said, we aren't at liberty to discuss the kids," the woman behind the desk explained, in the same monotone voice she'd exhibited the entire conversation. She stood and walked to the door.

Wanting to explode, Dani reluctantly followed her. "Thanks anyway."

Dani had no more than cleared the threshold than the office door closed behind her. "For nothing." Wow, no wonder Shayne had grown up so cold if this was any indication of the care and attention he'd been given.

Seething, she made her way down the stark hallway to the exit. A thin woman nodded as Dani approached, the woman from the office, the one who hadn't spoken. She looked like she hadn't had an easy life. But as Dani passed, the woman stuffed a folded slip of paper into her hand, turned, and walked away.

Dani blinked and stared after her. She opened the note, read it, and then turned back. But the woman was gone.

* * *

Dani took a seat at a table in the corner of the coffee shop with a clear view of the door. She sucked in her breath as the woman from the orphanage entered and approached her table.

Dani extended her hand. "Hello, I'm Dani Cochran."

"I'm Mildred Helm." Ms. Helm's soft voice seemed in contrast to her lanky appearance. "Shayne Kelley, hmm?"

"Yes ma'am. Anything you can tell me would be greatly appreciated."

"Why?" Ms. Helm asked.

Undercover Heart

Dani wasn't sure how much to divulge. "He and I are working with a group of at-risk kids at my school. I need to understand him."

"I don't see what one has to do with the other," Ms. Helm said.

Dani hesitated, but if she expected Ms. Helm to be upfront, so should she. She closed her eyes and took a deep breath. "I'm in love with him. Okay?"

Ms. Helm tilted her head. "Does he love you?"

"I think so. But he builds these walls. I can't tear them down without understanding why they're there in the first place. Shayne isn't exactly talkative."

"Never was." Ms. Helm chuckled.

Dani clinched the edge of the vinyl seat, eager for any information that would shed some light on why Shayne was the way he was. "The only way I can help him is to figure out what's hidden behind those walls."

"He won't be too thrilled with you poking around in his past."

"I know, but I'm desperate," Dani said. Waiting. Hoping.

Ms. Helm waived away the waitress. "This conversation never happened, okay?"

Dani nodded. "Of course."

"When Shayne came to us, he was a very sweet, loving two-year old. I'd just started here and he was one of the first kids I dealt with. I watched helplessly as a little more of him died with each setback. The system failed him. Not that out of the ordinary."

"How? His father thought he'd been adopted. They already had the family and everything."

"Things happen." Ms. Helm shrugged. "We only had Shayne a few weeks before the social workers arranged for him to live with the adoptive parents while they completed the legal technicalities. Ten months later, just before the final papers were filed, the wife kicked her husband out. That brought the adoption to an end."

Tears stung Dani's eyes. He'd been rejected twice. "So there must have been other families who wanted a child? I've seen pictures. He was a beautiful little boy. I don't understand."

"Afterwards, Shayne regressed, significantly. He stopped talking. Not a single word for over two years."

Dani covered her mouth, trying to swallow the lump in her throat.

Ms. Helm finally continued. "A perfect three year old boy, who just checked out. Wouldn't respond. Refused to be held. Didn't play with other children. It's difficult to place a child with psychological issues."

Dani tried to digest the words. As painful as the image was, she had a perfect visual of him. "He still seems so—so alone."

The older woman shook her head. "Think about what it would be like if you were snatched away from the people you loved and landed in a place where there are a hundred other children competing for what little attention there is to be had. Don't misunderstand, we care, but there's just so much to do and so little time. The infants don't realize the difference and are almost always adopted. It's the ones who've known some sort of family who feel the loss the deepest."

Dani gulped and almost wished Ms. Helm would stop.

"Add a stream of foster homes that dangled what he'd lost in front of him like a piece of brightly wrapped Christmas candy, which was never quite in reach."

Undercover Heart

"Nobody could get through to him?" Dani asked.

"Some kids become pleasers, doing anything they can to be prettier, smarter, sweeter, etc. They think the problem is them and if they become better, then they'll be worthy of love." Ms. Helm paused. "Others retreat so far into their shells that nobody can reach them. Shayne took that to the extreme. He not only resisted, but actively fought everyone who tried to help."

"A therapist maybe?"

"The child psychologist who worked with him said to leave him alone. All people need to be touched and he'd come around eventually. I thought his theory stunk. I feared we were going to lose Shayne, so I'd put the other children to bed and try to rock him. Shayne wouldn't cuddle no matter how hard I tried. I became too attached. They transferred me to the older kids."

Dani hugged herself, rubbing her hands up and down her arms. She appreciated Ms.Helm's candor. After spending less than an hour in the cold, stark orphanage, Dani realized Shayne wasn't just afraid of hurting her. He was terrified of being hurt himself. The walls he built were for more than protection, they were for survival.

He was desperate for love, even if he wouldn't admit it. The cold, detached face he presented to the world was a front. "Has he always gone by the name Shayne? James always called him Jamie or Jameson."

Ms. Helm came as close to a laugh as Dani had heard from her. "About the time he started school and began to talk a little, he started asking questions about his parents. When he learned his father's name was James, he refused to answer to anything except Shayne."

The last doubt Dani had about loving Shayne shattered. Even if he walked away in the end, she couldn't not love him. Her heart ached for that child, for the little boy who had been Shayne Kelley. It ached even more for the man he'd become.

* * *

The light on her answering machine flashed when Dani walked into the house. To her amazement, along with three messages from Patty, there were four from Shayne. With each one, he sounded more frantic. He left his cell number and demanded she call the instant she heard the message.

He picked up on the first ring and didn't even wait for her to say hello. "Where've you been?"

His blunt approach could use some finesse, but his concern was flattering. "What's wrong?"

"I tried to call all day. Don't you ever answer your cell phone?"

"It's dead," she grimaced. "My car charger quit working. But I'm fine. I just went with Felicia to Beaumont to visit her folks. No big deal," she lied. He'd be furious if he knew about her trip to Houston.

"Charge that damn phone and keep it with you. You could've let me know."

Dani couldn't keep the grin off her face. "I didn't have your cell number."

"Your sister didn't even know where you were."

"You called Patty? Did you talk to James?" she asked, changing the subject.

"A minute. He apologized for acting like an ass."

"And?"

"I didn't have time to deal with him. If you hadn't answered, I was about to head for Galveston."

Undercover Heart

"So come anyway," Dani coaxed. "Spend the night in my bed."

She caught his moan. "As tempting as that sounds, there are other places I have to be."

"Well, at least I have your number now." She waited for his response.

He paused. "Next time you leave town, let me know."

"That works both ways. When are you coming down?"

"I'll see you Tuesday in class. Things are starting to heat up here."

Dani nibbled on her bottom lip. That sounded dangerous. "Take care of you, for me."

There was a slight pause on the other end. "You too."

Dani couldn't wait for class Tuesday to see Shayne. More to the point, she couldn't wait for class to be over so she could be alone with him.

She didn't even let him dissuade her when he said he had places to go after class. "I cooked a pot of homemade spaghetti sauce last night. You have to come." She grabbed her satchel and locked the classroom. "Nobody can resist the Dani Cochran Special Recipe."

"Nobody?" He sighed. "Guess the bad guys can be bad one more night without my help. Let me make a quick call."

For the first time in their relationship, Dani assumed the role of sexual aggressor. Her only fear was that she'd move too fast and scare him away in her effort to make him feel her love. Still, she couldn't stop. She had Shayne's shirt unbuttoned before they were even in the bedroom. As she fused against him, Shayne slid his hand up the back of her blouse and tilted his head for a deeper kiss. She struggled with their clothes, fighting to get closer.

Shayne cupped both sides of her face. "Easy. There's no rush." He backed away and started undressing. Dani peeled off her clothes then helped him, kissing her way down his chest.

Driven by desperation, Dani poured her heart and soul into making Shayne feel.

After their lovemaking, Shayne cradled her against him and closed his eyes. "I'm running on two hours sleep."

Dani pulled the sheet over them and cuddled into his side. She nuzzled her nose into his neck. "Then sleep."

"Wake me up in an hour," he said, but his eyes were already closed.

As a lover, he was aggressive, yet sensitive. He teased her about her pink floral sheets, yet he looked fantastic tangled in them. Dani had never thought of herself as particularly passionate, yet she couldn't get her fill of Shayne Kelley.

With one finger, she pushed the hair out of his face and watched him sleep. He didn't realize that he was giving himself away by being so comfortable here. Even when uptight, she could get him to relax. Shayne Kelley would not be an easy man to live with, but if he thought she'd give up, he was in for a very long wait.

The sun was just setting when they got up. Dani put the spaghetti on low to heat while she filled the tub and added bubble bath from the fragrant assortment of bottles cluttering the back of the vanity. Shayne looked skeptical, but she threatened to push him in if he didn't join her.

They stayed in the tub till the water turned tepid, bathing each other, caressing, and cuddling. It wasn't the freshly painted rooms or the diminishing stacks of boxes that made the house feel like home, it was having Shayne here.

Dani leaned back against his chest. "All we need is a rubber duck."

Shayne leaned around to see her face. "A rubber duck?"

"Yeah, you know, like you used to play with in the tub?"

"I don't think I ever had one."

Realizing her blunder, Dani shifted in the tub, turned, and straddled his legs. She kissed him gently on the lips. "I'm sorry."

"No big deal. I didn't even realize I was supposed to have one." He rubbed bubbles down the tip of her nose.

Evidently the lack of the duck bothered her more than it did him. Dani leaned forward, rubbing her bubble-covered breasts against his chest. "Well, you have me instead."

"Much better." His brow wrinkled. "I'm curious though. What were you planning to do with the duck?"

Chapter Sixteen

Shayne wasn't eager to leave after dinner. Instead they sat in the glider to relax and listen to the surf.

Dani leaned back, stretched her feet out, and rested them on the rail. "I missed you so much. I didn't realize how much I looked forward to at least a phone call."

Too close. They'd gotten too close. He propped his bare feet beside hers on the railing. "Yeah? You were the one out of pocket."

She seemed even more thoughtful than usual. "Shayne, I love you."

He winced, but remained seated. "We've had a nice evening. Don't start this."

"Start what? I just said I love you."

"You say that so easily. I'll bet you've said it to every guy you ever slept with."

"Wrong. Not that I've slept with that many, but I've dated quite a bit. Even in high school though, I never felt strongly enough about any guy to tell him I loved him." Her hands clenched and unclenched. "You're the only man I've ever said those words to."

That terrified him even more than the words. "You know damn well what I think about love."

Dani raised one eyebrow, but thankfully, didn't take

up the argument. Instead, she scooted closer and wrapped her arms around his waist. "Right, you don't believe in it." She nuzzled his neck. "Want to go back to bed?"

He eased an arm around her waist. "Is sex supposed to prove you love me?"

"Couldn't hurt." She nipped at the top of his ear.

Her hand rested against his fly and her breath tickled his neck. "Dani, I enjoy being with you, but I'm not going to fall in love."

"Know what I think? I think you're more naive than I am."

His mind said grab her hand, but he was mesmerized as she slid his zipper down. "What makes you think that?"

"You still haven't figured out that love is what makes our relationship sizzle." She slid her hand inside his fly making rational thought impossible.

His eyelids drooped and he grabbed her hand and held it against his hardness. "Lust."

Dani wrapped her hand around him. "That too."

Shayne had never been as content or as confused as he was in Dani's bed, lying in her arms beneath the squeaking ceiling fan. The times they were together were the best in his memory. She cared about him more than he intended for her to, yet he couldn't break it off and quit coming here. Whether he wanted to admit it or not, it was too late. This one was going to hurt when it ended, but it would end. They always did.

He couldn't resist waking Dani up the next morning for a goodbye kiss. "Gotta jet. Bad guys are up and running."

Dani saw Shayne on Thursday afternoon, but he was

getting involved with the students at college and had less and less time to hang out at her house. That or he was using his job as an excuse. It probably wasn't her smartest move exposing her feelings. Maybe it was too early or maybe he'd never understand. But he needed to know. Or she needed him to.

Patty and James planned to drop Kyle off on Friday afternoon for Dani to watch for the weekend while they took Molly to a dance competition in Austin. She prayed he didn't do anything crazy in his parents' absence.

By the time Kyle had been at the house an hour, he'd met a girl at the community pool. Against her better judgment, Dani believed Kyle's promise that he would behave and left them swimming. If she wanted Patty to trust Shayne, then Dani needed to do the same with Kyle. She went back to the house to start dinner. When she went to call Kyle to eat, there was no sign of him or the girl. Dani panicked.

Pearl kept Chastity while Felicia came to help in the search, but there were over forty houses in the subdivision. Two kids at the pool said they thought Kyle had left with a girl, but didn't know for sure if it was him or who the girl was. He could be anywhere. The Highlands were on the road between Galveston and Austin and she didn't want to worry them. Not sure whether to involve the authorities yet, she called Shayne's cell.

He sounded much calmer than she was. "Don't worry. This is Kyle. He'll be back. They're probably making out somewhere."

"But, what am I going to tell Patty and James? They trusted me."

"And they've done such a wonderful job controlling him. In their custody, he made his way to Dallas. He's a resourceful kid. He'll be fine."

Undercover Heart

Dani tried to keep her voice calm. "I'd feel better if you were here."

"It may be a couple of hours. I need to cancel some plans." Shayne sounded put out with having to readjust his schedule for Kyle.

"Thanks."

"Chill. He'll be back by the time I get there."

Dani and Felicia took turns keeping an eye on the pool. Dani put on her roller blades and cruised down the seawall, hoping to spot Kyle. He was nowhere in sight. She coasted to a stop and wiped her forehead with the back of her hand. Did she expect Kyle to just materialize?

When Dani heard Shayne's Mustang pull up, she and Felicia were standing on the deck, watching dusk fall over the beach.

Shayne walked up and put his hand on her shoulder. "No sign of him?"

Leaning into him, Dani tried not to cry. "No."

Shayne motioned toward the door. "You girls take a break. I'm going to make a quick tour."

Dani didn't want to leave her watch, but Felicia insisted. "Come on, let him take over for awhile. You need to calm down."

Opening the door, Shayne gave Dani a push. "Fix yourself a drink. Cool off and relax."

He returned to the house after a run around the area. As soon as he got back, Felicia went to pick up Chastity. Dani knew she was expecting a call from her husband tonight.

Dani joined Shayne by the window. Her nerves were on end. What if something had happened to him?

He massaged her shoulders. "It's getting dark. I'll bet the girl's parents will be getting home soon and Kyle will show up."

Dani made sandwiches, but she couldn't eat. Iced tea was all her stomach could handle. "I should call Patty."

"He'll show up. I'm sure they could use a break from this crap."

Standing, he pulled her against him. His arms offered reassurance. She leaned her face against his chest and tried to relax. Just his presence helped.

Dani heard the door open and they turned to find Kyle slinking into the house. She pulled out of Shayne's arms, stomped across the room, and jabbed a finger in Kyle's face. "Where have you been?"

He ignored Dani's fury and cut his eyes at Shayne. "I see you called big brother to save the day."

Dani was beginning to understand James' frustration with Kyle. "I asked where you were."

Kyle shrugged. "Out."

"Kyle, you disappeared for almost six hours and all you have to say for yourself is 'out?' You're fourteen. You can't just take off without letting me know where you are." Dani was trembling she was so angry.

"I'm sure you two found other things to fill the time besides worry about me."

"We've searched everywhere. You know better than this. Your parents are going to be furious."

He kept a cautious eye on Shayne. "So don't tell them."

"Then tell me where you were all afternoon?" Dani said.

Undercover Heart

"I don't have to answer to you. You aren't my mother." Kyle smirked. "Actually, I don't answer to her either."

Shayne stepped between Dani and Kyle, leveling his gaze on the kid. "Dani, why don't you go tell Felicia he came back?"

Looking from one of James' pigheaded sons to the other, Dani decided to let Shayne deal with it. She slipped her feet into flip flops and let herself out of the house.

When the door closed behind Dani, Kyle smirked. "I know you're screwing her. It's so obvious."

Shayne kept his voice low. "I don't know what you're so pissed off about that you have to keep acting like a shithead, and frankly I don't care. You can do whatever you want to your folks, but Dani hasn't done anything to hurt you and you aren't going to put her through this bullshit."

"What are you gonna do about it?"

Shayne raised one eyebrow. "You do not want to fight with me."

Kyle looked him up and down. "If you think you're scaring me, you're wrong. I do what I want. Want to know what I was doing this afternoon?"

"Screwing some little girl probably, but no, I don't want details."

"I'll tell you details, if you tell me details. Just like brothers."

Before the kid had time to react, Shayne grabbed his shirt front and slammed him against the wall, lifting him off the floor. "We aren't brothers, and even if we were, Dani is your aunt. You are a guest in her home and you will show her respect."

Kyle stared him in the eye and struggled to be let down. He tried to knee Shayne in the groin, but Shayne nailed his leg against the wall with his knee. He held the glare until Kyle dropped his gaze.

"All right, but I'm not doing it for you. I'm doing it for Dani."

He allowed Kyle's feet to touch the floor again. "Fine."

Kyle pulled the hem of his shirt down and flexed his neck. "What's for dinner? I missed lunch."

"You missed dinner too. We've eaten."

"So I'll go buy me a couple of burgers."

Shayne shook his head. "We can't even trust you to go to the pool. What makes you think we'd trust you to get a burger? Take a shower and hit the sack."

"Right. It's not even ten o'clock."

"Act like a kid and people treat you like a kid. Shower."

Kyle hesitated a moment before escaping to the bathroom.

Shayne sat on the sofa so he could keep an eye on the door. At least there was no bathroom window for him to sneak out of.

Dani returned, glanced at Shayne, and then noted the closed bathroom door. "Is everything all right?"

"He's taking a shower and then he's going to bed. He wanted dinner, but I told him he missed it."

"Good. If he thinks I'm going to be his short-order cook after this stunt, he's crazy."

When Kyle came out and saw Dani, he grinned. "Got anything for a sandwich?"

Shayne shook his head. "Top bunk." There were only two bedrooms in the house. The spare room was full of boxes and an old set of bunks the last owners had left.

Smiling, Kyle tried to win Dani over. "Couldn't I just watch a little TV and grab a snack? It's early."

Shayne didn't give her a chance to answer. "Go to bed."

"You don't look ready for bed." Kyle smirked.

"We're not. We're just tired of listening to you. Top bunk, now," Shayne instructed.

"I don't do well with heights. I'll sleep on the bottom."

Shayne leveled him with a glare. "Top. I'm sleeping on the bottom."

"I might barf on you," Kyle pointed out, with all the charm of an arrogant teenager.

Shayne stood. "Keep it up and you're gonna miss breakfast."

As Kyle stomped away, Dani waited for Shayne to sit. The amount of commotion the kid made just climbing into bed would rival a herd of elephants, but she followed Shayne's lead and ignored his attempts to make them angry. She turned out the light in the kitchen and sat on the sofa with Shayne. "Think he'll try to run away?"

"I'm not giving him the chance. The kid just got a new best friend, whether he wants one or not. He tries to run and I'll handcuff him to the bunk."

By morning, Kyle was starving. He ate everything Dani set in front of him and wanted seconds. She filled him up with pancakes and bacon, partly as a stall tactic to keep from unpacking boxes. One part of her wanted all her parents' stuff unpacked and dealt with. The other wasn't ready to face all the bittersweet memories and the reality that she'd never see them again. But she'd been in her house a year. It was time to face reality. Maybe having her parents' things around would help fill the void of not having them here.

By Sunday night, this place would look like home. Shayne kept Kyle busy helping him install the rest of the locks, then they rented a truck and the three of them moved the bedroom suite Dani had in storage. He didn't give Kyle a chance to rest, but kept him on his feet, loading and unloading the truck.

She cooked lunch and Shayne allowed Kyle a short break for a sandwich and fries and then they continued moving mattresses into the house. Next they dismantled the bunk beds and helped arrange the bedroom until it suited Dani. She tried not to tear up as she looked at her parents' furniture and knick-knacks.

Shayne wasn't surprised at Dani's sentimentality, but even Kyle seemed moved by some of the memories. What had happened to make the boy so rebellious? Dani came across a box of photo albums and stopped to show Shayne pictures of her parents.

The kid smiled. "Things were different back then."

"Yeah, they were."

Kyle turned the page and found some shots of himself at about age five, straddling James' shoulders. "Dad's too serious now--when he's even around."

She gave him a gentle pat. "He's just trying to earn a living. He makes a lot more money at this job, even though he has to travel."

Kyle tore into another box. "Whatever."

Undercover Heart

Shayne had a momentary twinge of sympathy for him, but not enough to ease up. They didn't quit until they had the old bunks hauled to the Goodwill store, returned the truck, and the boxes either unpacked or stacked out of the way. Even though he and Kyle had done the heavy lifting, Dani looked beat. They all cleaned up and headed to the pier for dinner.

Kyle studied the menu. "I'm starved. I think I'll have the Captain's Platter."

Shayne recognized the ploy. "That's a lot of food."

"I missed two meals yesterday."

"Tell you what. Order whatever you want and I'll pay for it. Whatever you don't eat, you reimburse me. How's that?" Shayne offered.

"Great."

Shayne and Dani had long since finished their dinners by the time Kyle stuffed down the last shrimp. He looked miserable. As they made their way to the house, he was pale and complaining of a stomachache. Between being exhausted and stuffed, he went straight to bed without even being asked.

Dani shook her head and teased. "Think you overdid it?"

Shayne leaned forward and gave her a quick kiss. "Look at it this way, we don't have to worry about him sneaking out. He doesn't have the energy."

Dani handed him linens for the sofa and started to her bedroom. "You're bad."

"That's not what you said last Tuesday," he whispered as she walked away.

Sunday morning, Kyle turned green at the mention of breakfast. He sat on the sofa and groaned as Shayne and

Dani ate. After breakfast, they picked up where they'd left off organizing the house. Kyle worked, but at a slower pace. As the day wore on, he began to get his strength back. Shayne sent him to carry some boxes to the shed at the back of the carport.

Shayne was hanging a new blind when Dani came in from the deck. "Do you smell smoke?"

He no more than stepped out on the deck than the distinctive smell of pot filled his nostrils. He rounded the corner just in time for Kyle to drop the joint and stomp it into the loose sand. "One word from me to your probation officer and your ass is in juvie."

Kyle raised one cocky eyebrow. "What are you talking about?"

"Why are you so intent on getting into trouble? You crave attention or what?"

Kyle shoved past. "I just do what I want."

Shayne grabbed his arm. "You going to hand over the marijuana or you want me to search you?"

For a minute Shayne thought the kid might fight him, but slowly he pulled a bag from his pocket. Maybe enough grass for one more cigarette and a couple wrappers. "Are you going to turn me in?"

"Is that all you have?"

Kyle nodded.

"Pick up the cigarette you just ground into the sand and come on."

Kyle picked it up, but dug his heels in. "Shayne, shit man, you're not going to turn me in."

"I hope the old man's there for you. Lucky for you he has a good job because your legal fees are about to

Undercover Heart

skyrocket."

"I won't do it again. I swear."

"Get in the car." Shayne pushed the button and the Mustang alarm chirped.

Kyle didn't take a step. He glanced up at Dani, standing helplessly on the deck and his chin quivered.

"Do you want me to cuff you? Get in the damn car." Shayne figured Dani was afraid of how he'd handle her nephew, but he didn't have time to deal with her feelings at the moment.

Kyle wiped the tears out of his eyes with the heel of his hand and crawled into the passenger seat. "Give me a break."

Shayne stashed the pot in the console and started the engine. He backed out and headed down Seawall Boulevard. Kyle had developed a case of the hiccups. Shayne drove past the turn to head back to Houston. He wasn't sure why, but he didn't go to the Galveston police station either.

Considering his options, he drove until the road finally ended, took a right and pulled off into the sand. Kyle had stopped crying, but he wasn't saying a word.

"Get out." Shayne opened the door and stepped out of the car.

Kyle looked like he might pass out, but he followed Shayne around to the front of the car. "You gonna beat the shit out of me?"

There was nothing to block the wind out here and the blowing sand stung Shayne's face. He shook his head so the breeze would blow his hair back. "What do you think I should do?"

Kyle shoved his hands into his pockets and stared out

across the water.

"I'm a cop and you're a kid on probation who chose to smoke a joint right under my nose. All I can figure is that for some unexplained reason you have a death wish. You wanted me to catch you."

"Go ahead. Turn me in. It doesn't matter anyway. Dad knows I'm stupid. My grades suck and I'm not smart enough to ever graduate high school." Red splotches and gritty tears covered his face. He poked at a broken shell with the toe of his sneaker. "There's nothing I'm good at, except screwing up. My life's going down the toilet. Girls think I'm a nerd. I've never even gotten to touch a bare boob, much less anything else."

"It won't be a girl you'll be hooking up with in juvie."

Kyle wrapped both arms around himself and sat down in the sand, crossing his legs like a pretzel. "I'm not even smart enough to know why I did it. Maybe I did want to get caught. It's not like my folks give a shit."

Shayne looked down at his half-brother. He hadn't realized Kyle's self-esteem was so low. Seemed that having a real family wasn't much different than living with foster families. "I cannot believe I'm doing this. I've never even been tempted to let someone off."

Kyle's head shot up and his eyes widened. "You're not gonna bust me?"

"Being a teenager's tough. You're not a kid anymore, but you're not an adult." Shayne grinned. "It sucks, doesn't it?"

Kyle leaned back against the bumper of the Mustang and swiped at his eyes. "No shit."

"I don't know what you're going through at home, but you're not stupid. I'm going to make sure James finds you a good counselor."

"No!" Kyle stood and brushed the damp sand off the butt of his shorts. "Counselors are lame."

"Counselor or juvie? Your choice."

"Shit! Why are you doing this?"

Shayne nudged his shoulder. "Because this is what I want in return for not calling your probation officer. You owe me. I went to a therapist from the time I was three. It's not so bad."

* * *

Dani gave him a quizzical look when they returned. Shayne didn't take time to fill her in. Instead he kept Kyle busy hanging blinds. They'd just finished the last one when the Highlands pulled in.

Shayne waited until everyone said hello and Molly was telling Dani all about her dance recital before he motioned James toward the back door.

Kyle sat at the kitchen table and stared a hole through him as he ushered their father out onto the deck.

"What's wrong?" James asked before the door was even shut behind them.

"You'd better sit down."

James tilted his head, but took a seat at the patio table. "This sounds serious."

"I caught Kyle smoking a joint."

"And?" James asked, closing his eyes almost as if he didn't want to know.

As much as he wanted to retain the authority of the added height, Shayne took the chair opposite James. "I gave him a choice. Either I turn him in and he goes to juvie or he agrees to see a professional counselor."

James looked up and met his eyes. "You're giving me the same choice, aren't you?"

Shayne nodded. "Nothing's worked. His self-esteem is at rock-bottom. He wanted to be caught. He's not stupid, but he believes you think he is. Get him a counselor. You might consider going with him after the sessions get underway."

"You think I don't know how to parent my son?"

Shayne shrugged. "Something's not working."

"And if I don't agree?"

"Then I'll go to his probation officer and Kyle is off your hands for a while."

Chapter Seventeen

Shayne placed his pool cue in the rack and grinned. "Next time you feel like throwing away twenty bucks, give me a call."

"I don't think so. Where did you learn to play?" Barry started racking the balls.

"More lucrative than going to class." Shayne opened the Student Union door and reached in his pocket for his ringing cell phone. "Shayne."

At the sound of the voice, Shayne stopped dead in his tracks. "Hold on." He put his hand over the phone. "Catch you later, Barry."

He waited until the kid was out of earshot then put the phone back to his ear. "Who the hell gave you this number?"

"That's not important," James said. "How about meeting me for dinner, say around six? I'm buying."

Shayne bit back a sharp reply. "I've got plans."

"When are you going to sit down like a grown man and talk to me? You can't avoid me forever."

"Watch." Shayne closed his eyes, gritting his teeth so hard his jaw ached. "I've got to go."

"I'll be at the Kemah Boardwalk, Joe's Crab Shack, in case you change your mind or your plans fall through."

Shayne clicked the phone and punched in Dani's

number. He didn't wait for her to say hello before he attacked. "Who the hell do you think you are giving James my cell number?"

"I didn't give him your number."

"Then how did he get it?"

"Shayne, I don't know. But calm down and listen to yourself. You're so good at telling everyone else to deal with their problems, maybe you should take your own advice. Maybe it's time you dealt with your father."

"I'm not one of your freakin' lost causes."

"This thing is going to keep eating at you until you resolve it. Just talk to him." Her voice softened and became filled with concern. "Please."

He hung up on her. He didn't need little Ms. Let-me-solve-everyone's-problems inserting her good intentions into his business.

The anger hadn't diminished by the time he reached the Mustang. He opened the door and slid in without waiting for the heat to escape. The black leather upholstery scorched through his jeans and he couldn't even touch the gearshift. "Shit!" His jeans smelled like someone was ironing them. Or maybe that was his skin blistering.

For once, he didn't have any plans for the night, but no way in hell would he spend the evening with James Highland. He wasn't done with Ms. Cochran either. Where did she get off? 'Talk to your father, Shayne.' The woman had no right to butt into his business. What did she know about it anyway? She'd never lived a single day without the comfort of a family. She didn't understand the concept of rejection and the mental bullshit that went with it. 'Take your own advice.' Her words haunted him.

Screw it!

He drove half way to Galveston with every intention of

Undercover Heart

telling her off before he grudgingly admitted she was right. Avoiding the man sure as hell hadn't worked. The best way to put his father behind him and get on with his life was to confront him, hear him out, and then tell him to go to hell.

Shayne walked into Joe's Crab Shack an hour later and scanned the room. James Highland sat in a corner booth with an attractive blonde. Figured. He should be shocked, or at least surprised, but he wasn't. He started to turn and leave when James looked up and recognized him. He could walk out and that would be the end, but it was past time to face this situation, tie it up, and move on.

James stared at him and now the blonde had turned, her gaze assessing his appearance. Shayne strode across the restaurant and stopped beside their table.

"This is Karen, a friend from work."

I'll bet she's a friend. Shayne nodded at the woman. She ran a French tipped fingernail down the collar of her blouse, showing off a platinum set diamond ring. Her monthly hair salon bill probably ran more than his apartment.

The beige silk clung to her slender curves as she stood. Her glossed lips turned up at the corners. "Nice meeting you, Shayne. You look so much like your father." She widened her big brown eyes at James. "See you in the morning."

Every male in the room ogled Karen as she glided out of the restaurant. Shayne took the seat she'd vacated across from James. "Don't preach to me about morals."

"It's not what you think. Needed a friendly ear."

"Your wife hard of hearing?"

James took a deep breath. "Patty doesn't understand my need to get close to you. She gets defensive when I mention our relationship."

Shayne raised one eyebrow. "Wives never understand, do they?"

James shook his head. "You don't understand."

"Who gave you my cell number?" Shayne wanted to trust Dani that she hadn't given it out, but he had to know.

"Nobody." James shrugged. "It's in Kyle's cell phone contact list."

The kid was resourceful, he'd give him that. "Great."

James held up a hand. "Maybe you don't need to discuss the past, but I do."

"That's the first really honest thing you've said." At least he was aware that this whole getting to know each other exercise was more to relieve James' guilt than do Shayne any good.

"Let's start over. We got off on the wrong foot from day one. Can we just have a civil, honest conversation for a change? You've shut yourself off from people and I have to take some of the blame for that."

Bullshit. "Okay, let's be honest." James' face stiffened, but Shayne didn't give a shit. "You're off working while your wife takes responsibility for the house and kids. You need a shoulder to cry on and turn to some lady fifteen years younger than you. Your son is fighting like hell to get your attention and the only way he's found that works is to run away and smoke pot. By the time you wake up, he's going to be so far down the friggin' road you won't be able to help him."

James placed both palms on the table and glared into his face. "Wait a minute here."

"Molly will do the same thing once she realizes she's not getting any attention either. When bringing her a new doll won't cut it anymore. Your wife sees me as competition for what little bit of time you make for family. And you think

Undercover Heart

I'm the one who has problems with commitment."

"I told you, Karen's just a friend."

"A friend who shows up on a Wednesday night in a sexy little blouse and smelling like a perfume counter to hold the hand of a married coworker."

James' gaze lingered on Shayne's face and torso. "You can't tell me women don't throw themselves at you every day."

Shayne's jaw tensed. "The ones that do don't stick around long." He arched one eyebrow. "Must be my charming personality."

James grinned. "You said it, I didn't."

Shayne returned the grin. "But I'm not married. And just because a woman's available doesn't mean I'm interested."

The waitress bopped up to the table wearing a black skirt and a red and white striped blouse. She flashed a bright smile at them and opened a menu in front of Shayne. "Hey there good-lookin', can I get you something from the bar? Happy hour. All drinks half price."

He closed the menu and handed it back to her. "Shiner."

James smiled at the waitress and waited until she left. "It's always so easy, isn't it?"

"What?"

"Women. Getting them to fall for you."

Shayne shrugged. "Nothing much is easy for me."

James took a swig of his beer. "Patty and I are worried about Dani. We love her like a daughter. She sees the good looks, but she doesn't understand how it is with you. You know she's taking this relationship more seriously than you are and you know she's going to be hurt."

"Damn! I finally get it." Shayne felt his jaw drop. "I know why you automatically jump to the worst possible conclusion. You think I'm like you. You cheat on Patty, so it only stands to reason that I'd do the same thing to Dani or whoever I become involved with."

James opened his mouth to speak, but Shayne cut him off. "That's the way it was with my biological mother," Shayne stated, rather than asked. "She fell for the golden boy bit and you took advantage."

James combed his fingers through his hair and tried. "She was a sweet, small town girl. Captain of the drill team. We'd been in classes together since grade school. It just happened."

"You were kids. Why didn't you take care of the problem? You couldn't have been happy about the pregnancy."

Now that Shayne was willing to discuss the past, his father looked a little uneasy. "No, not at first. She was scared to death. I figured either her father or mine would beat the crap out of me once she told her folks."

"You didn't go with her to tell them?"

James shook his head. "Her mother figured it out and told her dad, who immediately called my father." He stared at Shayne. "Never once did we consider abortion. We didn't love each other, but we were friends and we wanted to do right by you."

"Do right by me. What the hell does that mean?" Shayne leaned back in the booth and waited for the waitress to set the beer down and leave.

James didn't speak until she was out of earshot. "Raise you. Provide for you. But we had no idea how hard that would be. We reached a point where we couldn't even

Undercover Heart

have a civil conversation. I'd go by her parents' house to pick you up and she'd bite my head off. Her grades fell because she had to miss so much school. Finally our high school counselor suggested we consider adoption. It was the hardest decision I ever made."

Shayne took a gulp of beer and narrowed one eye. "Life is never easy."

"Life?"

"Relationships. Women," Shayne explained.

"Was it that horrible in foster care?" James waved the hovering waitress away.

Shayne took another swig and smirked. "A week before my sixteenth birthday my foster mother decided to give me an early birthday present. The faithful, loving, wife who couldn't wait until her husband's Mercedes pulled out of the driveway before she invited me into her bedroom for a morning of fun and games."

James' mouth gaped open. "I hope those foster homes are the exceptions."

"Sure, those were the ones who'd passed all the inspections and were certified as safe, healthy environments for children."

James swallowed. "Were they all that bad?"

Shayne stared out the window at the bay, let out a deep sigh, and adopted a calmer, rational tone. "No, there were some decent ones." He took another drink and studied the green bottle. "The thing is, those were almost worse. The families were permanent. I was temporary."

* * *

The shrill ringing of the telephone jarred Dani out of a sound sleep early Saturday morning. It was Shayne calling to say he wouldn't be down until Sunday, if at all. She was surprised he'd called at all after their last conversation.

"Houston more interesting than I am?"

"Right, chasing a drugged out juvenile delinquent on an overpowered crotch rocket through the middle of Houston at three this morning is my idea of fun."

She didn't like thinking about the danger Shayne's job put him in. "Did you talk to James?"

"Yeah." He took a deep breath. "Sorry I jumped down your throat. Kyle somehow got my number and James confiscated it off his phone."

The last thing she'd expected was an apology. "That figures."

"Just let me handle my own life, okay?" He let out a breath. "Sorry. I'm beat and now I have to go in and fill out a damn mountain of paperwork."

Someone pounded on her door.

"What's the commotion?" he asked.

She glanced out the bedroom window. "Calvin and Mario are ready for work and I'm not even dressed."

"Be careful. See you tomorrow. Maybe."

The two boys worked with her all morning, moving everything out of her bathroom, even removing the cabinet doors, getting it cleaned and ready to paint. At noon, Dani made sandwiches, had them work another couple hours, then told them to take a swim. She paid them for the time worked, but refused to let them work both days of their weekend. They needed at least one day to relax. The plan was that they'd also work Monday and Wednesday afternoons after the weather cooled off painting the outside of the house.

The boys left early and Dani had nothing scheduled

for the evening. She opened a drawer for a clean pair of shorts and found Shayne's swimsuit. She loved his things mixed in with hers. Just this morning she'd reached for a pair of jeans in the closet and realized they weren't hers. He was beginning to feel comfortable here whether he'd admit it or not. Every time she noticed the box of condoms in the nightstand drawer, she grew moist.

Sunday Dani was up to her elbows in peach-colored paint when Shayne pulled up to the house. At least he'd been calling more often. She grinned when he came in without knocking and found his way back to the bathroom where she was working.

She greeted him with a kiss, but kept her distance, not wanting to get paint on his shirt. He placed a palm on each side of her face and planted a penetrating kiss on her lips.

"Wow, you're in a good mood." She spread her hands across his back and hugged. "I missed you."

Shayne cradled the back of her head, tilted her back, and kissed her thoroughly. "Same here. I wanted to come last night, but it was after one AM when I got in. I really shouldn't be here now." He pulled back, and glanced around. "You got a lot painted."

Dani stared at the purple streak running down one side of his hair. It had gel in it too, or something making spikes on top. In the mirror, she could see two distinct peach handprints on the back of his navy blue T-shirt. She giggled. "Including your shirt, but I promise I didn't do that to your hair."

He tugged at the hem and stretched to see the back of his shirt. "It was worth it." Taking a step closer, he wrapped her in his arms. "I locked the front door."

He slipped her shorts off and lifted her onto the vanity, positioning himself between her legs.

Dani giggled, watching him drop a couple of cellophane condom packages on the counter and struggle with his jeans. "So your ex-girlfriend was right. You like a bit more variety than a bed."

He stared at her chest. "Huh?"

"That blonde from jail. She said you'd be bored with me in a week. So she's adventurous?"

Shayne kissed his way down her neck. "She was just getting under your skin. We made out in the backseat of a car one night."

"That little witch." She huffed. "Somebody ought to teach her a lesson about trying to cause problems in other people's lives. If I'd actually been your fiancé, I'd have been crushed."

"Think that was the idea." He slipped her shirt over her head and ran his hands up her sides to fondle her breasts. He bit the top off the condom package and she groaned as he roughly entered her. His eyes never left her face as he began to move. "Feel good?"

"Oh. Don't stop." She wrapped her legs around his hips and leaned her head back. "If I had known sex with you was going to feel like this, I'd have pushed James to hire that investigator sooner."

"I'm sure you've had other lovers." He cupped her hips and held tight for the next thrust.

Dani sighed, leaned forward, and nuzzled her nose into his neck. She had, but at the moment she couldn't visualize making love with any other man besides Shayne. "Not like you. You're a fantasy."

He never broke the rhythm as he stared deep into her eyes. "I've never been anybody's fantasy."

Moving with him, Dani's vision clouded over with passion. "I'll bet you've been plenty of girls' fantasy." She

Undercover Heart

buried her hands in his stiff, long hair.

He seemed too engrossed to argue. At the moment, all that mattered to Dani was that they were together. He belonged in her arms. How he came to be with her seemed irrelevant. Her body tingled with sensation. Giving up on conversation for the moment, she attempted to teach him about love as he continued to instruct her on the art of sex.

Dani wanted to cook dinner, but Shayne insisted on bringing in fast food and helping her work on the house. They devoured a pizza and he sanded the cabinet doors while she finished painting the walls. At ten he gave her a long kiss and started for the door.

He couldn't just leave.

"I think you should give up your apartment and stay with me. It's only an hour drive, and you have to be here on Tuesdays and Thursdays anyway," Dani rationalized.

"I'm not about to put you in danger."

Dani started to argue, but took one look at his face and realized her blunder. His reason for refusing had more to do with his need for space than her security. The barrier might not be as strong as before, but it was well in place.

Shayne had refused to move in, but he might show up any time. They were becoming more at ease with one another with every visit. He arrived one evening with a porch swing and a sack of tacos. He only stayed long enough to eat, install the swing, and make love in her freshly painted bedroom.

As a lover, he could be slow and sensuous one time, wild and crazy the next, and everything in between. Dani splurged on new sheets, a red bikini, and an entire wardrobe of sexy underwear. If he lost interest, it wouldn't be for lack of effort on her part.

They put new tires on her folks' old ten speeds and rode down the seawall one Saturday. Shayne had mentioned checking out the pier and souvenir shops the weekend before.

Dani took off her yellow floral ball cap, yanked the rubber band off her ponytail, and shook her head while Shayne chained the bikes to the wooden railing. Geez it was hot today. Tendrils of damp hair clung to her face and neck.

Shayne leaned down to check out the huge conch shell perched out front of the wooden pier that supported the historic souvenir shop. "Think this thing's real?"

She shrugged, noticing that the back of his shirt was soaked with sweat. "It's been here for decades." Rebuilt after each hurricane and renovated numerous times, the souvenir shop out over the water had been in Galveston since Dani's earliest memory.

He finger combed his sweaty hair back and pushed his sunglasses up on top of his head. "Well, if it is, I hope I never run into his daddy."

Hand in hand, they wandered up the wooden steps into the shop.

Dani stopped and let go of Shayne's hand. Amber was standing behind the register, ringing up a sale for a lady and two small kids. "I had no idea you worked here."

Amber looked from Shayne to Dani, wrapped the last seashell and stuck it in the bag. "Girl's got to take care of herself. It doesn't pay much, but it's something."

The woman took the bag, smiled her thanks, and grabbed her kids.

"Hey, whatever it pays is that much more than you had, right?" Shayne said.

Undercover Heart

Amber nodded. Her lip piercing was missing today. "Yeah, and it's something to do."

He stretched to look out one of the windows at the waves crashing against the wooden piers holding the building high above the surf. "Cool."

Dani waved to Amber and followed Shayne. "When Patty and I were kids our parents brought us to Galveston every summer. Coming here to pick out a souvenir was a must, a tradition."

"So what are you buying today?"

"I'm going to get that." She pointed to a plastic pail filled with sand tools. "We can build sandcastles."

Shayne discovered the back part of the shop, where there was an open air deck suspended over the surf and wooden Adirondack chairs to sit. "I think I'll go for a beer. You want one?"

Dani felt refreshed after a beer and resting her legs after the long bike ride.

Shayne paid for the toys, waved goodbye to Amber, and they pedaled down the seawall in the direction of home. She spotted an outdoor burger place to cool off before attacking the last leg of the trip.

By the time they finally reached the house, Dani was panting and exhausted. "We must have ridden twenty miles."

Shayne was already stripping out of his sweat-soaked shirt and heading for the surf. "At least."

The sun had begun to set and the beach had calmed to a sedate reprieve, with the exception of the squawking gulls as they circled and prepared for the evening. After a refreshing dip in the ocean, Dani dumped out her new sand toys. "I bet I can build a fancier castle than you can."

He didn't respond, but did grab a bucket and shovel.

She glanced over at his project. A tall wall and a moat surrounded his simple, bucket shaped castle. "Slightly paranoid there, aren't you?"

He studied her intricate little work of art. She'd put her creativity into using her new tools and everything she could collect off the beach to decorate it, from seashells to driftwood.

"The bad guys are going to carry you away if you don't put more effort into security."

She winked. "You applying for the job?"

He raised one eyebrow, and returned to digging his moat. She smiled. She loved him when he was relaxed and funny. Who was she kidding? She loved him when he was uptight and acting like a jerk.

Slowly, Dani stood up and dusted the sand off her hands. "Actually, yours doesn't look all that secure either. It sort of looks like an upside down bucket with some water and a ring of sand around it."

With a laugh and a quick kick, she destroyed his castle and darted into the waves. Shayne was right on her tail. How did the man move so fast? She'd waded barely butt deep when his arms locked around her and pulled them both under the next rolling wave.

She came up spluttering, deliriously happy as they walked deeper into the surf arm in arm. She grabbed his shoulders and wrapped her legs around his waist to hang on as she devoured his salty lips. "I'm onto you."

"Literally." Shayne met her kiss and slipped both hands beneath her bikini bottom, cupping her butt and crushing her against him. As the next wave crashed into them, he spread his legs, barely managing to stay upright.

Dani pushed her dripping hair out of her face, reached between them, and slid his trunks down just enough to free him. He lifted her until she was riding his body. The waves pounding paled in comparison to their bodies. Nobody could fit her this way, make her feel as alive and wild as he did. In the water, his typically clear blue eyes reflected flecks of green and brown. Accented by wet tendrils of blond hair washing across his forehead, his eyes were a kaleidoscope of shades. Instinctively, she shifted to kiss his temple.

She moved with him, with the ceaseless rolling of the waves, even as she braced herself for the next wave to rush over them.

"Dani! We gotta stop."

She grasped his hair when he tried to pull away, as she rode another type of wave closer and closer to ecstasy. "Yeah, we should." She fought for breath as they rode over a large swell. "But the timing is safe."

Hard to tell whether her meaning penetrated, but he didn't pull away. She drowned in wave after wave of passion. His demanding mouth was so hot and warm against hers. All she could taste or breathe was the salty taste of Shayne. The wave exploded and so did she as salty sea water sprayed into her face. Shayne turned her back to the oncoming waves and never broke rhythm, surge after surge. His eyes closed as he shuddered and emptied himself into her.

He was still inside her and she didn't want him to pull away. "Let's do it again, right here, right now."

Shayne took a deep breath and held her tight as the next wave threatened his balance. "You're insatiable."

I'm in love. She wanted to tell him over and over. How he was the most wonderful thing that had ever happened in her life. How she wanted to spend the rest of her life with him. How she'd happily follow him anywhere, if only he returned her love.

But she knew he didn't, or at least he wouldn't admit it. She clutched tight around his neck and nuzzled into his chest, enjoying the feel of him.

Shayne was losing ground. Her thighs jittered like Jell-O just from being wrapped around him, while he took the brunt of the surf. Slowly she untangled her legs and buried her toes in the shifting sand. She held tight to him until she steadied enough to support herself. *I'm hopelessly in love with a man who doesn't believe it exists.*

They strolled back down the beach and stopped to shower off at the bottom of Dani's stairs. Shayne waited while Dani took her turn under the spray, then rinsed off while she pulled a large white T-shirt over her bikini.

When they reached the top of the stairs, Pearl was on the deck, her two young grandsons in tow. She struck a match and beamed at Dani as she and Shayne came up the steps from the beach. "Thought I'd get the grill going. Kids are getting a little hungry."

Dani froze. "Ohmygod, the neighborhood cookout. I forgot."

Calvin, Mario, and Amber sprawled at the deck table with soft drinks and a bowl of chips. Calvin tilted his head, nudged Mario, and studied Dani's legs.

The grill flared to life and Pearl motioned toward the door. "You two have time to grab a quick shower. I brought potato salad and chocolate chip cookies."

Shayne nailed Calvin with a threatening stare that had the boy at least feigning interest in his soda rather than Dani's curves. He saw the quiet, romantic evening he'd visualized disintegrate into a table full of potato salad.

Dani gave each of Pearl's grandsons a hug. "I've got hotdogs in the fridge ready to cook. You guys hungry?"

The smaller boy bounced up and down. "I want three."

Undercover Heart

His older brother didn't bother to answer. He was dragging a small piece of white rope around the deck at breakneck speed with the cat jumping and pouncing behind him. The little red-headed girl Shayne had met on his first visit raced to keep up.

Shayne followed Dani inside and waited as she pulled a whole grocery bag of hotdogs out of the fridge. He took two giant plastic bowls she handed him and set them on the counter.

Was the woman clueless to how sexy she looked? Her T-shirt fell off one shoulder, exposing her bathing suit strap, tied behind her neck. The damp bikini had soaked through the thin cotton, making it virtually transparent as it clung to her skin.

He took the hotdogs from her. She wasn't going back out on the deck looking like that with those hormonal adolescents around. "I'll take these out to Pearl. You get out of that wet swimsuit and hit the shower."

Standing on tiptoes, she planted a kiss on his lips. "You may frighten teenagers with that dark scowl, but it doesn't work on me." She headed toward the bathroom before he could respond.

"As long as it works on your oversexed, underage painters," he said to her departing back.

He carted all the food out and left Pearl in charge. Dani almost ran him down coming out of the bedroom. Dressed in faded denim shorts and a black tank top, she gave him a gentle shove. "Hurry up in the shower. I need you to man the grill," she instructed with a kiss as they passed in the hall. She'd piled her wet hair on top of her head with a clip and the black tank top she'd chosen was even sexier than the bikini.

It was going to be a long night.

This whole neighborhood cookout seemed to have

been planned ahead, yet Dani had failed to mention anything about it to him or he'd have made himself scarce for the evening. Not his idea of a fun-filled Saturday night.

Dani's friend Felicia and her husband showed up. Shayne watched Dani as she placed paper plates, plastic flatware, and bowls of chips and dips on the patio table. More to the point, he watched Calvin and Mario watch Dani, like two sex-starved juvenile delinquents. The whole situation with those two working at her house had him on edge. She seemed oblivious to the natural sexual way she looked, but guys sure as hell noticed. He could just imagine their graphic thoughts.

No one arrived empty handed. A couple of neighbors brought coolers of iced soft drinks and beer. There must have been at least thirty people there and they had enough food to feed three times that many.

He wanted to be angry at Dani for not telling him about the plans, but she seemed to be enjoying herself so much. The woman was in her element, making sure everyone had plenty to eat and drink. Two of the men turned on the floodlight and set up a volleyball net in the sand.

Amber grabbed Shayne's hand. "Come on, we can get in a game before desert."

He was too exhausted from his earlier escapades to get excited about a vigorous game of sand volleyball. "You guys go on. I'll umpire."

"Afraid I'll kick your ass, Agent Kelley?" Calvin asked, twirling the volleyball on one finger.

Shayne stood from his deck chair and snagged the ball. At least the game would divert their attention from Dani. "You and what army?"

Undercover Heart

Chapter Eighteen

The outside painting project hadn't progressed as fast as Dani had hoped. Calvin and Mario tended to horse around as much as they worked. But with her help they were making headway. It should have been finished last weekend. But if they accomplished as much next Saturday as they were getting done today, then it should be done.

Dani hopped off the ladder and motioned to Mario. "I've got a cold pitcher of lemonade in the fridge. When you guys finish that section, come upstairs and take a break."

Ten minutes later, balancing a tray containing a tall pitcher of lemonade, three glasses, and a plate of homemade brownies, she turned to set it on the table and bumped into Mario. The tray tilted and the pitcher toppled and bounced off her right shoulder. "Whoa!" she squealed as the icy liquid drenched her T-shirt and shorts.

Mario grabbed the tray before the remaining contents hit the floor. She swiped at the sticky liquid. "What a mess. Let me grab a towel. Maybe you guys should just get a couple sodas out of the fridge."

She headed for her bedroom, holding the soggy shirt away from her skin. Forget a towel, she needed dry clothes. She collected a clean shirt, bra, and shorts from the bureau and headed for the bathroom to wash off the sticky lemonade. Bumping the door shut with her foot, she yanked her shirt over her head, unhooked her bra, and pitched them over the shower rod to dry. The shorts followed a similar path. She grabbed a washcloth and reached to turn the sink

234

faucet on just as the door opened.

Standing only in her panties, Dani quickly swiped her fresh blouse off the counter and held it in front of her. Her hands shook as they clutched the blouse. Breathe.

Mario stood in the doorway, looking almost as embarrassed as her. Calvin came up behind him and both boys' eyes were as wide as saucers, but they didn't look away.

She tried to push the door, but Mario was half in and half out. "Excuse me," Dani said, grasping the blouse like a lifeline.

Snapping out of his daze, Mario darted down the hall. Dani heard the rumble of Shayne's Mustang outside. Calvin bolted after his friend as if the slamming car door was a gunshot. A minute later, and that might not have been so far from reality.

Dani shut the door and glanced in the mirror at her beet red face. "Shit." She'd covered her chest, but the reflection of her backside had been glaringly visible. Had they barged in on her on purpose or was it an accident?

She heard the refrigerator door open and two distinct tops pop on soft drink cans before the front door opened.

"Hello," Shayne called out.

Without wasting any time, Dani washed off and pulled on fresh clothes. By the time she made her way to the living room, neither Calvin nor Mario were anywhere in sight.

Shayne glanced at her. "What the hell's going on here?"

"Nothing. I just dumped a pitcher of lemonade down the front of me." She plastered a smile on her face and headed toward the kitchen. She did not want to find out how Shayne would react if he knew about the bathroom incident. "The house is looking nice, don't you think?"

Undercover Heart

His eyes narrowed. "You're as jumpy as Calvin and Mario. They practically got stuck trying to squeeze out the door at the same time."

"You make them nervous now that they know you and I are a couple."

"They were fine the other night at the cookout."

She ignored his frown and breezed past to clean the floor. "Are you off for the weekend?"

"Yeah." He propped one shoulder against the doorframe and watched her like she was a drug dealer. "You aren't going to tell me?"

"There's nothing to tell." Oh yes, he'd definitely overreact. She picked up the tray of brownies from the table, snatched the empty plastic pitcher off the floor, and carried it all into the kitchen. "And stop looking at me like a cop."

"Then stop acting like a criminal."

"What are you talking about? I've got to mop this up before ants carry us off." She dropped everything on the counter and turned. Judging by the dark storm brewing in those blue eyes, he wasn't buying it. Wiggling her way into his arms, she tilted her mouth up for a kiss. "I'm fine, Shayne."

* * *

Monday morning Dani took a mental roll call of her students. Was Tad running late? Mario and Calvin were in their seats early, heads buried in their work. Neither one had come back inside Saturday, but they'd gotten a remarkable amount of painting done in the hour and a half they'd worked after the bathroom escapade.

Dani still wasn't sure what to make of the whole incident. If it was truly an accident, they would have immediately turned and left the room. But Calvin in particular had stood and drank his fill. If Shayne hadn't pulled up, she wasn't sure what might have happened. The more she thought about the look on Calvin's face, the more concerned she felt.

Amber tapped her pencil on her desk and looked at Tad's empty seat. "Where's the whiz kid? Weird that Calvin and Mario are more studious than your star pupil."

Dani wandered around the room to check everyone's progress. "If you're smart, you'll concentrate on preparing for your final instead of worrying about everyone else."

"Yeah, if I had to waste my entire summer in here, I'm damn well going to pass," Calvin said.

Mario winked at his buddy. "Amber hasn't figured out yet that she needs an education to survive. She's still waiting on Freddy to get sprung."

"Settle down and concentrate on your work. It's too late in the semester to waste your time insulting each other. Finals are Thursday."

Where was Tad? She was supposed to report to the board if anyone missed class. At least Tad wasn't one of the kids in trouble with the law, just the school. The kid had good grades. His problems were personal, not scholastic, and she didn't want to get him into more trouble with the police.

When Tad still hadn't arrived by 10:00 AM, Dani pulled out her folder and carried it to the hall. Maybe he was sick and his parents had forgotten to call in. She was unable to reach his mom, but his dad said if she'd hold off reporting him, he'd find Tad and have him in class by noon.

The kids had sat down with their sack lunches when Tad, accompanied by both parents, stalked into the lunchroom. He shuffled up to Dani, staring at his feet. "Thank you, Ms. Cochran, for not turning me in."

Tad's father nodded toward the hallway door. "Could we have a moment of your time, Ms. Cochran?"

Undercover Heart

Dani followed the couple into the hall and listened while Tad's mother explained that they were in the midst of a divorce. Tad simply wasn't adjusting.

Tad stepped up behind his mother. "Tell the truth, Mom. He kicked you out."

The woman rubbed her forehead and looked exasperated.

Her husband stepped in. "Not here. We can discuss this tonight, son."

"Discuss what? Her new bed partner? I'll skip that sordid little chat, if it's all the same to you. T-M-I."

It was sad to see a grown man blush. Tad's father squeezed his son's arm. "I said, we'd talk tonight. Your priority for the rest of the day is to get through your studies. You will do what it takes to get out of this nonsense you've created. You will show up for class the rest of the week on time and ready to work. You will give your teacher and your mother the respect they deserve. You will not continue on this self-destructive path. Do we understand each other?"

Dani took the business card Tad's father handed her. "I wrote both our cell numbers on the back. If he isn't in his seat five minutes before class starts, call."

Dani kept an eye on Tad. Granted, he was diligent about his work during the afternoon, but anger seethed just beneath the surface. After class, he stayed behind as the others left. Once they were the only two in the room, he gathered up his books.

As he passed her desk, he paused. "I thanked you earlier because my parents insisted, but I don't give a shit what they think or want. I'll be in my seat the rest of the week, but I'm doing it for me, not them."

Dani raised an eyebrow. "You *should* do it for yourself. But I got the impression that they both care very much what happens to you."

He shrugged and slung his backpack over one shoulder. "My mom's a...mess."

"The fact that she showed up today tells me she cares about what happens to you."

Smirking, Tad headed for the door. He turned. "Yeah, but not as much as her new girlfriend."

Whoa! Dani wasn't sure what she could say about that one that could possibly make a difference. "Sometimes things change and it's out of our control. You have to adjust." Dani froze, her own words hitting too close to home. She was supposed to start her period last week, and she'd been telling herself it was just stress causing her lateness.

"Yeah, well, if this is my new reality, the only way I see to come out on top is to become a divorce lawyer." Tad smirked.

"That's resourceful." She put her own worries aside and stepped around the desk. "At least your parents are there for you."

"Yeah, I guess." Tad shuffled his feet. "Until Mom started sleeping with Lana."

"Just because your parents are no longer in love with each other, doesn't mean they don't love you. You need to make the best of your new situation."

"Don't worry. I know how to play it."

She searched her mind for brilliant advice. "Your choice. Look, you're a very intelligent boy. But even with scholarships, law school is expensive. You might need their help."

An almost evil grin spread across his face. "Choices. You're beginning to sound like the cop. Use them for what I can get out of them. Now there's a choice." He started out the door.

"Tad, the smartest thing you can do for yourself is to stay out of trouble."

He shoved his fingers through his hair. "I intend to. But not because of my parents. From here on, I take care of myself."

* * *

Dani spent Friday shopping for Shayne's twenty-sixth birthday on Saturday. He had no idea she knew, but she was determined to make this a birthday he'd remember.

She cruised through the aisles at Wal-Mart for any last minute things she might have forgotten. She needed condoms to add to one of the gifts, but the display of early pregnancy tests stopped her short. She still hadn't started her period.

Reading the labels, she selected one that said it could show accurate results within the first week. Her hand shook, but she dropped it in the cart. What if she really was pregnant? She was only a little over a week late, but her cycle had been regular since she turned sixteen. One lousy time. She'd always wanted children, but this was the absolute worst way for it to have happened. Shayne would freak out.

Don't panic. It was probably just stress.

Dani wrapped each gift in a different color and tied them with bright ribbons. She set the table with her mother's china and crystal, chilled a bottle of wine, and placed the birthday cake on a glass pedestal. If this didn't impress him, she had an ecru lace teddy hanging in the closet.

Shayne finally called about two o'clock from a pool hall where he and some other guys were wasting a Saturday afternoon. Dani glanced around at the decorations. "So finish the game and come see me."

"This will probably break up in a couple of hours, but there's a party tonight."

Dani didn't want to give away her surprise, but she couldn't stand it if he didn't show up. "I'm cooking. Dinner's at six."

"You sound like a wife," he commented. "What's for dinner?"

"You'll never know unless you show up." *Please let him give in.*

"I'll probably get fired, but..." He took a deep breath. "I think I can make six."

"See you then."

The afternoon flew by. Dani made one final trip around the house to make sure everything looked perfect. She showered and took extra time with her appearance. After all, she didn't want to be overshadowed by the other gifts.

She adjusted the neckline of her sundress and took a long look at her reflection in the dresser mirror as she heard the Mustang. She glanced around the room one final time and waited by the door with a camera to capture his reaction.

He opened the door and leaned forward for a kiss. His lips barely brushed hers before he backed off in awe. His gaze journeyed around the room, taking everything in. Dani flashed a couple of pictures, bringing his attention back to her.

"What's all this?"

She wrapped her arms around his waist and gave him a long, penetrating kiss. "Happy birthday, Lover."

Undercover Heart

"How did you know today was my birthday?"

"I've known it for years."

"How?" Shayne closed his eyes. "Never mind."

Dani grinned. "This is your night."

"Wasn't that one of those bad old TV shows?" Shayne stepped further into the room and dropped his duffel bag on the chair. "You did all this for me?"

"I did most of it. Felicia went shopping with me and Pearl provided the flowers for the centerpiece."

Shayne glanced at the flowers, but he couldn't smell them over the yeasty aroma of baking bread. He draped his arm around her shoulder. "I'm in shock."

"Wait till you see what we're having for dinner. The grill is lit, but I still have to cook the steaks. Everything else is ready." She pushed him down in the recliner and handed him the paper. "Just take it easy, birthday boy. Dinner will be served in a half hour or so."

Shayne put the newspaper aside, leaned back in the recliner, and looked around the room at the bright streamers, helium filled balloons boasting everything from 'Happy Birthday' to 'Let's Get Lucky', and a birthday cake topped with blue candles. He remembered a couple of other birthday parties, one present maybe, but nobody had ever gone to such an extreme. The coffee table was covered.

Realizing how much Dani had put into this made him cringe with guilt. Even though he'd reminded her repeatedly that this wouldn't progress beyond an affair, he'd known from the beginning she was more involved than she should be.

Summer was almost over. Time for his next assignment. As the time drew closer to end the relationship, the reality of how much Dani had risked worried him. She cared too much.

Who was he kidding? He cared too much. He'd let his guard down and he was going to pay the price. The worst part was, Dani would be hurt in the process.

Turning his head, he studied Dani as she came in from the deck. There was a childlike innocence about her, blended beautifully with a feminine temptress. She wore a bright yellow strapless sundress which exposed her tan shoulders and her feet were bare. Her dark hair was twisted on top of her head with a giant clip. His fingers tingled with anticipation of caressing the silky tendrils that had worked free.

The woman was destroying him!

Standing, he strolled into the kitchen and slipped his arms around her waist from behind, inhaling her scent. The peaches and cream fragrance of bubble bath, mixed with dinner, smelled sexy as hell. Until this moment, he'd never thought of food as smelling sensuous, but it definitely held its own appeal.

"You happy?"

Shayne rubbed his face against her silky hair and nibbled at her earlobe. "Absolutely."

She popped a bite of peeled carrot into his mouth. "Hungry?"

He continued to caress and tease. "Umm-hmm." He tilted her head back so he could kiss her throat. Sex was beginning to hold more appeal than dinner.

Dani leaned back against his chest. "We have all night."

He kept his arms wrapped around her stomach, kissing and nuzzling her at every turn while she tossed the salad. She didn't seem to mind.

Inhaling the aroma of grilled steak, he followed her when she headed for the deck. "Smells good."

Undercover Heart

She placed the salad on the table and went after the steaks from the grill. He pulled out her chair and Dani sat. He sat across from her and rolled the little paper whistle she'd placed in the center of his plate between his fingers.

An off-key whistle shrieked and Dani's paper tube unrolled, bumping into his nose. She grinned. "No frowning tonight. It's against the rules."

"Okay." He still couldn't believe she'd done all this for him.

Dani rushed through the meal, as anxious as a little kid on Christmas morning to get to the gifts. She made him sit in the middle of the living room while she piled the presents around him and snapped more pictures.

He opened a pair of roller blades first and turned them over to spin the wheels. Emerald green satin sheets to fit her bed came next and he wiggled his eyebrows at her. "Gee, these look a little big for the bed in my apartment."

She winked as he unwrapped a package containing the rubber duck.

"That duck thing really bothers you, doesn't it?"

"Open the box!" She laughed when a dozen or so cellophane wrapped condoms fell out in his lap. "I didn't know what kind of rubbers you liked."

She grinned as he opened a drill, plugged it in, and pulled the trigger. "Men seem to get some sort of thrill out of the sound of power tools," she commented, flashing another picture.

Tired of playing the role of model, he stole her camera and snapped a couple pictures of her. She handed him the last gift. A tiny silver-framed baby picture caught him off guard.

Dani leaned forward and gazed at the frame. "Beautiful baby. You look about a year and a half."

He couldn't stop staring. "Where did you get this?"

"I stole it from James." Dani didn't sound ashamed in the least. "He has a whole box full anyway."

"Of me?" Shayne was stunned. "Why would he keep a box of old pictures of a kid he gave away?"

"Because he loves you. I'm not sure he has a clue how to show it, but I know he does."

Shayne narrowed one eye. "Yeah, it's kind of hard to swallow when he gave me away and didn't show up again for twenty-four years."

"You never give up."

"He actually called me this afternoon. Kyle went to his first therapy session yesterday. Surprise! They want to talk to James and Patty. Go figure," he said with a sarcastic grin.

"They aren't bad parents."

"They have their heads stuck up their asses. Maybe the counselor can pull them out."

"They'll be fine. This is just a rough phase."

He set the picture frame on the table. He did not want to argue about his father tonight. "Come here."

She pounced into his arms knocking him backwards into the pile of discarded wrapping paper. Rolling on top, he decided it was time to move past the birthday presents and enjoy Dani. He molded against her and covered her mouth with a hard kiss. His hands worked their way up her sides to palm her round breasts.

She tried to escape his lips. "I can't breathe."

He rubbed his nose against hers. "Breathe me," he suggested, returning to her full, soft mouth.

Shayne shoved one hand up Dani's thigh to her hip,

Undercover Heart

taking the yellow dress to her waist. He kissed his way down her neck, pulling the elastic neckline lower to expose her dark nipples. Her breasts were so plump and round, he thought, as he took one into his mouth. He'd never experienced anything as warm and luscious as her body beneath his. He kissed lower, taking the offending dress with him on the sensual journey, kissing, touching, and caressing every inch of her. Her clothes ended up on the floor with the wrapping paper and Shayne took her big toe into his mouth.

Dani laughed and tried to pull her foot away. "That tickles."

He tugged both feet, one on either side of him and positioned himself, resting intimately between her thighs. "Nobody ever did anything like this for me."

"You mean like this, or a birthday party?" she questioned indicating their position on the floor. She slipped her arms around him and squeezed his ass through his jeans.

"Either." He fumbled with his zipper and pushed his jeans low enough to free himself.

Shayne made slow, easy love to Dani amidst the paper. In the time they'd been together, Dani had proven to be an ideal match for him sexually. They fit together too perfectly. But why did she have to think she was in love?

Chapter Nineteen

Shayne woke up Sunday morning with Dani cuddled against his side, unable to move. His arm was numb from being trapped beneath her neck while her arm rested casually across his chest. The breeze from the ceiling fan creaking above the bed stirred her hair which tickled his chest. She looked as wild and sexy as a baby tiger. He glanced at her teddy, hanging by one strap on the bedpost and smiled as she stretched and nuzzled his chin with the top of her head.

She felt so right in his arms. He didn't want her to, but she did. He'd sworn he'd never let anyone get close enough to hurt him again and he'd done a good job of it, till now. He pushed a strand of long, dark hair out of his face.

Of all the women in the world why did he have to fall for James' sister-in-law? Leaving her was going to hurt like hell. Dani and this house offered more comfort than any place he'd ever been or anyone he'd ever been with. Still, the college semester ended last week. Why was he putting off ending the relationship?

Her phone rang and Dani stretched, rolled away from him, and grabbed the receiver.

He stared at her heavy breasts. The woman tantalized him, body and soul.

While carrying on the conversation, she glanced up and followed the direction of his gaze. Without missing a word, she reached down and lowered the green satin sheet

Undercover Heart

to below his waist, caressing his body with her eyes. Her finger looked pale in comparison as it trailed over his chest down to that one part of his anatomy always shielded from the sun.

He remained perfectly still and let her work her magic. He couldn't resist reaching out and squeezing the inside of her thigh, amused at her attempt to keep her voice calm long enough to get rid of whoever was on the phone.

Finally she dropped the receiver back into the cradle and pounced on him, tickling and kissing. "I was trying to carry on an intelligent conversation."

"That's rude when you have company. Anyway, you were seducing me."

Dani ran her foot up the inside of his leg. "You know, if you'd just move in, you wouldn't be company."

"You'd get tired of me. I'm a lousy roommate."

"Try me." Sitting up, she shook her head. "We have to get up. Some friends are meeting on Bolivar beach to play volleyball. I said we'd come."

He wrinkled his nose. "Not a good plan."

"Sure it is. We've got to ice down drinks and buy hotdogs. Come on. I'll race you to the shower," she challenged, already running for the door.

He bolted out of bed and tripped over the pile of sheets, unceremoniously dumped beside the bed in their rush to put on the new satin ones. Dani kept the house clean enough, just not quite organized. She'd never finish all her projects. Still, that was what made it Dani's home.

The ferry trip across the bay was a kick. It was the first time he'd ever driven his car onto a boat. They got out and stood at the rail with the rest of the passengers. Dani tried to spot porpoises, although they didn't see any. The sun bounced off the iron deck and sweat ran down his back by the time they docked on the other side.

She greeted her friends with hugs, listening to all the gossip since she'd bought the beach house last year and moved out of her condo. He exchanged pleasantries with two girls who shared the condo down the hall from where Dani had lived.

The little blonde's eyes held a bold invitation. "Are you and Dani exclusive?"

"We hook up when we can," he told her in answer to her smoldering gaze, hoping she'd take the hint.

Needing an escape, he grabbed Dani's hand and led her into the surf. They didn't come out until one of the guys started the grill.

Shayne opened a package of wieners and frowned at Dani. "Did I mention I don't like hotdogs?"

She took the plastic package and started lining wieners up on the grill. "Then starve," she said with a kiss.

He consumed three. Unbelievable how good things could taste on the beach that were hardly edible at home.

Dani watched him down the last bite. "Sure glad you don't like hotdogs, or there wouldn't be any left for everyone else."

The beach was cleaner and less crowded than the ones on the island. They hung the volleyball net and everyone had room to spread out and play. A jock type positioned himself beside Dani in front of the net. Shayne had been watching him for the last half hour. Everywhere she went, the guy managed to be in the same place. Dani moved away, but the jerk kept crowding her.

The other team served and as she bounced up to return the ball, the guy moved into position so that she landed against him. She either didn't notice or didn't mind as she stepped back up to the net. How the hell could she not

Undercover Heart

notice how guys interpreted her outgoing friendliness? She might be oblivious to what the guy had in mind, but Shayne wasn't.

Shayne stepped forward, slipped a possessive arm around Dani's bare middle, and planted an earth-shattering kiss on her lips. The jock frowned and backed up. He held his position between Dani and Don Juan.

She sidled closer to Shayne and whispered. "That wasn't very subtle."

He patted her bottom. "Wasn't trying to be."

They watched the sun set on the trip back across on the ferry. Exhaustion was taking hold. Shayne unloaded the car and dumped the sandy paraphernalia on the washer. Since his summer classes had ended, he was in no particular hurry to leave. The juveniles had completed their summer regimen. Dani had to get up early and go to school the next morning to organize her classroom for the fall term. Still, they showered and retired to the porch swing.

"I'm not ready for the semester to start," she complained.

"I'm glad it's over."

Dani paused. "Are you enrolling for fall?"

"No. The guy's a novice. When I finally got an invitation, he shook my hand and was ready to close the deal. Hopefully the next assignment will be more of a challenge."

Dani closed her eyes and tried to breathe. "So are you moving on?"

"Did I tell you the Houston P. D. offered me a job?"

Her whole face lit up and he felt even more like an ass. "Are you considering it?"

"I guess the idea of staying in one place is beginning to sound appealing, but not Houston. Too close to the old man."

Reaching for his hand, Dani entwined her fingers in his. "It's also close to me."

Yeah, that was part of the problem. Too damn tempting. The longer he let this drag out, the worse Dani was going to be hurt. The worse they were both going to be hurt. "Dani, you remember when we started this, I warned you not to get involved."

"Sorry. My mind listened, but my heart won out. I love you."

Her words made him want to crawl under a rock. "The three most abused words in history."

"Not if they come from the heart."

Didn't sound like she was going to let him off the hook tonight. Leaning his head back, Shayne tried to figure out how to turn the conversation around. "Would you just let it drop?"

"No, I won't. Your actions contradict your words."

"Because we sleep together?"

"More than that. You're happy here. If you weren't, you wouldn't keep coming back. The more we're together, the more I love you." She leaned forward and her lips met his with a tantalizing kiss. "Do you have any idea how fantastic you are?"

Shayne swallowed the lump obstructing his breathing. "Caring about people is disastrous. They just walk away."

"I will never, never walk away. I know it's hard for you to trust. But life is about taking risks. I'm tired of being alone. I want a home with you." She moved over and straddled his legs. He couldn't avoid her penetrating eyes. "Please take

Undercover Heart

the job in Houston."

He couldn't stand up without dumping her on the deck. "No. If you don't expect anything from people, then you aren't disappointed."

Dani lost her battle with tears. "You won't take a chance, even for me?"

He blinked back tears. This was it, the end. He hadn't planned it to be tonight, but it was happening. He didn't want to quit coming here. He enjoyed being with Dani, yet her loving him threatened his norm, or the norm as he'd defined it. He had to escape, but she was still in his lap. "I can't. Not even for you."

Dani shivered and he hated himself for hurting her. He looked away from her eyes. They made him feel like a swine. She took his face between her hands and forced him to look at her. "I don't know how to tell you this, but I can't not tell you."

He gulped, the dread building with every second she didn't speak. "Tell me what?"

She let out a breath, staring so deeply into his eyes that he felt exposed, like she could see inside his soul. She wasn't just upset, her terror mirrored his.

Why didn't she just say it? "Not going to tell me what?"

Her eyes were swimming in tears. "I'm pregnant," she whispered so softly he barely heard the sound.

Shayne's world stopped. She couldn't be pregnant. He'd always been careful. Shit! Except. Except that day in the surf. He stared into her liquid brown eyes. His hands closed around her slim waist. There was no room for a baby there. He couldn't feel anything different. "You're sure?"

Dani leaned forward and rested her forehead against his. "I'm a week late and I'm always on time."

Pamela Stone

He lifted her off his lap and stood. He couldn't sit there and let her destroy him. His heart raced a hundred miles an hour as he fought for control. Pacing across the deck, he leaned against the rail at the opposite end and gulped salt air into his lungs. "One damn time." He spoke more to himself than her.

She followed him across the deck. "Shayne, it's okay." She looked like she was going to burst into tears.

His mind raced, reliving that afternoon they'd built sandcastles and had sex in the surf. "Have you taken a pregnancy test?" Dani slipped her arms around him, but he pushed her away. "Have you?"

"I took an early detection test."

He eased out of her reach and moved back across the deck. "Positive?" His voice sounded harsh, but he couldn't help it.

"Yeah, but it's so early. Hard to be sure." She swiped the back of her hand across her cheek. "I'll feel better after I make an appointment with my doctor."

Shayne fought for breath. He couldn't just sit here. He couldn't leave. Bad guys didn't faze him and this one woman had him shaking.

"I haven't been late since I was a teenager."

His teeth clenched.

Dani flinched, but he couldn't touch her. Not now. Not tonight. He pushed away from the rail and headed for the front door. "I've got to get out of here."

She followed him into the house and dogged his heels as he gathered up his things and started out the door.

"Shayne, wait."

"Make the appointment and call me." He paused, but

253

Undercover Heart

couldn't look at her. "Just let me go now. Please."

"Fine!"

She glared as he passed, but he didn't slow down.

"For a tough guy so good at telling other's to deal with their problems, you suck at it. You ever plan to stop running away from yours?"

* * *

Dani couldn't get in to see the doctor for over a week and felt lucky to get that appointment. But a little more doubt faded as each day passed. Those nine days were the longest of her life. She worked on her classroom during the day and worried over Shayne and the baby all night.

Nobody she could talk to would understand. Patty and James would lecture her. Felicia liked Shayne, but even she didn't believe he was the guy for Dani. Pearl thought he was adorable, but women from her era believed getting pregnant without the benefit of marriage was a disgrace. The only person she could really talk to about it was Shayne, and he didn't show up all weekend. When she called him, he insisted on picking her up after class on Tuesday and accompanying her to the doctor.

She went to church on Sunday, but seeing the families, mothers and fathers with their small children, only made her feel worse. Shayne probably thought she got pregnant to trap him. Had she? Certainly she hadn't made a conscious choice that day. But maybe, maybe subconsciously that's what she had wanted. It didn't matter anyway, the result was the same.

Her four remaining students had managed to pull through summer school. She just hoped she'd helped them in other ways.

With only a week break, the regular semester started. The room full of children were restless and reluctant to be confined in a classroom when the temperature outside hovered above a hundred degrees. Dani had a difficult time keeping them in their seats. The heat made her nauseous and she almost lost her lunch when two boys got into a fistfight in class and one ended up with a bloody nose. Somehow, she managed to finish the rest of the day and Shayne was waiting in the parking lot when she walked out.

He opened the Mustang door without touching her.

He looked so stern, Dani said little more than, "Hello," and granted him his silence.

The doctor confirmed her pregnancy, and handed her prescriptions for prenatal vitamins and something for the nausea. Dani had mixed emotions. She'd already fallen completely in love with this child, yet it caused so many complications with Shayne. If they had any chance of making this work, he couldn't stay only out of obligation. Reluctantly, she trudged back to the waiting room.

Dropping a copy of Parents magazine on the table, next to the artificial African violet, Shayne stood. He looked out of place in the muted pastel waiting room. She studied his face, searching for any sign of acceptance.

Silently he mouthed the word, "Yes?"

"Yes," she whispered.

He pulled out his wallet to pay the bill, but Dani handed the receptionist her insurance card.

He remained distant and polite. Dani swiped at a tear, yet in a way she was thrilled about the baby. Her emotions were confused. Shayne drove back to the school in silence and parked next to her Volkswagen.

Did he plan to just drop her off in the parking lot, as if there was nothing between them? "I have food at home for dinner. Will you come by and talk?"

The creases between his brows spoke volumes. He

Undercover Heart

nodded his acceptance.

Just the thought of driving the few blocks home seemed like more than Dani could handle. Her hands shook as she got out of his car and crawled behind the wheel of her VW. She kept one eye focused on the rearview mirror, half afraid Shayne wouldn't follow, half afraid he would.

What happened to fairytales? Life would be so perfect if he'd just sweep her into his arms and tell her how much he loved her and wanted this baby.

That was one ending she could rule out.

She left him in the living room long enough to go change into a loose dress. Maybe it was all mind games, but already tight clothes bothered her. Shayne had poured two glasses of iced tea by the time she was changed.

"You all right?" he asked, handing her a glass.

"I'm fine. How about you?"

"I thought I was prepared." One dark eyebrow rose. "Maybe not?"

She stared, memorizing his features. His youthful appearance was offset by an edge of maturity beyond his years. "I already pretty much knew." Tearing her gaze away, she opened the refrigerator. "How about a turkey sandwich? I can't stomach anything hot."

"Whatever."

It felt strange to be so formal and stilted with one another when they'd shared so much here. She built sandwiches and refilled the tea glasses, relieved to have something to busy her hands.

Shayne chewed, but he didn't seem aware of what he ate.

She was always hungry lately, but food didn't settle if

she ate too much at once. She put half her sandwich in the refrigerator and sat back down across the table from her baby's father.

It took all her control to keep her voice from shaking. "I love you so much I ache. There isn't anything in this world that would make me happier than spending the rest of my life with you and our child. But, I'm not a teenager. I have an education and a career. I'm perfectly capable of raising this child on my own. And willing." She couldn't read his expression. Today might be the last time she ever saw him. "If you and I have any chance for a future together, you can't feel trapped. I won't do that to you."

Shayne took a deep breath. "That's not it."

She stared into his face, desperate for some clue into his thoughts. "Then what? Talk to me."

"I don't think..." He stared at her. She was so innocent. He wanted to protect her, yet there was nothing he could do. "I don't think I want to bring a child into this screwed up world."

Dani's eyes flashed. "That's a cop out. The world is only as screwed up as you let it be. We can make it whatever we choose to, for us, for this baby."

"Will you even consider an abortion?"

She turned as white as the refrigerator. "I want this child." One hand cradled her belly and tears trickled down her cheek, threatening to melt his soul. She swiped at the tears. "Not fair."

Shayne stood and stepped around the table, pulling her up and into his arms. He held her tight against his chest. "You're right. That wasn't fair. Look, I'm reeling from this. Can we just take a little time and think, let things sink in?"

"I've done nothing but think for nine days. I don't know

what else I can do to convince you how much I love you, how much I'd like to make our relationship work. But at this point, I'm tired." She pushed away and put a couple steps between them, shoving her hair back and drying her eyes. "Every time I make the slightest headway, you put up another wall. So take whatever time you need. But I'm having this baby. With or without you."

He wanted to reach out and comfort her, but until he made up his mind, he didn't have the right. He clenched his fists. "I did not want to hurt you."

"I know." She straightened her shoulders. "I want you to understand that I did not do this, nor will I ever do anything to hold you if you don't want to be with me. If you decide to make this work, then do it because it's what you want, not under any false sense of obligation. I will be fine. I don't need you."

Dani showed strength he hadn't realized she possessed. "I've got an early flight tomorrow to California. I'm not sure when I'll be back."

"All right." She didn't ask why he was going. She didn't make a single demand. He'd rather she screamed or hit him. Anything but this calm acceptance.

"My phone should be in range if you need anything."

Dani nodded and repeated the words she'd said to him before. "Take care of you, for me."

"You too." His hand came up to touch her, but he let it drop.

* * *

Shayne's week sucked. Old feelings surfaced that he'd managed to keep buried for years. Hell, taking a slug in the gut had less of an impact than Dani's pregnancy. He couldn't let this kid grow up without a father. And the thought of Dani eventually marrying someone else sent him into a

Pamela Stone

cold sweat.

In spite of his battling emotions, his interview with the Carmel police department went well. Hey, putting on a convincing act was part of the job. That he could handle. By the end of the day, they were anxious to name a start date. The job was a significant increase in money. He'd be hiring and training a team to do pretty much the same work he'd been doing for seven years.

Now all he had to do was accept the offer. But for the first time in years, he didn't know what the hell to do. Dani and the baby dominated every waking thought and he couldn't sleep. He even caught himself scanning the local real estate section for a house Dani might like. Luckily he had some money put back, because houses in the Carmel area were outrageous.

If it wasn't so sick, it'd be comical the way he picked up the phone to call her at least twice a night, and then changed his mind. He had to get his head straight.

The last evening in California, Shayne drove down the Pacific Coast Highway and took a long walk on the beach. He missed Dani. As much as he hated to admit it, she'd gotten to him. He didn't even want to think about going through life without her. Not that having a baby was the best start to a relationship, but being together seemed right. The waves crashing against the jagged rocks held nothing against the churning in his stomach.

Could they make this work?

His return flight to Dallas was booked for Saturday morning. By the time he caught a connection to Houston, it would be too late to drive to the island. Maybe he'd go anyway.

The airport in Dallas was bedlam. Flights headed south were delayed or canceled because of a tropical storm in the Gulf. He let a lady with a toddler have his seat in the

Undercover Heart

lounge area and leaned against a pillar where he could watch the television monitor.

The storm that had been brewing in the gulf the last few days had changed directions and was now headed for the Texas coastline. Although the center of the storm was predicted to come ashore east of Houston and Galveston, the airport in Houston was experiencing massive weather delays from the wind and rain.

He pulled out his cell and dialed Dani's house. "Is the weather as bad down there as it looks on the news?"

"Just rain and wind. Nothing major." He stuck one finger in his other ear so he could hear over the roar in the terminal. She didn't sound concerned in the least. But then, Dani never worried about her safety.

He had a bad premonition, and if there was one thing he trusted, it was his instincts. "It's only going to get worse and you need to go inland. Get off the beach."

"Hello, Shayne. Nice trip?" she said cheerily, starting the conversation as if she'd just answered the phone.

He took a deep breath. Okay, so he'd come on a little overprotective. "Hello, Dani. My trip was fine. Now pack up a few things and head to Houston before the storm makes landfall."

"I've weathered these things before. I'll be—" The line went dead. When he called back a recording said all circuits were busy. "Dammit."

Chapter Twenty

*D*ani lit another candle and listened to the wind pound against the house. She'd forgotten to charge her cell phone again, but she had plenty of candles and two good flashlights.

It was sort of cozy and romantic with the power out. She placed the candle in the center of the dining table and looked around the room. Maybe she'd overdone it a tad. But the candlelight calmed her.

She was still trying to figure out Shayne's frustrating phone call. It was just a tropical storm. What was he so worried about? She'd weathered others.

And what was he doing in California? Had to be an assignment. Maybe that was good. She certainly couldn't live close and see him on a regular basis when he didn't love her.

And if he did admit that he loved her, the one conclusion she'd reached during his absence was that if she and Shayne had a chance, they needed to live on their own and away from James and Patty. A fresh start.

She twisted the blind open and watched the raging storm. Lightning streaked across the horizon and broke the darkness. Sheet after sheet of rain marched across the beach, almost horizontal in angle. The palms on her one lone tree whipped and turned backwards. The brunt of the storm would pass by around midnight and she wouldn't be surprised if by morning, the sun was out. Texas weather.

Undercover Heart

What was she going to do about Shayne? What could she do? The man had to make up his own mind. Either he wanted to be a part of her life or he didn't. She loosened the drawstring on her light cotton slacks and rubbed one hand across her flat belly. Would this child ever even know his, or her, father?

She jumped as a loud pounding sounded at the door. Nobody in their right mind would be out in this. Before her heart started beating again, the door burst open.

She squinted into the semi-darkness. "Mario?"

He slammed the door and shook like a wet dog, slinging water everywhere. "Expecting someone else?"

Goose bumps ran up her arms. "What're you doing here?"

Yanking his soggy shirt over his head, he didn't answer for a minute. "You said we could always come to you if we needed anything."

Dani wiped her sweaty palms on her thighs and tried to squelch her dread. "Is something wrong?"

He kicked his soppy tennis shoes off and took a couple steps toward her, wearing nothing but his wet jeans. "Nothing's wrong that you can't fix."

Instinctively, she stepped back, trying not to stare at the snake tattoo covering his right breast and shoulder. "You shouldn't be here." Until tonight, it had never dawned on her how big this kid was. Six feet tall and pushing two-hundred.

He continued to approach. "You look nervous, teach. Where's your cop friend?"

"Shayne's not..." *Okay, Dani, think smart.* "He'll be down as soon as he gets off. I actually thought it was him when you knocked."

"You suck at lying. Ain't been here all week. Why

would he show up tonight?"

Mario moved close enough for Dani to smell the cigarettes on his breath. Then she got a glimpse of his dilated, glassy pupils. He was high. "You should leave."

He grabbed the back of her neck. Before she could react, he pressed his mouth to hers with so much pressure, her lip gnashed against her teeth.

She shoved him away and scrambled across the room, but he lunged forward, grabbing her arm. He locked both arms around her and trapped her against him. She tried to wedge her arms between them, pushing frantically against his chest. Fear skittered up her spine.

Dani kicked at his shin and scratched his chest. "Let me go!"

He squeezed tighter, shoving her face against the snake tattoo. "Come on. You said you cared about me. Not saving it for the narc, are you?" He grabbed a handful of hair and yanked her head back, assaulting her mouth with another kiss. "I've watched you all summer, prissing around in those skimpy clothes, making me and Calvin hot. You want it."

She willed herself to stay calm. Think rational. "Mario, don't do this. Do you want to end up in prison? Let me go now or I will press charges."

"Too late for that, teach. Let's get these clothes off you." He twisted the neck of her T-shirt around his hand and ripped it down the front.

Dani clawed at his face and tried to grab his hands away, but Mario was already going for her bra.

"Quit fighting. You been eyeing some young meat all summer. You staged that whole game the other day so we'd get a look at your tits." He tried to rip the front of her bra, but the elastic held. Thank God.

Undercover Heart

Mustering all her strength, she plowed her knee into his groin.

Mario grunted and released her to grab his crotch. "Bitch!" Pain shot through her jaw as his fist connected and he shoved her onto the couch.

She hit with a thud and caught the full impact of Mario's weight as he landed on top of her. Out of nowhere, a metal object glinted in his hand. With one quick flick, he cut the elastic on her bra, then held the knife to her throat and struggled to shove her pants down. "So you want to fight?"

She couldn't let this happen. Tears blurred her vision as she realized how ineffective pleading would be.

To hell with that.

While he was distracted untying her pants, she knocked the knife away. Wiggling and struggling, they both tumbled to the floor, wedged between the sofa and coffee table. The sudden fall snapped her pants' drawstring.

Mario yanked them down below her hips. His laugh sounded possessed as he grabbed her hair again and forced his tongue down her throat. She bit hard, but he was so high, he didn't even seem to notice.

"Look, bitch. You want it rough, I'm an expert at that." He put his knee in her stomach and his fist smashed into the side of her face. "Like the taste of blood?"

Pain exploded in Dani's head. The room swirled and the world faded away. All she could think about was the baby. She'd survive the rape, somehow, as long as her baby wasn't hurt.

The front door blew open and the musty smell of rain filled the room. The cool air helped clear her head.

"Help me!" she screamed and tried to see around Mario's shoulder, but she was trapped beneath his bulk and his hand had a death grasp on her panties.

"Oh crap! Mario, stop, man. You'll fry for this."

She breathed a sigh of relief at the sound of Calvin's voice. Until it registered that he was Mario's best friend.

"Change your mind? Decided you want some too, huh?" Mario twisted around and looked at Calvin. That was all the distraction Dani needed. She fumbled for her mother's heavy blue onyx bowl on the coffee table and cracked it against the back of Mario's skull.

He collapsed in a lifeless heap on top of her.

Dani struggled to her feet, yanking her slacks up. "You have a cell phone?" she slurred through swollen lips.

Calvin stood frozen to the spot.

"Calvin! Call 911," she demanded, shaking uncontrollably.

He pulled a cell phone out of his pocket, but didn't dial. He kept staring at her.

"I'll do it." Dani clutched her torn shirt together and grabbed the phone. She punched in the emergency number and swiped at tears as she tried to explain the situation to the dispatcher.

A sharp pain sliced through her abdomen and her face throbbed. Please, God. She couldn't lose this baby. She closed her eyes and pressed one hand to her stomach, sinking to the floor. "I'm pregnant."

* * *

Shayne didn't step off the plane in Houston until almost midnight. After a two hour delay taking off and then circling Houston until the weather let up enough so they could land, he just wanted off the damn plane. He shouldered his duffle and dug his cell phone out of his pocket. He turned it on and watched the screen for a signal. One message. Maybe Dani'd finally returned his call.

Undercover Heart

When the caller identified himself as a lawyer, Shayne almost hung up before he heard the name Danielle Cochran. He pressed the phone back to his ear and all the blood drained to his feet. All he could decipher from the cryptic message was that something had happened at Dani's house and this guy was Calvin's attorney. He bolted toward the exit, dialing the number on the message.

Shayne hit the emergency room door at a dead run. Hell, he could have gotten here faster in a boat. The roads were flooded and the rain hadn't let up. He pushed his dripping hair back out of his face and stopped at the desk. "Danielle Cochran. Where is she?"

Unaffected by his anxiety, the receptionist tapped a couple keys on the computer and shuffled the papers on the desk, finally pulling out a pencil. "Cochran with a C?"

Before he could strangle her, James walked up. "What're you doing here?"

"Is Dani okay? Where is she?"

James glanced at Shayne's soaked jeans and shirt. "We got here half an hour ago. They haven't even been out to tell us anything."

Shayne considered whether to kill him or the receptionist first. "Thanks for calling me," he said sarcastically.

James put his hands on his hips and shrugged. "What's the point?"

Well, if he hadn't known where he stood with his father before, he knew now. "I'm not fighting with you."

Shayne glanced at the packed waiting room and noticed Patty watching their exchange from a sofa in the corner. He turned back to the lady at the desk and pulled out his badge. "I want an update on Danielle Cochran."

She scrutinized the badge and shrugged. "I'll see what I can find out, but with the storm and all, it's a funny farm tonight. Can't make any promises."

"Anything would be more than I have now." He ignored the Highlands and paced. His clammy clothes clung to his skin. He grabbed a Styrofoam cup and filled it with coffee then went to stand by the window. At least the hospital had electricity. The car radio said half the island was dark.

He had a sketchy picture of what had happened, but the thing that worried him most was that Calvin kept apologizing. Apparently they hadn't known Dani was pregnant. Shayne reminded himself that Calvin had also said Dani was okay enough that she'd called the cops herself.

"Family of Danielle Cochran."

Finally. Shayne turned from the window and hurried forward to meet the doctor. James and Patty pushed in beside him.

The guy looked hardly old enough to be out of med school. He finally focused on James and extended his hand. "I'm Doctor Zimmerman."

"James Highland, her brother-in-law. How is she?"

"Her face looks bad, but it'll heal. No broken bones, just some deep bruises."

Shayne's nerves were shot and Dr. Zimmerman wasn't telling him what he needed to know. "The baby?" Dani would never get over it if she lost the baby.

"Are you the father?"

Shayne ignored Patty's quick intake of breath. "Yes."

"That's the most serious worry right now. Ms. Cochran is still having severe abdominal cramps. She took a strong blow to the stomach. For now, we're keeping a close eye on things. It's very early in the pregnancy. The positive is that even if she miscarries, I don't foresee a problem with her having other children."

"Does she know that?"

Dr. Zimmerman shrugged, but looked more tired than concerned. "She's aware of the situation."

"Please, can we see her?" Patty asked.

"I'll take you in, but she's been through an ordeal. At this point, she's withdrawn and it's best not to talk." He raised both eyebrows. "Don't stay long. If she becomes agitated, you'll have to leave."

Shayne followed the Highlands into Dani's room and stood back as Patty rushed to the bed. With the way they'd parted, he wasn't sure how Dani would react to him. Patty leaned over and kissed the dark lump on her forehead. "Hey, baby. Everything is going to be okay."

Dani didn't respond. Her gaze met Shayne's and he tried to read her thoughts. Her face was bruised, one eye black and swollen closed. Her bottom lip was split and the top so swollen it almost touched her nose. Mario was going down, and if Shayne had his way, he was going down as an adult. By the time he got done, the kid wouldn't see freedom for years.

Patty continued to fuss over her sister, smoothing her hair and straightening the sheet. James stood close behind, one hand resting on his wife's shoulder.

Dry eyed, Dani didn't push them away, but she didn't respond. Didn't they have enough sense to notice that she didn't need this right now? Every so often, she glanced at him, but he wasn't about to get into any conversation with the Highlands as an audience. Especially when he wasn't sure where he and Dani stood.

Doctor Zimmerman came in and checked her IV. "I've ordered a mild sedative to help you sleep."

Dani's hand went to her stomach. "But—"

The doctor patted her hand. "It's safe."

"We'll be right here," Patty said. "You rest."

"No." Dani pulled the sheet up. "I want to be alone. Go home to the kids."

"But, you might need something during the night. Wake up afraid or disoriented."

She closed her eyes. "I don't want any of you here."

"Okay." Patty gave her hand a quick squeeze and nodded. "Whatever you want. We'll be in the waiting room."

The Highlands walked out, but Shayne didn't leave his stance against the far wall.

"You too," Dani said.

He walked across to the bed and tried to take her hand.

She yanked it away. "Don't touch me."

Standing back, Shayne shoved his hands into his front pockets. "Just relax and let the medication work."

The doctor adjusted the IV. "Sir, she needs to rest."

His instinct was to refuse to leave, but Dani just pulled the sheet up to her chin and closed her eyes.

He'd never felt so helpless. His lady and their child were lying here suffering and there wasn't a damn thing he could do, not even comfort her.

He wasn't surprised to find James and Patty waiting in the hall when he left her room.

Undercover Heart

"You want to explain?" James asked before the door had even shut.

James' tone snapped Shayne's last nerve. "Not to you."

James stepped forward and grasped Shayne's upper arm. "Did you get her pregnant to spite me?"

"We're not having this conversation tonight." Shayne shoved his hands in his pockets to keep from punching his father. "Here's the bottom line. It's not your problem. Dani and I are both adults and we'll work this out."

"Oh, so you're going to marry her and stand beside her through this? Raise your child? Not as easy of a decision as you thought, is it? Because you have to make a commitment to someone besides yourself and you can't do that."

Of all people, he resented James talking to him about commitment. He kept his voice low. "We both seem to have a problem with commitments, don't we, Dad? I don't make them and you don't keep them." He turned to Patty. "I'm staying tonight. If it makes you feel any better, I intend to take care of her."

Shayne sat in the chair beside Dani's bed, watching her sleep, listening to the sound of the rain pound against the window, and trying not to gag on the sterile antiseptic smell of the hospital.

Dani looked calm, peacefully sleeping through his turmoil. The hospital temperature was icy against his damp clothes, yet he ignored the chill and studied her bruised face. From time to time she'd frown and put her hand on her stomach, but then relax again.

They couldn't lose this baby. It would destroy Dani. Her heart was so tender and this child--his child--was already a part of her. On the flight home, he'd finally admitted to himself just how much he wanted this woman in his life. But it wasn't until he'd been faced with the possibility of losing the baby that it had hit him how much he wanted that too. Not that it didn't scare the hell out of him, but he intended to be the father he'd never had.

His gaze followed a nurse as she came in for her nightly rounds. Her rubber soles squeaking on the polished tile floor echoed in the quiet. He touched the screen on his phone to check the time. Four AM. Dani arched her neck and groaned as the nurse checked her blood pressure and heart rate on the monitor. Methodically, the nurse offered a sympathetic smile as she adjusted the IV.

He watched the door close behind her then looked back at Dani. She was staring at him as if she wasn't sure he was really there.

Shayne stood and moved to the side of the bed, but he didn't touch her. "Hi, beautiful."

She put a finger to her swollen mouth and winced. "Hi."

"Are you hurting? Anything I can do or get for you?"

Her eyes closed and she shook her head. "No. Why don't you just say it and get it over with?"

"Say what?"

"I told you so." She took a deep breath and let it out, then opened her eyes. "You did. You warned me about everything. Don't take the job with the troubled kids. Don't hire Mario and Calvin. Lock the doors. Keep my cell phone charged. Quit taking everyone in. And the list goes on and on, I'm sure."

He sat on the edge of the bed and took her hand. "The only thing you did was be trusting and supportive. And that's nothing to feel guilty about. You're an incredible lady."

Undercover Heart

"And it nearly got me raped, didn't it? Mario had a knife, Shayne. A knife to my throat!" She swiped at her eyes, then jerked her hand away when it hurt. "How could I not see what he was capable of? Well, no more. I'm never trusting anyone again. You're right. People suck."

He hated that Dani's awakening to reality had to be so brutal. Unknowingly, Mario had inflicted more mental blows than physical. "Not all of them. You showed me that there are some people who put others before themselves. People who go above and beyond to help people they don't even know."

He closed his eyes a second. "Don't blame yourself for the actions of some drugged out juvenile. Mario was out of his mind."

"Don't make excuses for him. I want him locked up."

"He will be. At seventeen, the kid already has an impressive list of priors." Shayne ran his thumb up and down her fingers. "By the time this is over, I intend to see that he serves some serious time."

Putting one hand to her stomach, she buried her head back against the pillow. "What about Calvin?"

"I only talked to him on the phone. He kept repeating that he made the right choice. He apologized. The kid's scared to death."

Dani stretched her legs and kept rubbing her stomach. "Must've talked about what they were going to do to me, pictured it. Planned it. But Calvin couldn't follow through. Guess he got scared, but if he hadn't shown up, I couldn't have fought Mario off. He's so big and he didn't even seem to feel pain."

"Drugs do that."

"Yeah, well I was a fool to think caring about them could make a difference. It doesn't change anything."

"Wrong." He reached over and placed his hand on top of hers. "Dani, your love changed my life. Hell, maybe it saved my life."

She gripped the sheet and her stunned expression said more than words.

"I love you." He closed his eyes then opened them. "God, I don't want to go through life without you. Give me a chance to be a husband to you and a father to this baby. Please."

She stared at their entwined hands, resting on her stomach. "You don't have to say that just because I got hurt or I'm pregnant."

He leaned over and gently brushed his mouth to her swollen lips. "Are you kidding? I nearly blew it. For the first time in my life I've found someone I want to spend my life with and I'm scared shitless of losing you. Scared of never having a shot at being a part of a family, our family."

Dani reached up and ran her palm down his cheek. "What were you doing in California?"

"Job interview. Building a team like ours for the Carmel PD. How do you feel about relocating?"

He searched her face, but he couldn't read her thoughts. How could he even ask that? She loved her little beach house and her sister.

Her eyes bore deep into his, still she didn't speak.

"You, me, our baby, and California." She kissed the tip of her finger and placed it against his lips. "I'm hallucinating."

"No, I'm dead serious." He rubbed his hand across her stomach.

She smiled. "As long as we're together we can make it our home."

Undercover Heart

"Can I hold you?"

Dani winced as she scooted over bit by bit to make room. "Only if it's permanent. I love you. But you come back and it's for good."

Shayne eased down beside her, resting one hand lightly on her belly. "Just try to get rid of me."

Dani slowly opened her eyes to sun peeping through the stark hospital blinds, the storm from the night before had passed. She smiled at Shayne, stretched out beside her on the narrow bed, his hand resting on her stomach. Poor guy hadn't gotten much sleep last night. Her eyes adjusted and found a nurse beside the bed.

Running a hand through Shayne's hair, Dani woke him. "We have company."

He opened one eye and looked around. "Okay." He yawned and eased off the bed. "Sorry."

The nurse waited until Shayne moved aside and then plugged in a machine she'd rolled in on a cart. "I'm here to do a sonogram."

Shayne moved in close and watched the screen with Dani. There wasn't much to see so early in her pregnancy, but the blob definitely had a heartbeat."

Dani squeezed Shayne's hand and stared at the screen, afraid to ask. Afraid not to. "So, everything looks okay?"

The lady nodded. "I don't see any problems, but the doctor will take a look and give you an official report when he makes his rounds."

As the nurse left, James and Patty came in.

James noted Shayne's rumpled clothes and shook his

head. "I don't even know what to say anymore."

"Okay, then let me." Shayne rubbed the sleep out of his eyes. "Let's talk facts."

Until now, Dani had never noticed that Shayne was an inch or two taller than his father.

"You willingly gave up all parental rights when I was two. At twenty-six, I don't need or want a father."

James started to interrupt, but Shayne held up his hand. "Before you get pissed, just hear me out. Dani and I are getting married. If you'll accept me as her husband, I'm willing to accept you as her brother-in-law."

Dani held her breath. She knew Shayne was making the gesture for her. Because she wanted peace in the family. Please let James recognize how much effort this took for him.

James studied his son. "What if I say no?"

"Then I take Dani and leave with a clear conscience."

"Leave?" Patty asked.

James narrowed one eye. "Do you love her?"

Shayne's eyes never left his father's. "Yes."

"Then what else can I ask for?" James reached and shook Shayne's hand. "Welcome to the family."

Patty turned to Dani. "This is what you want?"

For the first time, Dani didn't sense anything more than sisterly concern in Patty's tone. Dani rubbed her belly and attempted a smile. "Maybe we'll have a little boy, just like his daddy."

Shayne crossed his eyes and groaned. "Paybacks can be hell."

THE END

Rocking Horse Cowboys (Available Now)

"No damn way!" Dylan McKeon blinked at the lawyer then turned his glare on his mother. "Did you instigate this?"

Daisy grinned back at him with all the innocence he knew his mother did not possess. "I'm as surprised as you, sweetie. Who'd have thought your father would do such a thing?" Judging by the upturned corners of her glossed lips, she did.

"Why would Dad leave half the ranch to Jordan?" It made no sense. Jordan had walked out of Dylan's life over two years ago and he hadn't seen neither hide nor hair of her since. Dylan turned back to the lawyer. "Is that all? What other death bed insanity did he pull?"

His father's attorney and longtime drinking buddy ran a finger down the paper and flipped the page. "A few specified items and his vast music collection he left to Daisy." He nodded to Mom. "All other personal property, vehicles, farm equipment, livestock, bank accounts go to Dylan McKeon, his only son. With the one specification."

Dylan swallowed the bile in his throat. No way in Hell he was going to allow Jordan Harris to reap a cent off of his or his father's hard work. "Fifty percent of the McKeon family's ranch? We'll see about that."

Pamela Stone

Partners By Design (Available now)

What? What did he want from her? Savannah strained her neck to study his face, decipher his thoughts. Navy blue eyes burned into hers, but he waited. Why didn't he touch her?

I shouldn't want him to touch me.

His hands were inches from where her shirt gaped open. If she turned just slightly.

Tilting her head against his shoulder, she nuzzled in and rubbed her nose against his neck, inhaling a whiff of rain, sweat, and musky aftershave.

We can't do this.

Don't turn me away.

His mouth covered hers, lips parted, inviting her inside the warmth. His fingers undid the two buttons she'd managed to fasten on the shirt then squeezed her breast. He slid his other hand beneath her hair, his fingers pressing hot as he repositioned her for a deeper kiss.

She tugged on his damp hair, pulling him closer and feasting on his mouth, starved for the once-familiar taste of Logan. His ten o'clock shadow scratched her chin and ignited her peaked senses.

Thunder rumbled and clashed across the sky and sheets of rain washed over the truck. Deep in the floorboard her phone vibrated, but she tuned it out.

Logan tasted so right. The years melted away. She was sixteen again, and carefree, and alive. She'd missed this. Missed him.

Logan Reid was the long awaited sequel to her own personal teenage love story. The one she'd replayed in her mind so many times she'd never forgotten a single line of dialogue or erotic sensation. But she'd rewritten the ending hundreds of times.

"Come home with me."

Her eyes popped open and she blinked at Logan. Familiar yes, but not the young boy of her fantasies.

They weren't teenagers and she was not going to let him destroy her again. In desperation, she pushed away and tugged her shirt together. "What made me ever think we could be friends?"

Circling her waist with his hands, he pulled her back against his bare chest, and rested his chin on top of her head. "You were the best friend I ever had, Savannah." His lips nibbled her ear and his breath tickled her neck. "You were everything good that ever happened to me."

His words cut deep into her memories. She'd felt the same. But that was before he'd left her cold and alone with not a single word of explanation beyond, 'It's over.'

About the Author

Pamela Stone spent twenty plus years in the technology field before becoming a romance writer. She is a native Texan whose mom encouraged the importance of wardrobe, dance, and piano lessons and whose father added go-kart racing, slot cars, water skiing, and a pony to the mix. Toss in a wild imagination, lazy walks on her grandparents' farm and another grandmother with a shed full of romance novels to while away hot afternoons.

Writing is pure escapism for Pamela. Childhood imaginary friends grew into teenage fantasies. Later as a mother of two young boys, she began writing to keep in touch with the adult world. She continued writing as a method to wind down in the evenings from long days spent in Corporate America. Anybody notice a pattern here? Not enough adult socialization - write. People overload - write. Either way, she claims that writing keeps her sane. Cheaper than a therapist and tons more fun.

She still resides in Texas with her childhood sweetheart and husband. She loves writing romance and sold her first novel, Last Resort: Marriage, on Friday the 13th, June 2008. How's that for luck!

Pamela loves to hear from her readers and can be reached through her website at:

www.pamelastone.net

Made in the USA
San Bernardino, CA
20 July 2015